ST. MARTIN'S

MINOTAUR

MYSTERIES

FORTUNE
LIKE THE
MOON

ALYS CLARE

St. Martin's Paperbacks

First published in Great Britain by Hodder and Stoughton, a division of Hodder Headline PLC

FORTUNE LIKE THE MOON

ISBN: 0-312-97632-1

Printed in the United States of America

St. Martin's Press hardcover edition / May 2000
St. Martin's Paperbacks edition / April 2001

St. Martin's Paperbacks are published by St. Martin's Press, 175 Fifth Avenue, New York, NY 10010.

10 9 8 7 6 5 4 3 2 1

For M. D.

Thank you.

O Fortuna!
velut Luna
Statu variabilis,
semper crescis
aut decresis

Oh, Fortune!
Like the moon, changing,
Forever waxing and waning . . .

From *Carmina Burana,*
'Cantiones profanae';
author's translation.

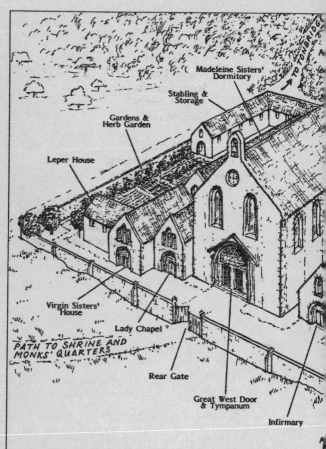

Madeleine Sisters' Dormitory

Stabling & Storage

Gardens & Herb Garden

Leper House

Virgin Sisters' House

Lady Chapel

PATH TO SHRINE AND MONKS' QUARTERS

Rear Gate

Great West Door & Tympanum

Infirmary

HAWKENLYE ABBEY

TO TONBRIDGE

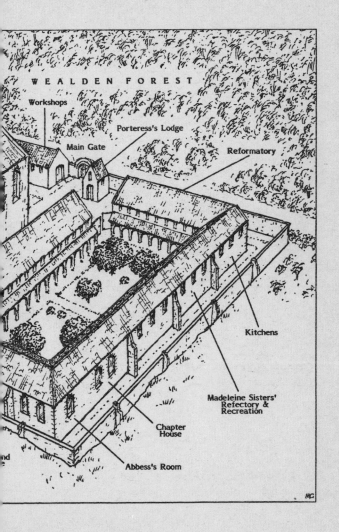

WEALDEN FOREST

Workshops

Porteress's Lodge

Main Gate

Reformatory

Kitchens

Madeleine Sisters'
Refectory &
Recreation

Chapter
House

Abbess's Room

MC

PRELUDE

Dead, she was a pattern of black, white and red on the sparse, short grass of a dry July.

Black for the fine wool habit, still quite new. It bore none of the darns in the front panel of the skirt that told of years spent kneeling in prayer, and the rear hem was still pristine, not yet worn by careless contact with stone steps. White for the wimple and barbette which had framed the face, although the wimple was no longer secured around the throat and chin but torn away. White, too, for the pale, pale skin. For the face, frozen into the expression of abject terror that it would wear until the flesh rotted from the skull. For the shockingly exposed legs and loins, from which habit and underskirt had been thrown back. In death she was immodest, poor lass, lying there with her thin white legs wide apart. It was as if her corpse had been arranged deliberately so as to make a pleasing pattern, for the outflung arms matched the angle of the spread legs.

Red for the blood.

So much blood.

Her throat had been cut, with the same eye for symmetry that had arranged the limbs. The slash began exactly under the right ear lobe and ended precisely under the left, and it gaped open to its widest immediately beneath the small and somewhat feeble chin.

Her bare neck and throat were soaked with blood, and it had trickled down in several fine streams on to the collar of the habit, where it was absorbed by the wool.

There was blood, too, on the white legs. A great deal of blood, glistening on the dark pubic hair and smeared on the inner thighs.

The morning sun came up over the horizon, and the greyish light of dawn quickly grew stronger, brightening the black and the white so that the contrast deepened. Sunlight shone on the dark crimson blood, making it shine like a jewel. A ruby, perhaps, as dazzling as the one set in the gold cross that lay a few paces from the horror-struck, dead face.

The daylight waxed, and from somewhere quite near a cockerel began to crow, repeatedly, as if determined to be heard.

3

In a nearby building a bell rang, its summons followed by sounds of life as people set about beginning the day.

A new day.

The first of the infinite number that the dead woman would not see.

The First Death

Chapter One

Richard Plantagenet, trying and failing to attend to two things at once, lost his temper, threw a pewter mug half full of ale at a manservant, leapt up out of his chair and, flinging himself forward, stubbed his toe on the protruding end of a stone floor slab.

His furious oath, echoing up to the rafters and down again, had the effect of silencing everyone in the hall, and left even the least observant in no doubt as to the King elect's frame of mind.

'Are you all right, sire?' one of the attending clerics asked bravely.

'All *right?*' bellowed the King, hopping on one foot as he massaged the toes of the other, ineffectually, he discovered, since he was wearing his boots. 'No, Absolon, I am not all right.' He paused, as if summarising the many causes of his discontent, and the reddish eyebrows drew together in a ferocious frown of concentration. Bishop Absolon, fearing the worst, hastily stepped back a pace. But Richard, instead of giving way to his frustration–borne anger, mastered it, returned to his chair, sat down again, and said, in a surprisingly meek tone, 'Please, Absolon. Continue.'

As the priest launched into the seemingly endless reasons why Richard's coronation must take place so soon, and why every single tiny detail must be so exhaustively discussed, one or two people standing nearest to the new King noticed that, although he had tucked the communication from England inside his tunic, he had not forgotten about it. The short, strong fingers kept returning to it, blindly finding it and touching it as a man in peril grasps his rosary.

Had any of the clergy surrounding him and badgering him with their suggestions, their requests and their demands known him well, this action of Richard's would not have surprised them. For the letter was from his mother, and Eleanor of Aquitaine, newly released from her admittedly comfortable imprisonment and truly free for the first time in fifteen years, was in England preparing the way for the coming of her favourite son.

Neither Eleanor nor Richard, although desiring it most fervently, had expected that Richard would inherit his father's throne. Who would have, indeed, when he was the second of Henry II and Eleanor's four surviving sons, with an elder brother who not only thrived but enjoyed the special favour of his father? Indeed, so great was Henry II's faith in his eldest son that he had the lad crowned while he himself still lived and reigned. Richard, it seemed, must content himself with the duchy of Aquitaine, his inheritance from his mother. No mean gift, certainly. Except the man who ruled Aquitaine would be a duke. Not a king.

But the Young King died. At the age of twenty-eight, full of the characteristic Plantagenet vigour and apparent ruddy health, suddenly he took sick of a fever. A fatal fever.

Henry II, grieving for his heir and his favourite, had to come to terms with the disruption of his careful plans for the secure future of his dynasty. Cursed with feuding offspring and a meddlesome wife who, far from reminding her three belligerent sons of their filial duty, actually *encouraged* them in their machinations against their father, grudgingly he recognised Richard – the apple of his mother's eye, damn the man! – as his heir. To the throne of England.

Six years later, Henry II was dead.

The last winter of his life was a dreadful one. He had rid

himself of Eleanor and her infernal, everlasting interference by shutting her up in Winchester and putting a guard on her, but he couldn't mete out the same treatment to his heir, much as he would have wished to; apart from anything else, Richard had an army. He had forged an alliance with Philip II of France, and the two of them had been harrying Henry throughout northern France.

It was enough to make anyone depressed and weary at heart, even a king. Especially a king. Henry's long winter of hard riding in foul conditions had led to an anal fistula, badly abscessed, and he was resting at Le Mans, trying to build up his strength, when Richard and Philip attacked and forced him to flee the town. Their peace terms were a humiliation for Henry, and grief was added to bitterness when he learned that his youngest son, John, had joined forces with his brother and the French King.

He retired to his castle at Chinon, very sick, and in such pain that he could neither walk nor sit comfortably; they'd had to carry him out to sign the peace treaty. His abscess had opened, and blood poisoning followed quickly. He died on Thursday 6 July, and those who knew no better said it was from a broken heart.

At the height of the hot summer of 1189, then, Richard Plantagenet became King of England. He had been born in England – his much-travelled mother hadn't let pregnancy slow her down, and she'd given birth to Richard when staying at Oxford – but, since childhood, he had only visited England briefly. He hardly spoke English, and had only a vague notion of what the land and her people were all about. Home, to him, was Aquitaine, and his court was at Poitiers; the very name by which he was usually known in France was Richard the Poitevin.

The paramount need now was not so much to educate Richard on the subject of his new kingdom. It was to educate his new subjects about him. And on the spot was the very person to fulfil the task; energetic – even more than usual, after fifteen years a virtual prisoner – and utterly sincere in her devotion and loyalty to her son, Eleanor, in her sixty-eighth year, set about preparing the way for Richard.

She had little time. Richard was due to arrive in England in August – was even now just across the channel – and it was being suggested that his coronation should be early in September; the third, they said. Perhaps it was this sense of rush that made her normal good sense desert her, for, to general surprise and quite a lot of dismay, she announced that, in Richard's liberal and humane name, the jails of England were to be emptied, and those awaiting trial or punishment given their freedom.

The move was, perhaps, a gamble, a typical Eleanor, typical Richard, gamble. If it worked, then hundreds of genuinely grateful ex-prisoners would infiltrate English society to its depths – literally its depths – spreading the message of how wise, how Christian, was this new king. And, indeed, the majority of those pent up were imprisoned for no greater crime than infringement of England's strict and ruthlessly applied forestry laws. If it failed, though, if just one released felon abused the great gift of his freedom and reverted to his old ways, then what would be the public reaction? Would they say this Richard was a fool, believing you could release a criminal and, naïvely, that gratitude would lead to honesty? Would they say, even more damagingly, that this new reign which, so they were told, promised so much, was starting under a cursed star?

Yes. They would.

They would, and they did. It had happened.

The communication from England which Richard kept touching that hot July day in northern France was Eleanor's account of an unusually brutal murder which had just been discovered. In some area of this blasted new kingdom he was about to inherit called the Weald.

Weald. What *was* that, Weald? What did it mean? More to the point, where in God's name was it? His mother had mentioned some town. Ton something. Ton what? Some place she was interested in – some place she actually knew, whatever the relevance of that might be – because there was a convent there. Some abbey, on the lines of her beloved Fontevraud. What had she said about the place? That it was ruled, as was Fontevraud, by a woman?

God's boots, Richard thought, an abbey ruled by a woman.

He itched to get the letter out and reread it, more thoroughly this time. But Absolon was still droning on, and behind him three more bishops had lined up to have *their* say. And a papal legate was expected to arrive later in the day.

Richard sighed, trying to fix his mind on what the priest was saying. But concentration was proving elusive; he was distracted by Absolon's left hand, gesticulating in emphasis, by his beard, with a single long, untrimmed hair that sprang out from the rest, by the old man's yellowing teeth.

From the courtyard outside sounded the excited whinny of a horse, instantly answered by another. Someone emitted a laugh, quickly shushed. My men, Richard thought, are going hunting.

He stood up again, stepping down from his raised chair, this time careful to avoid the upthrusting slab. With a courteous bow to Absolon, who was standing with his mouth open, displaying several rotten teeth, Richard was about to murmur his excuses.

He changed his mind, and left the hall without another word. He was, after all, King.

He did not ride out with his men. Not, in any case, with the hunting party, whose boyish high spirits would have been as damaging to concentration as Absolon's ramblings. Instead, he summoned one of his squires and a handful of the older men, one or two knights among them, leading them off into the forest at a pace which they had to exert themselves to follow. They rode for some miles, and then, as the others loosened rein and allowed their horses to amble along beside the small stream that flowed through the woods, Richard drew apart.

He dismounted, and settled himself on a grassy bank fragrant with wild flowers. And, as his tethered horse began to tear up mouthfuls of the lush pasture, at last returned to his mother's letter.

It made no better reading this time. In fact it was rather worse, since, now that he wasn't trying to listen to two people talking to him at the same time, he could give it his full attention.

The facts themselves were repugnant. A young nun, less than a year into her noviciate, raped and murdered, throat cut, body left exposed to anyone who passed. Poor, innocent child – in fact the woman was twenty-three, but his mother liked the sound of a ringing phrase – slaughtered for no apparent reason, unless it were robbery. A jewelled cross had been found nearby, and there was conjecture that the murderer had been disturbed, frightened into throwing away his spoils.

The location of the murder could not have been more inconvenient. The victim was a member of the community of Hawkenlye Abbey, and the abbey was situated a mere handful of miles from the town of Tonbridge. With its position on the Medway, at the place where the main London to Hastings road crossed the river, any horrified gossip that reached the town from the abbey would spread like fire in a cornfield up to London. To be received and discussed by the kingdom's men of power, who would not hesitate to form opinions and pass judgement.

'And there will be gossip,' Richard muttered, 'there always is. And how can it best be contained? Who, in God's name, can advise me in my dealings with this barbaric place?'

'Sire?'

He turned at the address, having thought himself out of earshot of the others. One of the older men stood before him – one of the knights – and, as Richard looked at him, he knelt.

'Don't kneel there, man!' Richard said impatiently. 'It's muddy.'

'Oh. So it is.' The man looked resignedly down at his one soaked knee. 'Next to new and clean on,' he said, not quite quietly enough.

'I'm honoured,' Richard said laconically.

The man's head flew up. 'Sire, please, I didn't mean . . . Of course I would dress in my best for you! I only meant—'

'It is of no significance.' Richard waved away the excuses. He was trying to remember who the man was, and why the sight of his tall frame and tough-featured, appealing face should somehow be reassuring . . . 'What is your name?' he asked abruptly.

The man fell on one knee again. The same knee, either, Richard thought with mild amusement, because this was how he habitually did it, or because he would thus avoid soiling both legs of the new hose. 'Josse d'Acquin, sire,' the knight said, turning his cap in his hands, then clumsily dropping it. A shame; it, also, looked new, and was in the latest fashion. A detail which, somehow, did not seem in keeping with the man. Perhaps he had made some attempt to smarten himself, knowing he would be in the company of the court set.

'Well, Josse d'Acquin,' Richard said, 'I have been trying, and so far failing, to recall how you and I are acquainted. Will you enlighten me?'

'It was years ago, sire,' the man said eagerly, 'it's no surprise your grace doesn't remember, why, we were nothing but boys, really, you, your brothers the Young King, God rest him, and Geoffrey, my, he was only fifteen! And you, sire, scarce a year older! As for us, the pages and squires, well, I was one of the oldest, and I wasn't much more than thirteen.' Throwing care to the winds, he shifted his position so that his not inconsiderable weight was borne on both knees, then went on, 'Back in Seventy-three, it was, sire, and you and young Henry were in a right pother with your father, God rest his soul—'

'Amen,' Richard responded piously.

' – over his refusal to give you more of a say in the running of things, in particular your own estates, and—'

'We fought together!' Memory had returned to Richard, full-blown and complete with sights, sounds, deeds and powerful emotions of a time sixteen years in the past. 'We encountered a scouting party of my father's and Henry said we should make a run for it, since you and the other squires were so young and we did not have the right to involve you in something so one-sided and foolhardy, and—'

'And the lads and I said, we're with you, we *want* to fight, we're aching for a chance to draw blood, and—'

'And so we launched a surprise attack, disarmed and unhorsed four of them, at which the rest fled!'

'Four?' Josse d'Acquin had a humorous face, and his generous mouth was quirking into a smile. 'Sire, I would stake my life on its being six.' He glanced at Richard. 'At the very least.'

'Six, seven, eight, think you?' Richard was smiling, too.

'What a day,' Josse mused, sitting back on his heels.

'Indeed.' The King was staring at him, absently noting the muddy puddle water seeping into the seat of the hose and the hem of the elaborately bordered tunic. 'I never forget a face,' he said. 'Knew perfectly well I'd met you before, Josse.'

Josse bowed his head. 'Sire.'

They remained quite still for some moments, as if suddenly turned into a painting. Some knightly illustration, with the loyal servant waiting, head bent, for the command of his lord. Of his king.

The King, in this case, was thinking. Wondering, in fact, if the vague and general pleas for help which he had been sending up, immediately before this character from the past had reappeared, might just have been answered.

Deliberately Richard stilled his mind, allowed himself to be a receptacle.

After a moment, he had, he was quite sure, received the message he was waiting for.

He reached down and lightly touched Josse d'Acquin on the shoulder. 'D'Acquin,' he began, then, less distantly, 'Josse. Oh, get up, man, you've got your backside in a puddle.' Josse scrambled to his feet, instantly bending into a sort of half crouch; both he and Richard had noticed he was almost a head taller than the King.

'Josse,' Richard went on, 'you're a local man? Of Norman stock, yes?'

'My family estates are at Acquin, sire. Near to the town of Saint Omer, a little to the south of Calais.'

'Acquin?' Richard ran swiftly through his mind to see if he'd heard of it, decided he hadn't. 'Ah. I see. And what of England, our new kingdom over the water? Are you familiar with England?'

'*England,*' Josse echoed, in the manner of someone saying, a *pigpen.* Then, as if instantly regretting it as less than tactful, when the land's throne had just been inherited by the man standing in front of him, he said with patently false enthusiasm, 'England, yes, indeed, sire, I know it quite well. My mother, you see, was an Englishwoman, born and bred in Lewes – that's a town in the south-east – and in my youth she insisted that I get to know her country, her language, her people's ways, that sort of thing.' He smiled faintly. 'People didn't say no to my mother, sire.'

'I know that sort of mother,' Richard muttered feelingly. 'So, England and the English hold no fears for you?'

'I wouldn't say that, exactly, sire.' Josse frowned. 'There's always fear attached to the unknown. Well, not fear, more apprehension. Well, maybe not even that, but—'

'A sensible amount of wariness?' Richard supplied.

'Precisely.' Josse smiled openly now, and his teeth, Richard observed, were a great improvement on Bishop Absolon's. Then, as if remembering where the conversation had begun: 'Sire? Why do we speak of England?'

'Because,' Richard replied simply, 'I want you to go there.'

Chapter Two

Josse had gone to Richard the Poitevin's court because of fond memories from the past, not because of hopes for the future. It had been enough, or so he'd thought, to be in that stimulating, action-packed company, where the restless energy of Richard seemed to permeate right through court society, so that you just never knew, from one day to the next, what was going to happen.

And, whenever the court hadn't had to up sticks and follow Richard off to some distant part of his territory, there was the sheer exuberance of life back in Aquitaine. Richard, brought up in the expectation of inheriting those rich, colourful lands, had thrown himself into the ways of the people, cultivating the love of music, song, the poetry of the troubadors, and the free thinking that characterised his mother. He was utterly her son, and wealthy society in the Poitevin court faithfully reflected the character and habits of both of them.

As he set out on the dusty, crowded London road out of Hastings, Josse reflected how dramatic a change had happened to him, purely because he'd obeyed a sudden whim and joined the group that rode off with Richard that day in Normandy. He didn't flatter himself with the notion that Richard had chosen him for this delicate mission because of any strengths Josse possessed; only an irredeemable egotist could think *that*. Why, the king had even had to be reminded of who Josse was!

No. It was nothing more than having been in the right place at the right time.

Something, Josse admitted modestly to himself, that whatever guardian angel it was who guided his footsteps was quite good at arranging.

He was, without a doubt, very pleased to have been entrusted with the job. Richard had briefed him fully, or as fully as he could, when he himself had only Queen Eleanor's first report to go on. What emerged most powerfully, for Josse, was that Richard seemed genuinely disturbed at the thought of this magnanimous gesture, this releasing of prisoners, going wrong. Being misinterpreted.

Mind you, Josse thought as he edged his horse to a canter and hurried past an overloaded waggon that was creating clouds of choking dust, mind you, it always did sound a cockeyed notion. Me, I agree with that Augustinian canon in Yorkshire – what was his name? William of Newburg? – who was heard to remark that, through the so-called clemency of this new king, a crowd of pests had been released on the long-suffering public to commit worse crimes in future.

But maybe the King and his good lady mother weren't as familiar with the sort of scum that habitually languished in England's jails as Josse was. Josse was quite unsurprised at the concept of one such released felon reverting to his old ways; the surprise, in fact, was that they weren't all at it.

As the long, bright day wore on, he became hotter, dustier, thirstier, sweatier, and more out of sorts. By mid-afternoon, he was beginning to wish he'd been anywhere but standing before the King when this notion of sending an agent to investigate the murder had been conceived.

If only I were back in Aquitaine, he mused as he encouraged his weary horse up the gentle but long slope to the High Weald, I would be relaxing in a shady courtyard, jug of fine wine at my elbow, perfumed air in my nostrils, music playing softly in my ears, prospect of an evening's entertainment ahead. And a damned good dinner. And that pretty widowed lady, the one with the secret smile and the irresistible dimple, to seek out and pursue . . .

No. Best not to fantasise about her, since, in the absence of Josse, she would undoubtedly have turned her tempting dimple elsewhere by now.

Instead he turned his thoughts to his own lands. To Acquin, and his sturdy family home. Perhaps the squat buildings and the thick-walled courtyard were not exactly elegant, but they were safe. The gates were solid oak and barred with iron, and, in times of threat, there was room within the spacious yard not only for the family but for the majority of the peasants whose right it was to look to their lord for protection. Not that it happened often: Acquin, hidden in a fold of the sheltered valley of the Aa river, was well enough off the beaten track for danger, usually, to pass it by.

Occupied with thoughts of his brothers, his sisters-in-law and his many nephews and nieces, Josse was surprised to discover he was at the summit of the low rise he had been so laboriously climbing. Drawing rein, he stared out across the Medway Vale, opening up before him. Up to his left somewhere, on the fringes of the great Wealden Forest, was Hawkenlye Abbey, his ultimate destination. Waiting for him, together with its abbess. Richard had seemed quite in awe of its abbess, when he told Josse about her. The sudden proximity of both the abbey and its mistress concentrated Josse's mind with swift efficiency; straightening his back, collecting his dozy mount, he stepped up the pace to a brisk trot and set off down the road to Tonbridge.

He had decided not to arrive at the abbey until he had found out what people were saying about the murder. Discovered what conclusions public opinion was forming, seen if Richard was right about the blame being thrown on to one of these damned released prisoners. Josse had to admit, it did seem a likely answer. It'd be what he'd have thought, had he not just been promoted to investigating agent and therefore not permitted such rash and shallow judgement.

Tonbridge was much as he remembered it from a brief visit a decade or more ago, except that it was busier and more populous. The fine castle, up there on the rise overlooking the Medway crossing, was still held by the family of the man who had founded it: Richard, Lord of Bienfaite and of Orbec, had been the great-grandson of Richard, Duke of Normandy, and had fought beside his cousin William of Normandy at the Battle of Hastings. His reward, when William ascended the throne, was generous indeed; the castles of Tonbridge and of Clare, in the county of Suffolk, were but the pickings of some two hundred English manors.

Either from a wish to be stylish or from lack of imagination, the family were enthusiastic followers of the new fashion of calling each successive eldest son by his father's name; an unenlightened stranger coming to Tonbridge and wishing to enquire of its lord could be fairly safe in asking after Richard. Richard FitzRoger, the current lord, had inherited from his father in 1183; now, six years on, Josse observed, there were distinct signs that the family continued to flourish.

The traffic thickened as he entered the town. A poorly packed mule train had disgorged the contents of a parcel of what looked and smelt like badly tanned skins, and the two youngsters who appeared to be in charge were rapidly losing control of their mules and their tempers. Picking a way round the confusion, Josse wondered how quickly order would be restored, and what penalty the lads would have to pay for the chaos. Perhaps they'd be lucky, and escape with a couple of clips round the ear.

The up side of having a powerful family as lords of the region meant that law and order were, in general, better maintained here than in some less well-policed areas of the kingdom. Josse would have liked to know what the lord and his officials made of the murder up at Hawkenlye. Were they conducting investigations of their own? Would it be better, as far as Josse was concerned, to keep his own counsel, and disguise the fact that he came directly from the new king?

Yes, he decided. Undoubtedly it would. He could think of nothing more guaranteed to arouse the resentment and animosity of the lord and master of Tonbridge Castle than the arrival of some usurper who thought he knew more about local characters and conditions than did a man born and bred there. A *foreign* usurper, to boot – Josse had no illusions that having an English mother would carry much weight around here.

He adopted his usual practice when travelling, and approached the inn with the most comings and goings. Situated some fifty or sixty paces back from the river, the tall gates that gave on to the street stood wide open, and Josse could see through to the yard within. There were signs that the row of stables was in the process of being mucked out; although it was possibly a little late in the day, at least the inn servants were getting round to it in the end.

A thin-faced man carrying a well-loaded hayfork gave a preoccupied nod when Josse enquired about lodgings. Putting down the fork and taking Josse's horse, the man directed Josse to a doorway across the yard, its stone step worn into a dip by the passage of thousands of pairs of feet. Inside, in a long, stone-flagged passageway, a well-endowed woman, fractionally the wrong side of middle age, was shouting orders to two awe-struck girls.

'. . . and don't take all day about it, I've plenty for you to do down here! Yes?'

Realising that the 'Yes?' was directed at him, Josse said, 'I believe you may be able to offer me a room for the night and a meal, madam?'

She looked him up and down. 'Not from these parts, are you?'

'No.' He wondered how she knew. He didn't often speak English, but he was pretty sure he didn't have a strong accent.

'Thought not.' She was nodding as if in self-congratulation. Pointing a work-reddened hand at his tunic, she said, 'We don't get dyes bright as that hereabouts, that's for sure, even what with us being so close to London and the pretty taste of its people.'

She raised sharp, light-brown eyes to his face. 'You've been travelling in the south, I'd say.'

'You'd say right.' He smoothed his fingers over the embroidered border. 'I'm rather pleased with the work myself.'

'Hm.' She was looking askance at him, as if an appreciation of a nice piece of cloth was not entirely manly. 'Well, I've lodgings, aye. You pay up front, mind, I'll not have foreigners disappearing at first light and vanishing into the blue with their bills unpaid!'

Foreigner. There, he'd been right. He smiled, and reached for his purse. 'How much do you want?'

His room was adequate, although there were two more narrow cots in it; if the inn opened its doors to any more guests that night, he'd be sharing. Not that it bothered him greatly. As long as they didn't snore.

One of the girls brought him a bowl and a jug of warm water – you couldn't have called it hot – and he set about removing the dust of the road. Then, in view of the fact that he'd been travelling continuously for several days, he allowed himself the luxury of an hour's sleep. He had the soldier's knack of being able to switch off almost at will, which was just as well since the inn was full of the racket of a bustling, busy evening, and the road outside seemed to be inhabited by carts with squeaky wheels and people who didn't know how to speak below a bellow.

He woke up feeling much better. Mind alert and eager, he went down to start mingling with the locals.

'Makes no sense, to my mind, this mass release of robbers, thugs, rapists and that. Aye, thank you, sir, I don't mind if I do.' Responding to Josse's enquiring glance and the finger pointing at the empty ale mug, the man pushed it towards the tap boy for a refill. He was the first person Josse had got into conversation with, and hadn't needed much encouragement to start talking.

Lubricating him with a second draught of ale might elicit a few interesting revelations.

'See, like I told my missus,' the man leaned back against the wall, settling himself comfortably as if preparing for a long session, 'it's just no good expecting people to change, now, is it? I mean, once a thief, always a thief, that's my motto.'

'Well, that's one way of looking at it,' Josse conceded. 'But we're talking about murder, here, aren't we? Is it really certain that the nun was killed by a released prisoner, when most of those released were imprisoned for lesser crimes? Violation of the forestry laws, that's what I'd heard.'

The man looked at him pityingly. 'I'd like to know who else'd have done such a foul deed. I mean, stands to reason, doesn't it?'

'Yes, I suppose so,' Josse replied, who didn't suppose anything of the sort.

'You tell me what else is more likely,' the man went on, warming to his theme, 'than that one of them ruffians feels his sudden freedom going to his head – *and* his other bits, if you get my meaning' – he shot a sly sideways glance at Josse, and placed a finger alongside his nose – 'and, coming across some young thing in a habit out walking by herself in the middle of the night, he can't resist launching himself on her, pulling up her skirts, revealing all that smooth young flesh, them plump white thighs, then having his wicked way with her.' The man's eyes were bulging with lust, and the protuberant Adam's apple in his scrawny neck moved up and down swiftly as he swallowed a couple of times. 'Then, when she starts screaming out for help, he slits her throat, both to shut her up *and* so's she won't be able to point the finger of blame at him. There you are, sir, that's what happened.' He took another long swig of ale, burped, and added, 'Hexactly that.'

'Mm, I imagine you've got it about right.' Josse mastered his dislike and leaned companionably against the neighbouring piece of wall. 'I suppose King Richard's clemency isn't going down very well hereabouts, then? Not now this brutal murder has happened?'

'I don't know nothing about no King Richard,' the man said. 'King Henry, now, he did all right, and his Queen's a lovely woman. Pity it's not still the pair of them holding the reins, that's what I say.'

'They speak highly of King Richard.'

'Who does?' the man responded. 'Nobody knows aught about him. Not round here, anyway. You ask anybody' – he made a wide gesture, as if to embrace the entire population of the tap room – 'he's an unknown quantity, that's what he is!'

'Matthew's right,' said a newcomer waiting to be served. There were several nods and grunts of agreement from nearby drinkers. 'It's all very well for Queen Eleanor to set off round the country telling us what a fine king he's going to be, and I don't blame her for that, him being her son and all.'

'God bless Queen Eleanor,' someone said, and there were several equally loyal and laudable echoes.

'But seems to me this here hasn't really been thought through.' The newcomer put his head closer to Josse, as if afraid unfriendly ears would overhear. 'Now there's no proof, and I'm not one to condemn a man before he's even been tried, but—'

'Before he's even been arrested,' put in another voice, greeted by a few brief eruptions of laughter.

' – but it's suspicious, like, isn't it? Nice peaceful community up there in Hawkenlye, no trouble, no violence, for more years than you could count, then all of a sudden the doors of every jail in the land get flung open, and some nun minding her own business, no threat to nobody, gets raped and murdered, throat cut from ear to ear like a slaughtered pig!' He folded his arms as if his conclusion were inarguable. 'I mean, who else would want to kill a nun?'

Who indeed, Josse thought. 'Surely it's not a bad thing for a new king, and, as you imply, one who's rather an unknown quantity, to begin his reign with a gesture of clemency?' he suggested, testing the water. 'A very Christian gesture, at that. Didn't Our Lord, after all, condemn those who didn't visit those who were sick and in prison?'

One or two of the more pious among the company crossed themselves, and someone muttered, 'Amen'.

'*Visiting*'s one thing,' a new voice said darkly. 'Ain't sensible, even for a Christian, to go letting 'em all *out*.'

'And it's hardly fair on us,' said the plump woman who had let Josse his room, appearing behind the counter and beginning to fill a vast jug with ale. 'Us women, I mean. We won't lie safe in our beds at night knowing this villain's abroad! Who's going to be next?' She stared round the room with wide eyes, as if afraid some murdering rapist was about to leap out at her. 'That's what I say!'

'He'd have to be desperate,' someone behind Josse muttered, too quietly for the woman to pick up. Several men standing close heard, however, and there were a few sniggers.

'He'd have to find it first,' came a hoarse whisper. 'Be a case of fart and give me a clue, I reckon.'

'Be a well-travelled path when he *did* get there,' someone else added. 'Dear old Goody Anne, she didn't earn herself the money for this place by sewing fine seams or peddling her wares in Tonbridge Market.'

'She peddled them *behind* Tonbridge Market,' the original speaker said. 'On her back in the bushes!'

Josse joined in with the general laughter. Anne couldn't have been totally unaware of the ribaldry, and she didn't seem to mind. Maybe the respectable trade of innkeeper which she now practised hadn't entirely ousted the odd foray into her former profession. He glanced at her. She was still comely, even if she was a little on the large side. Good luck to her, either way.

He drew back from the counter and found a place on the bench that ran around three walls of the tap room. The evening's company was quite well away now – it had, after all, been a hot and dusty day, and there was nothing like a draught of ale to soothe a rasping throat – and he listened to several conversations going on around him.

You would have thought, he reflected some time later, that there had never been a murder around here before. Surely it couldn't be that rare an occurrence? Tonbridge was a busy place, always had been. The market attracted all sorts, and there was the river, *and* the main London road, going plumb through the town. And only a few miles away was the Wealden Forest, and, as everyone knew, there were all manner of odd goings on in there. Even Josse, whose youthful spells in England had been spent a score or so miles away, knew of the forest's dark reputation. It was like all old places – its many former inhabitants had filled it with their own mysteries and legends, and nobody was prepared even to try to sort out fact from fiction.

Hawkenlye Abbey was on the fringes of the Wealden Forest. Were these men right, and was this murder simply a matter of a released criminal leaping on the first woman he came across, then fleeing into the sanctuary of the great tract of woodland?

Perhaps it was.

But passing judgement on that, Josse thought, is not what I'm here for. My job is to stop this whole sorry business tainting the start of King Richard's reign.

And how I'm going to manage that, the good Lord alone knows.

He sat on for another hour, sipping at his ale, not wanting to fuddle his wits by ordering a refill. Tempting though it was – Goody Anne, whatever she did when the lamps were out and nobody was looking, knew how to keep her beer.

Eventually, the company began to disperse. Few were thoroughly drunk, but most had consumed enough to make them garrulous. And, depressingly from Josse's point of view, few had a good word to say about the prospect of their new king.

How accurate an indicator was tap room gossip? Did it reflect what the population at large thought, or were more educated and thoughtful men reserving their judgement?

The thought provided a glimmer of hope, but, almost as soon as he'd come up with it, Josse dismissed it. There might very well be such wise and cautious men, yes, but they would undoubtedly be few in number. The great mass of the English people – the ones whom this whole exercise of Eleanor's and

Richard's had been designed to impress – were represented by the men who had been there in the tap room tonight.

Josse turned from that depressing conclusion to a plan of action for the next day. Stay on here in Tonbridge, and ask around some more? But that might bring his presence and his interest to the notice of the Clares. Did he want that?

No. If he were to fulfil King Richard's hopes, he ought to keep his head down. Work behind the scenes. Had Richard wanted a public investigation, he wouldn't have given the task to an outsider like Josse, he'd have sent word to the Clares to sort it out.

Josse put down his empty mug and got to his feet, nodding a goodnight to the few remaining drinkers. Climbing up to his room, he was relieved to find that the two other cots remained empty. He pulled off his boots and stripped off his clothes, slipping naked into bed and pulling up the light cover.

Then he blew out the lamp and closed his eyes.

He knew what he was going to do in the morning. He would ride up on to the ridge and locate Hawkenlye Abbey. One of the convent's nuns had been murdered, and he was ready, now, to go to the scene of the crime.

The men he had talked with and listened to that night had, although he was sure they didn't realise it, raised a number of questions, for which their hasty and simplistic version of what must have happened hadn't supplied answers. Josse let the questions float in his head for some minutes, turning them over, conjecturing a few possible solutions.

But it was too soon – far too soon – for solutions.

Deliberately emptying his mind, he turned over and was very soon falling asleep.

Chapter Three

The dead nun was named Gunnora. Her body had been taken back to Hawkenlye Abbey, and the infirmarer had done her best to disguise how she had died. With the wimple back in place, the dreadful slit throat was no longer visible, but it would have taken greater skill than the infirmarer possessed to do anything about the dead woman's terrified expression.

Abbess Helewise, emerging from the abbey church after her third session of kneeling in vigil beside the cadaver, wished the dead girl's family would hurry up and send word as to what should be done with the body. The coffin lid had been sealed now – thankfully – but, in this hot weather, the whole church, indeed the whole abbey, seemed to be corrupted with the stench of death.

It is not, Helewise said firmly to herself as she crossed the courtyard with brisk steps, good for morale. I shall have to do something about it.

It was all very well treating a grieving family with sympathetic tact – always assuming they *were* grieving, which was, Helewise had concluded, by no means certain. She had detected some strange attitudes there, in her dealings with them over Gunnora's admission to the convent. I have refrained from pressing them for a decision, Helewise thought, for possibly they themselves, in shock at this sudden death, do not yet know what they want to do. Whether it would be best to take their daughter home or leave her here with her sisters in God.

But there were others to consider. Helewise had a convent of living nuns in her charge, not to mention the monks in their nearby establishment and all those unfortunates of various stations who, for whatever reason, were temporarily accommodated at Hawkenlye, and she could not go on indefinitely allowing the very air they all breathed to be corrupted by the dead. And, when one looked at it practically – Helewise was very good at looking at things practically – the sooner Gunnora was decently buried, the sooner everyone could get over the horror of her murder and proceed with ordinary life.

Helewise ducked her head and left the bright sunshine of the courtyard, crossing the shady cloister and entering through the door in the corner that led to the small room where she conducted the business of the convent. Of Hawkenlye Abbey in its entirety, for she was not only the superior of her nuns, but also of the small group of monks who lived beside the holy spring a quarter of a mile away, down in the little valley beneath the convent.

She had held the post now for five years. She knew she suited the Abbey – false modesty was not one of Helewise's character traits – and she also knew that the Abbey suited her.

Frowning, she sat down at the long oak table which, at considerable effort and cost, she had brought with her from her former life, and, focusing her mind, began to go logically through the whole disturbing question of the life and death of the late Gunnora of Winnowlands.

The foundation at Hawkenlye was new, in terms of the construction of a major abbey, so new that it was still a blessed relief to be rid of the carpenters, stonemasons, and the endless crowd of workmen who, so it had seemed, were set on becoming as permanent a feature as the nuns and the monks. Building had begun in 1153, under the direct order of the new Queen of England, Eleanor of Aquitaine, and it had been because of a genuine miracle which had happened, right there on the very spot.

For time out of mind, there had been nothing more to Hawkenlye than a huddle of huts among the thinner tree growth at the edge of the great Wealden Forest. The forest was a lonely place, and many believed it to be haunted; there were tales of strange noises from the ancient iron workings, where men had laboured before history began, and more than one traveller lost down some long-forgotten track spoke of a phantom group of Roman soldiers who appeared to march off right through the trunks of a copse of birch trees . . .

Since the Romans had abandoned the old iron workings, little use had been made of the forest other than for the fattening of swine, on the abundant acorns and beech mast which littered the forest floor in autumn. The only time of year that the area could be called busy was the seven-week period between the autumn equinox and the feast of St Martin, when the woodlands were uncharacteristically crowded with people fattening their livestock before slaughtering them for winter provisions.

Into this strange and deserted place, on a hot day early one summer, came a band of French merchants, who had been on their way from Hastings to London when they were overcome by a mysterious sickness. They had been ill during the crossing from France, but, believing it to be nothing more than *mal de mer*, had proceeded towards London. By the time the group reached the ridge about the Medway Vale, however, all five were incapable of going any further. Delirious with fever, they were suffering excruciating pains in the limbs, and two of them had developed swellings in the groin. Their companions, terrified of contagion, found them what shelter there was in the primitive settlement at Hawkenlye, then abandoned them.

The Frenchmen were on the point of giving themselves up into the Almighty's hands when, to their amazement, they began to recover. They had been drinking from a little spring in a shallow valley near to where they had been left, a spring whose water was reddish, slightly brackish. And the least sick of the merchants, who had undertaken the arduous task of bringing water back to his companions, had a vision. Still burning with fever, head throbbing and sight blurred, he thought he saw a woman standing over him, on the bank out of which the spring flowed. She was dressed in blue, and in her long white hands she carried lilies. She smiled at the merchant, and he seemed to hear her praise him for his devoted care of his friends; giving them the spring water, she said, was the best cure.

The merchants, naturally, told their story far and wide. The more entrepreneurial of those who heard it set out for Hawkenlye, and soon a brisk trade sprang up in phials of the miracle water. The Church, alarmed both at the lack of reverence being shown in the face of a true miracle, and at the loss of potential revenue to themselves, stepped in and built a shrine over the spring, with a small dwelling nearby to accommodate the monks who were to tend it.

Rumour of the wonderful appearance of the Virgin Mary, in an obscure glade in the faraway Wealden Forest, reached the great Abbey of Fontevraud, on the Loire close to Queen Eleanor's home town of Poitiers. The Queen's strong links with Fontevraud stimulated her ambition to create similar communities elsewhere, and, at her coronation in May 1152, she was already planning the first English abbey on the Fontevraud model.

Synchronism is a strange phenomenon, with an intrinsic power which often leads to the irresistible belief that certain things are *meant*. Thus it was for Eleanor, who first received pressure from Fontevraud to adopt this fledgling community at Hawkenlye in the name of the mother house – for was this not most suitable, Fontevraud also being dedicated to the Blessed Virgin? – at the very time when, just crowned Henry II's Queen, she had the power to do so.

Hawkenlye Abbey was spectacular; both Eleanor and the Fontevraud community saw to that. The abbey church and the nuns' house, up on top of the ridge, were designed by a French architect and built by French stonemasons; the *pièce de résistance* of the master mason was the tympanum over the church's main doors. In common with many of his fellow craftsmen, he requested, and was granted, permission to adopt the theme of the Last Judgement; few who gazed upon his creation remained unmoved by its power.

In the centre of the domed space sat Christ in majesty, pierced hand raised, expression a combination of sorrow and severity. The blessed ones advanced towards him on his right, the Holy Virgin Mary leading them, St Peter ushering them gently along from the rear, sun, moon and stars above them bathing them in the heavenly light of righteousness. Angels blowing trumpets played a fanfare, as if welcoming the good to the eternal reward of being in the presence of God.

On Christ's left were the damned.

If the promised joys of heaven were not sufficient to persuade the sinful to mend their ways, then surely the picture of hell as depicted in the Hawkenlye tympanum would have done the trick. Satan's kingdom, in the eye of the master mason, was a place of unbelievable torment, with a particular torture, chosen for its appropriateness, reserved for each of the Seven Deadly Sins. Pride was personified by a king, naked but for his crown, being forced to walk on burning coals by two demons with pitchforks; Lust by a curvaceous woman whose breasts were being gnawed by rats whilst serpents slithered into her groin. Gluttony, rotund and fat-buttocked, was upturned into a barrel of excrement; Anger, face contorted with rage and agony, had his skull prised open and his brains sucked out by hunchbacked devils. Envy and Avarice, too busy coveting the worthless riches of others to look behind them, were on the point of being flayed alive by a quartet of demons with ropes and sharp knives in their long-taloned hands. Sloth, fast asleep on a pile of faggots, was bound by a fanged devil while another put flames to his pyre.

Tactfully, the Abbey's founders also employed local workmen alongside the imported Frenchmen. English wood-carvers, working with sound English oak, beautified the abbey church interior with their craft, and, kept under lock and key in the Treasury, was an English-made carving in walrus ivory of the dead Christ supported by Joseph of Arimathea, said to have been a secret gift from Eleanor herself. The shrine down in the vale also received loving attention, and even the simple lodgings of the nuns and monks were made adequately comfortable.

The new abbey was to be headed by an abbess.

There was considerable opposition to this novel concept, not least from the monks in the vale. But the precedent had been set, and set, moreover, in the community at Fontevraud. Founded by the Breton reformer Robert d'Arbrissel, who, among other revolutionary ideas, believed in the supremacy of women, Fontevraud had fought for and won its right to appoint an abbess almost a hundred years previously. And d'Arbrissel had been proved right; were not women, because of their experience in raising children and running homes, far better organisers than men? Should it, then, have surprised anyone that the same skills required for a noblewoman in charge of her husband's great estates adapted perfectly to running an abbey?

The Hawkenlye opposition did not stand much of a chance, and even that evaporated when Queen Eleanor herself paid a visit. A handful of senior nuns with the temperament and the experience to run her new abbey had been suggested to her, and she had made her choice with customary decisiveness and speed. Her first appointee was a success, so was her second. By 1184, when the need arose to select a fourth abbess, the precedent was established; Eleanor spared time from her busy schedule to return to Hawkenlye and view the shortlisted nuns, and she made her selection within minutes of meeting the successful candidate.

Helewise Warin, thirty-two years old, was as enchanted by Queen Eleanor as Eleanor was by her. From the moment of her appointment onwards, Helewise made up her mind that she would be the most efficient, most effective abbess that Hawkenlye had ever had.

This determination arose, to a large extent, from a laudable desire not to let the Queen down, not to make her, even for a moment, regret her choice.

But it also arose from Helewise's pride.

Pride had no place in a nun, she was well aware. And was she not reminded of the penalty, every time she entered the church and looked up at the Last Judgement tympanum? But, reasoned her intellect – another quality which a nun ought to suppress, especially when it was at war with obedience and humility – I am no longer merely a nun. I am an abbess, with an immediate community of nearly a hundred sisters, fifteen monks and twenty lay brothers dependent on me, and, in addition to them, the secular population of this small but thriving little place.

If pride led to her doing the job well, Helewise concluded, then proud she would be. The good of the community would undoubtedly benefit from her resolve not to let either the Queen or herself down. And if that pride was a dirty stain on her soul which earned her prolonged aeons naked and walking on flames in purgatory, then that was a price she would just have to pay.

Perhaps some kind soul would remember her in their prayers or have a Mass or two said for her.

Josse obtained directions for Hawkenlye Abbey. They were fairly vague, but he realised as he reached the summit of the rise that they had been quite adequate; from there, he could see the tall sloping roof of the Abbey church, and from then on, it was easy.

Nearing the entrance, he looked about him. The forest crept almost up to the road on his left-hand side, but on the right, the trees and undergrowth had been cleared. Some of the land was under cultivation, some was pasture. A small flock of sheep raised nervous heads as he rode by, and he noticed a nanny goat tethered to a post, a well-grown kid running around her. In the distance, where the cleared land gave way once more to the surrounding forest, he caught sight of a huddle of dwellings, from one of which a thin spire of smoke rose up into the still morning air.

The pasture land fell away into a narrow valley, in which Josse could see the roof of a small building with a large cross rising from one end. Beside the building was another one, longer and lower. From what he had been told of the Hawkenlye community, he guessed these must be the shrine of Our Lady's spring and the monks' house.

He was nearing the imposing gates of the Abbey. As he drew level with the enclosing wall, a nun emerged from a small room let into a corner tower, and demanded to know his name and his business.

He was prepared for this. Nobody required to know your identity or your bona fides when you checked into an inn in a market town, but riding into a convent was different. Reaching inside his tunic, he took out the papers which King Richard's secretary had issued. One of them bore Richard's personal seal.

It was enough for the porteress, who bobbed a sort of curtsey and said, 'You'll be wanting Abbess Helewise, I shouldn't wonder,' at the same time pointing towards a cloistered courtyard adjacent to the great Abbey church. 'You'll find her in there. Get one of them to show you the way.'

Them, he realised, meant a group of three nuns gliding from the cloister in the direction of the church. Nodding his thanks to the porteress, he dismounted, and, leading his horse, approached the nuns, one of whom took his horse's reins in a tentative and evidently reluctant hand, while another undertook to show him to the Abbess's room.

Looking all about him while trying not to make it obvious, he followed.

His guide whispered, 'Who shall I say?'

He told her.

Moving ahead of him with a small gesture of apology, the nun entered the courtyard under an archway, crossed the cloister and opened a door. She murmured something to the sole occupant of the room, but her voice was too quiet for Josse to make out the words. She beckoned Josse inside, then, her task completed, sidled past him and closed the door.

Abbess Helewise had looked up as the nun spoke. Now, as Josse stood before her, she sat perfectly still, studying him. Her face, framed in starched white beneath the black veil, was strong-featured, with well-marked eyebrows, large grey eyes, and a wide mouth which looked as if it smiled readily.

But she was not smiling now.

If he hadn't known it was impossible, he'd almost have said she was waiting for him; there was no suprise in the calm face, no expression of enquiry in the eyes.

'Josse d'Acquin,' she said, presumably repeating what her nun had said. 'And what, Josse d'Acquin, do you wish of us?'

He presented his papers and allowed them to speak for him. If Abbess Helewise was as impressed by the royal seal as her porteress, she gave no indication, but, opening up the letter which it secured, read right through it.

Then, folding it and smoothing it with a surprisingly square and strong-looking hand – somehow Josse had imagined nuns' hands to be invariably pale and long, more suitable to prayer than to cracking walnuts – she looked up at him.

And said, 'I had imagined someone like you would arrive, sooner or later. You wish, I have no doubt, that I tell you what I know of Gunnora of Winnowlands?'

'I do, madam.' Was that the right form of address for an abbess? If it wasn't, she didn't seem to mind.

Her face, tense with some inner strain, suddenly relaxed, and for an instant she almost smiled. 'Please, my lord knight, sit. May I offer you refreshment?' She reached for a small brass bell. 'It is' – now the smile was unmistakable – 'a long way from the court of King Richard.'

'I have not come direct from there.' He returned the smile, pulling up the indicated chair and seating himself. 'But, aye, refreshment would be welcome.' Another of Josse's soldierly habits was never to refuse food or drink when it was offered, on the grounds that you never knew when it was going to be offered again.

Abbess Helewise rang her bell, and asked the nun who responded to bring ale and bread. When these had been served – the bread was warm and unexpectedly delicious, and there was a sliver of some strong cheese with it which Josse guessed was goat – the Abbess began to speak.

'Gunnora had been with us a little under a year,' she said, 'and I cannot say that her admission to our community was entirely a success. She appeared to be devout, spoke with fervour, at our first meeting, of the certainty of her vocation. But—' The dark eyebrows drew together. 'But something was lacking. Something did not ring true.' She glanced at Josse, and, again, there was the faint smile. 'You will no doubt ask me to elaborate, and I fear I cannot. Except to say that, in general, Gunnora had the wrong character for convent life. She said the right things, but they did not come from the heart. As a consequence, she did not really fit in with us, and, knowing this, naturally, she was not happy.' Instantly correcting herself, she said, 'Did not *appear* to be happy, rather, for she confided neither in me nor, as far as I know, in any of her sisters.'

'I see.' He tried to absorb the rapid thumbnail sketch of the dead nun, and failed. He was having a problem of adjustment: until this moment, she had been just that, a dead nun. Now, suddenly, she was a person. Not a very happy person. 'Did she have any particular friends?' he asked, more for something to say than any real desire to know. Was it relevant if she did have?

'No.' Abbess Helewise didn't hesitate. 'Well, not, that is, until—'

She was interrupted by a knock on the door, followed almost instantly by the arrival of a plump nun of about fifty. 'Abbess Helewise, I'm so sorry to barge in on you, but – oh. Sorry.'

Blushing a hot, embarrassed red, the nun backed out of the room.

'May I present my infirmarer, Sister Euphemia,' the Abbess said calmly. 'Euphemia, come back in. This is Josse d'Acquin.' Josse stood up and bowed. 'He has come from the Plantagenet court. He wishes to hear what we may be able to tell him of poor Gunnora.'

'He does?' The infirmarer's eyes rounded 'Why?'

Abbess Helewise glanced at Josse, as if to say, shall I tell her or will you? Receiving no response, she said, 'Because, Euphemia, King Richard has doubly a need to understand what lies behind her murder. For one thing, she was of our community here at Hawkenlye, and his mother the Queen Eleanor has close contacts with our house. For another, it was in order to perpetrate the good and clement reputation of our new sovereign that a number of prisoners were released from jail, one of whom, it seems likely, committed this outrage on our sister.'

Josse could not recall either reason having been expressed in the papers from Richard's court. His opinion of Abbess Helewise rose.

The infirmarer was looking increasingly distressed. 'Abbess, it's about the poor lass that I need to speak to you! Only . . .' She looked pointedly at Josse.

'I'll wait outside,' he said.

'No,' Abbess Helewise said, in a tone that suggested she was used to people doing what she said. 'Whatever Euphemia has to say, I shall only have to repeat to you. You had better hear it from her own lips. Euphemia?'

Josse felt sorry for the infirmarer, who had clearly neither expected nor wanted an audience of more than the Abbess. 'It's not easy,' she hedged.

'I am sure it is not.' The Abbess was relentless. 'Please, try.'

'I *know* I shouldn't have done it,' the infirmarer burst out, 'and it's been on my conscience ever since. I can bear it no longer, truly I can't, believe me! I've just got to tell someone. I'll confess and do penance, I don't mind, it'll be such a relief. Whatever I'm told to do, I'll do it, with a good grace, no matter how harsh it is!'

'Quite,' the Abbess said when the infirmarer at last paused for breath. 'Now, what shouldn't you have done?'

'Shouldn't have gone looking at her, examining her. Only I meant well, really I did, and anyway, I let my curiosity get the better of me.'

'How?' asked the Abbess patiently. 'I think you had better explain, Euphemia. You speak of Gunnora?'

'Of course! I said, didn't I? I was laying her out – oh! Terrible it was, that great wound in her poor throat, made me fair weep, I can tell you.'

'You did well,' the Abbess said, more warmly. 'It cannot have been a pleasant task.'

'That it wasn't! Anyway, when I'd tidied her up at the top end, I thought I ought to—' she paused delicately.

'Go on, Euphemia,' the Abbess said. 'Our visitor is aware, I'm sure, of the other outrage perpetrated on our late sister. You were saying, you went on to wash the cuts and abrasions caused by the rape, and—'

'That's just it! There wasn't any rape!' interrupted the infirmarer.

'What?' The Abbess and Josse spoke the word together. 'There must have been,' the Abbess went on, 'the thighs and the groin were drenched in blood.'

'You must be mistaken,' Josse said gently. 'It's quite understandable, Sister Euphemia, after all, it must have been an appalling job.'

'I'm not mistaken.' Euphemia spoke with dignity. 'Sir, I may not know much, but I do know the female genitalia. I was a midwife, afore I entered the cloister, and I've seen more vaginas than you've had hot suppers. Oh!' Belatedly remembering where she was, she blushed again, a hand to her mouth. 'Forgive me, Abbess Helewise,' she muttered from behind it, 'I didn't mean to sound coarse.'

'I am sure you didn't,' Abbess Helewise said graciously. 'Continue. You were explaining to us your familiarity with the private parts of the female anatomy.'

'Yes, that I was. Well, see, the hymen was still there. In full, like.' Euphemia paused, but nobody spoke. 'She was *virgo intacta* when she died, Abbess. Nobody'd raped her, not then, not ever.'

'But the blood?' Josse said. 'What about the blood?'

'It came from her throat, I reckon,' Euphemia said quietly. 'Whoever did for her, he scooped up the blood from her cut neck and smeared it on her – smeared it down there. Left her there, skirts up over her belly, legs all open, covered in blood.'

There was silence in the room as they all thought about that.

Then the Abbess said, 'Someone killed her, and made it seem as though he had also raped her.'

'Because,' Josse added, 'murder and murder plus rape are two different crimes.'

The Abbess looked up and met his eye. Nodding slowly, she said, 'Two very different crimes.'

Chapter Four

'And now, if you please, Abbess Helewise,' Josse said when, Sister Euphemia having gone back to her infirmary, they were once more alone, 'I should be grateful if you would tell me everything you can recall of Gunnora's last hours.'

Helewise wondered if he had intended to sound so pompous. Studying him, observing the slight tension evident in the way he leaned forward in his seat, she decided in his favour. The man was nervous – perhaps uneasy at being inside a convent, it did affect some people that way, especially men – and his anxiety had given rise to an overformal tone of voice.

He was also, she had noticed, considerably too large for the delicate little chair he was sitting on. Well, it was hardly more than a stool, really, all right for a lightly built woman but not equal to the task of supporting a tall and broad-shouldered man. One, moreover, who appeared to have an innate restlessness, so that, trying to keep still on his inadequate seat, the effort was readily apparent.

It was up to her, Helewise decided, to put him at his ease. With that in mind, she arranged her face in what her late husband had been wont to refer to as her despot-after-a-good-dinner expression. Smiling benevolently at her visitor, she noticed brief alarm, quickly replaced by a tentative answering smile.

Oh, dear. Perhaps dear old Ivo had been right about the despot.

'How much do you know about the daily routine of a convent, my lord d'Acquin?' she began. 'I ask because, without a working knowledge of our life, it will be more difficult for you to remark on any oddities in Gunnora's final days.'

'I understand. Madam, I know little other than that your hours are determined by the saying of the offices, and that your prayers intercede with Almighty God on behalf of all mankind.'

It was nicely said, and she inclined her head in recognititon. 'Indeed, we follow the discipline of the Divine Offices, throughout the twenty-four hours of the day. Our rule, like that of the great foundation at Fontevraud, is modelled on the Benedictine Rule, although there are certain significant modifications. However, we are not like a strictly enclosed order, in that prayer within our own house is not our sole occupation. We serve the community in other ways.'

'As I was escorted in, I saw a sister helping a man to accustom himself to walking with a crutch,' Josse said. 'And I could be wrong, but I thought I heard a baby cry.'

An observant man, this Josse d'Acquin, Helewise thought, to have noticed so much in the brief seconds it would have taken him to cross from the gates to the cloister. 'You were not wrong. We run a hospital here, in the long wing beside the church. Sister Beata, whom you saw, has been caring for a poacher who lost his foot in a man trap. We also have a wing for the care and rehabilitation of penitential whores. It would perhaps surprise you, sir, to know how many former harlots are redeemed by motherhood into the wish for a purer life.'

'I am happy to hear it.' He appeared to have detected a reproof in her tone, which she had not intended, for he went on, 'I did not wish to sound as if I were prying, Abbess Helewise, when I mentioned the baby – it was merely that the sound surprised me.' In a convent, hung unsaid on the air.

'Please, there is no need for explanations.' She smiled at him again, this time more genuinely. 'One of the girls in our care gave birth last week. We, too, are still sometimes taken aback at the sweet sounds of her baby.'

'A hospital and a reformatory,' he said, visibly relaxing now. 'You have much work here at Hawkenlye.'

More than you think, she thought. Would it appear prideful to tell him the rest? Perhaps. But then she would be speaking for her sisters, who did the hard work. Who deserved recognition. 'We also run a retirement home for aged and infirm monks and nuns, and a small leper hospital.' He reacted to the last, as people inevitably did, and she said what she always said by way of reassurance. 'Do not be alarmed, sir. The leper house is isolated from the community, and we are fortuante in that three of our sisters elected of their own free will to be enclosed with the sick. They, and those of their charges who are able, join in with the spiritual life of the community by way of a closed-off passage leading to a separate chapel, which backs on to a side aisle of the church. You are no more in danger of contagion here than in the world at large, possibly less so, since our nursing sisters are expert at detecting the early symptoms of leprosy. If they have the least suspicion, the patient is put in a separate holding ward until—' No. No need to go into the clinical details. 'Well, until the sisters are sure.'

He was shaking his head, had been doing so for the last few seconds of her speech. 'Abbess, you misunderstand. My response to what you were telling me was not one of fear or horror.' He paused, then amended, 'Not entirely so, anyway. I cannot claim to be any more immune to the dread of the sickness than the next man. But actually what was passing through my mind was what a heavy burden of work you and your sisters bear. What a responsibility is yours.'

She stared hard at him, but could detect no insincerity, no attempt to flatter her, win her over. 'My nuns and I are greatly helped by the lay brothers, who live with the monks down beside the shrine,' she said. Credit where it was due. 'They are good men. Unlearned, but strong and willing. They remove from us the need to weary ourselves with hard labour.'

'I did not know about them,' Josse said. 'I was only told of the monks, who care, I believe, for the spring where the holy water flows.'

'Indeed they do.' She was careful to keep her tone neutral. No need to reveal to this sharp-eyed visitor that one of her most persistent problems was with the fifteen monks in the vale, who appeared to think that living so close to Our Lady's blessed shrine gave them an aura of holiness that everyone else ought to revere. A holiness that, so they seemed to believe, gave them immunity from hard work. They were, in Brother Firmin's own words, the Marys, adoring the Lord, or in this case His Holy Mother, while the Marthas – Helewise and her nuns – got on with being 'busy with many things'.

Instead she went on, 'You appreciate, my lord d'Acquin, the reason for our hospitals and homes?'

'Aye. You have a healing spring in your Abbey.'

'Yes. And, according to tradition, the original sick merchant to whom the Blessed Virgin appeared – you are aware of the story?' He nodded. 'The merchant said that Our Lady praised him for giving the spring water to his fevered companions, and she told him it was the best possible cure.'

'The monks, then, tend the spring,' Josse summarised.

'Yes. They see to the immediate needs of those who come to take the water. They provide shelter from the sun or the rain, a warm fire when it is cold, benches to sit on, simple lodgings for those who wish to stay overnight. They collect the water in jugs and pour it into the pilgrims' cups. They also provide spiritual counsel for those in need.'

Josse caught her eye. She knew what he was going to say before he said it. 'It sounds a relatively undemanding life, compared with that of your sisters,' he remarked.

He had picked up what she had tried so hard to ensure that he didn't. I must, she told herself sternly, be even more careful not to allow my resentments to show. 'The monks work devotedly,' she said, filling the words with sincerity.

He was still watching her, and the brown eyes held a certain compassion. 'I don't doubt it.'

There was a moment of silence, during which Helewise felt the very beginning of a sympathy between them.

Then Josse d'Acquin said, 'You have, Abbess, given me a

most clear picture of life at Hawkenlye Abbey. I think, now, that I am ready to ask again if you would tell me what you can of Gunnora's final hours here.'

Helewise sat back in her chair, and, after a moment to collect her thoughts, turned her mind back to that day, remarkable, surely, because, although it had been Gunnora's last on earth and the precursor to that terrible death, yet it had been so very *un*-remarkable.

'Gunnora had, as I believe I told you, been with us not quite a year,' she began. 'This means that she was still a novice. During a sister's first year, we prefer her to spend more time at her devotions than engaging in the practical work of the sisterhood – it is important, we feel, to ensure that our nuns are firmly secure in the spiritual life of the community. Trials and rigours lie before them, and we wish to armour them for the test by helping them to become safe in the Lord.'

'I understand,' Josse said. 'It sounds very wise. Besides, a year is not long.'

'Indeed not. There is much for a novice to learn.'

He twisted on his flimsy seat, making as if to cross his long legs; again, she had a sudden vivid impression of energy kept under strict control. The stool gave a squeak of protest, and Josse arrested the movement, slowly and carefully replacing his foot on the floor. Bringing her mind back – not without difficulty – to the matter under discussion, she heard him say, 'You also commented earlier that Gunnora wasn't really suited to convent life,' he said. 'Could you elaborate?'

'I did not mean to sound judgemental,' Helewise said quickly. Dear Lord, but she had. 'Only it seemed to me that Gunnora struggled more than most with the tenets of a nun's life.' He was still wearing his enquiring expression. 'Poverty, obedience, chastity,' she said. 'Different sisters have difficulty with each of those three. Young women who come to us in their late teens and early twenties have to fight a natural inclination towards the strong demands of the flesh, and older women who enter the Order after a life as a wealthy man's wife find it very hard to sleep on a plank bed and wear the plain black habit.

Many, if not all, of us find constant and total unquestioning obedience a heavy cross to carry.' She paused. 'Gunnora, God rest her soul, while not, I think, having problems with chastity, never ceased to fight poverty and obedience. So consistent were her infringements against the Rule that I find it virtually impossible to say with any honesty that she had made much progress in a twelvemonth.' She met Josse's eye. 'Soon she should have been taking the first of her final vows. I was not going to permit it, sir. I was going to tell her, as gently as I could, that I did not consider her ready.' Again, she hesitated. Would it be disloyal to go on? But then Gunnora was dead. And, to find out the why and the how, this man needed to know the whole truth. She added softly, 'And that, in my view, she never would be.'

He accepted that without comment. But she knew he had heard, knew he had understood the significance. His contemplative silence went on for several moments, then he said, 'And that last day, presumably, had its share of infringements?'

'Presumably, although they would not necessarily all have come to my notice straightaway, unless I happened to observe them. Gunnora was present at each Divine Office, outwardly one of the community, yet, as ever, giving that sense, that strong sense, that her thoughts were elsewhere.' She leaned towards him, trying to put across what she had perceived of Gunnora in terms that would have meaning for one who had not known the girl. 'Sir, she was here at her own wish, yet always you felt she considered she was imparting a great gift by favouring us with her presence. When things went well with her – and it would be wrong to suggest they never did – she would adopt a particular expression. A sort of superior smile, as if she were saying, there, I *can* do it if I so choose. And, if one of the senior sisters uttered even so much as a mild reproof, Gunnora would receive it with a face cut out of stone. There was clear resentment in her very immobility.'

Josse nodded. 'Aye. What in a soldier would be called dumb insubordination.'

'Yes!' The phrase fitted perfectly.

'She had few friends, I believe you said?'

'I did, although in truth the concept of friends is not one we recognise here. Partiuclar associations are discouraged, since it is too easy for a group of two or three close friends to exclude others, ignore the social needs of less outgoing sisters. However, what you say is right in essence. Gunnora was rarely sought out in recreation, rarely the first one to be chosen if a sister required a companion for an excursion outside the Abbey. Until shortly before her death, I would have judged that she spent most of her time in the secrecy of her own thoughts, and that it was precisely where she preferred to be.'

'What happened to change that?' Josse prompted.

'The arrival of a new postulant. She and Gunnora took to each other, although it seems hard to imagine why, when they were so different. Elvera is a lively young woman, and I am at present entertaining doubts as to whether what she has is truly a call from God, or a romantic notion that she cuts a dashing figure in a habit, administering holy water to the grateful sick.' She met Josse's eye, echoing his smile. 'It happens, sir. Out of the many girls and women who ask for admittance each year, at least a quarter eventually decide that the call existed only in their imagination.'

'What do you do with them?' He sounded genuinely interested. If, as seemed likely, he had been in command of men, then it followed that he would be interested in such delicate matters of administration.

'Everyone who comes knocking on the door is allowed entry, but at first all we undertake is to admit them for a trial period of six weeks, during which they are free to leave at any time. With the totally unsuitable, it usually takes no more than a fortnight. When the six weeks are up, those still with us are admitted as postulants, and their training as nuns begins. Six months later, they take a simplified form of the vows and become novices. If, after a year, all has gone well, they then take the first of their permanent vows.'

'And how long, Abbess, do you give this Elvera?'

She permitted herself a brief laugh. 'She may not even last the day.'

'Don't allow her to go till I've spoken to her,' he said quickly. 'If that's allowed?'

'Yes.' She did not think she needed to ask him why he wanted to talk to Elvera; he would no doubt tell her.

She was right.

'They were friends, you say, these two?' She nodded. 'So, a woman who had been quite content with her own company for nearly a twelvemonth suddenly becomes close to an apparently quite unsuitable new arrival. How new was she?'

'She has been here almost a month. She and Gunnora had known each other a little over a week.'

'Brief, for the birth of such an unlikely liaison.'

'It was. But already I had had to remind Gunnora several times that she must not seek out the girl so blatantly. And, the very morning of the day she died, I overheard Gunnora and Elvera laughing.'

'Laughing.'

Something about the way he said it suggested he had misunderstood. 'We don't forbid laughter,' she said gently. 'Only, as in every other walk of life, there is a time and a place. Yes?'

'Yes.'

'And by the hospital, outside the room where a grieving husband sits beside his dying wife, is not the place for girlish giggling.'

'No. Of *course* it isn't.' He sounded appalled. 'Gunnora, at least, should have had more self control, she'd been with you long enough, surely, for that?'

'She had.' The incident, small but distressing, was, Helewise thought, a perfect illustration of what she had been trying to put across. Gunnora abided by her own rules. Lived inside her head, and did not appear even to notice the needs of others.

Josse was muttering something. Noticing her eyes on him, he said, 'You reproved her, for the laughter?'

'Not I. But Sister Beata rushed out to hush the pair of them, shoo them away, and Sister Euphemia heard the disturbance. She, I understand, administered something of a tongue-lashing.

She cares deeply, sir, for her patients. And for the good reputation of her hospital.'

'I don't doubt it. And what of the rest of that day?'

'Gunnora's face took on its stoniest expression, and there was a dramatic air of suffering about the way she deliberately distanced herself from Elvera, from all of us, in fact. It was extraordinary' – Helewise was quite surprised to find herself making the admission – 'but she had the gift of actually making her accuser feel guilty, even when, as in this case, she was totally in the wrong, and whoever had remonstrated with her did so with every justification.'

'So, she spoke to no one during the evening?'

'I think not. I cannot speak for the entire evening, for I did not observe her continually. But I sat near to her at supper and opposite her at recreation, and she utterly rejected any attempt to draw her into conversation. She seemed relieved, in fact, when the bell summoned us to Compline and, immediately afterwards, to bed.'

'And no one ever talks after going to bed?'

'No. Never. Contact between one nun and another is not permitted in the dormitory.' No need, she was sure, to explain why.

'And no one ever gets up, wanders about, leaves the dormitory?'

'No. The answering of calls of nature is accomplished within each sister's curtained recess.'

'Ah.' He reddened slightly. 'Abbess, I apologise for these questions which touch on delicate matters so private to your community. But—'

'I understand the need. Go on.'

'Would anyone have heard a sister get out of bed? Leave the dormitory?'

She considered. 'I would have said yes, but I may be wrong. Our days are long, sir, and most of us fall asleep quickly and stay that way until we are called, first at midnight for Matins, and then at daybreak for Prime.'

'Gunnora was present at midnight?'

'She was. And absent for Prime, when the alarm was raised and the search parties sent out.'

'She left, then, in the small hours.' He closed his eyes, apparently as an aid to visualising the scene. 'Let us say that, intending this nocturnal expedition, she returned to her recess after the midnight office and made sure she stayed awake. Perhaps lay down fully dressed, so as not to risk making a noise when she rose again. Would anyone have noticed if she did that?'

'No. We do not peer into each other's sleeping areas. And, besides, the candles are blown out as soon as we are back in the dormitory.'

'So. Gunnora waited until everyone was asleep, then moved silently along the dormitory, past all the sleeping sisters, and—'

'Not all of them. Gunnora's cubicle was three from the door.'

'I see. She opened the door, and—'

'No, it was propped open. It was a very hot night, and we had elected to leave the door open so as to get a little more air into the dormitory.'

'Ah. Hm.' Again, the closed eyes. 'Abbess, might I be permitted to look inside the dormitory?'

She had known he would ask. She replied simply, 'Yes.'

She guessed what he was going to do. He asked her to arrange the long room — now quite empty — as it had been that night. She did so, propping the door with the same stone and arranging the flimsy hangings around the first few cubicles. The tidiness and immaculate order pleased her; she was glad this wasn't a day when some sister, in a hurry, had left her bedding even slightly disarrayed. Then she showed him where Gunnora had slept. He stepped inside the adjacent cubicle, and let the thin curtain fall again.

'Now, if you would be so kind?' he asked.

She went into Gunnora's cubicle. It was disturbing, to be where the girl had spent her last, lonely hours. She removed her shoes, then waited, making herself count to fifty. Then, as silently as she could, she tweaked up the hanging, slid under it and tiptoed along the dormitory and out of the door. She knew, as did all the nuns, that the third of the wooden stairs tended to creak, so she stepped straight from the second to the fourth. Then, still with exaggerated caution, she went on down to ground level.

She had just put her shoes back on when, some minutes later, Josse appeared at the top of the short flight of steps.

'I didn't hear you,' he said. 'I had my eyes shut, and I called out to you, and you didn't answer, so I knew you'd gone. I didn't hear a thing,' he repeated, 'and *I* was wide awake! I was listening out for you!'

'I know.' She felt strangely excited, affected by this small discovery that it was perfectly possible for someone to leave the dormitory unheard. She said, genuinely wanting to know, 'What now?'

The light in his face drained away, and he said sombrely, 'Now, please, you show me where she was found.'

Helewise led him out of the rear gate of the convent. It gave on to the track that wound down into the vale; after only a few yards, the rooftops of the shrine and the monks' house came into view. Soon after that, she branched off on to a lesser-used track, which became steeper as it neared the valley floor.

She had not been down here since they'd found Gunnora.

'She lay there.' Helewise pointed. 'Just off the path. Right in the open, which was odd.'

'Yes,' he agreed. 'You'd have thought whoever killed her might have tried to hide the body. A belated discovery of the murder surely would have helped him, if only to give him longer to get away.'

'It was more than not hiding her,' Helewise said slowly. 'It looked for all the world as if he'd been quite determined we would find her. She'd been – *arranged*.' It was the best word she could think of.

'Arranged,' he repeated.

'Her arms and legs made a sort of star pattern' – oh, it was hard, remembering! – 'and it seemed that some trouble had been taken to make the shape as perfect as possible.'

'Dreadful,' he muttered. 'Callous, and quite horrible.'

She didn't want to, but she knew she must tell him the rest. 'Her skirts were folded back so neatly. I noticed that.' Realising her omission, she said, 'I did not find her – two of the lay brothers did, only a matter of minutes after the search began. I was just coming down from the Abbey, and I heard them shout. I was the third one to look on her.'

'I see.' His voice held compassion. 'Go on. You were telling me about her skirt.'

'Yes.' She swallowed. 'The skirt and underskirt had been folded as one, and there were three folds. The first raised the garments to knee level, the second to thigh level, the third placed them across her belly. She was, as I think you know, naked from the waist down. And covered in blood.'

Her voice was shaking. She clenched her teeth, hoping he wouldn't ask her anything else until she had recovered her equanimity.

He didn't. Instead, he wandered slowly around the place where Gunnora had been found. It was impossible even for Helewise, who had seen her, to say exactly where the dead girl had lain; the small amount of blood that had trickled down into the grass had been ground in by the many boot and shoe soles that had trampled the scene. It was not, then, immediately clear what Josse was gaining from his long perusal. Perhaps he was just giving her some time.

Eventually he returned to stand beside her.

'There was something about a cross, a jewelled cross?' he asked quietly.

'Yes. They found it there, at the bend in the path.' She pointed.

'A rape that wasn't, and a stolen cross that was thrown away. Although it is difficult to see why, unless it was by accident, since the murderer was not being pursued.'

'Not by us,' Helewise said. 'It is possible that someone else saw him.'

'Someone who prefers not to advertise his presence here in the dead of night?'

'Quite.'

'Hm,' he said. And, again, walking a few paces away, 'Hmmm.'

She said, 'About the cross.'

He turned, alert eyes on her. 'Yes?'

'It wasn't Gunnora's. It was very similar to hers, same gold mounting, same size and colour of ruby. But Gunnora gave hers to me a few months ago, and asked instead to wear a cross of plain wood.'

'She did? Why?'

That was easy. 'As a demonstration of poverty, I think.' A very ostentatious show, Helewise had thought privately at the time, and not a very useful one since Gunnora had specifically asked Helewise to put the cross away safely for her. It would have been more convincing had she asked her Abbess to sell the pretty thing and use the proceeds for the poor.

'So she would not have been wearing her own jewelled cross when she died?'

'No.' It was still secure in Helewise's cabinet; she had checked. Now the other one, that was found beside her, was there with it. 'The wooden cross was still round her neck, but it had somehow slipped under her scapula. Probably only another nun would have thought to look for it.'

'A rape that wasn't,' Josse repeated thoughtfully, 'and, now, a theft that wasn't.' He stared at Helewise. 'Abbess, all we seem to be left with is murder.'

Chapter Five

They walked side by side back up the slope to the Abbey, on its ridge. He did not have to shorten his stride greatly; she was a tall woman.

Seen from this side, the Abbey presented a less stoutly walled aspect. Well, Josse reflected, that was understandable; the entrance through which he had first arrived faced the road, and, even if traffic was light, establishments of the size and prestige of Hawkenlye Abbey usually marked out their territory behind high walls and a solid gate that could be locked and barred at night.

Coming up from the pleasant green vale whose tranquillity had so recently been violated, however, the Abbey appeared less formidable, and the gate did not appear, Josse thought, to be any great deterrent to someone determined to break in. That, too, was understandable, since a section of the Abbey's community lived down there in the valley, and, presumably, required fairly free access to the main foundation.

Nevertheless, it was food for thought.

He stared up at the Abbey as they neared the gate. Now that he had been inside, he could piece together the layout of the various buildings. From down here, as from the road, the roof of the church dominated; running along one side of the church was what he now knew to be the hospital wing. On the other side was the long room where the nuns slept. It was sightly taller than the hospital wing; he recalled the short flight of steps he and the Abbess had climbed to reach the door. There would, he assumed, be a stair leading directly from the dormitory to the church, for the sisters' use when they were summoned from their beds for the night offices.

The large group of buildings forming three sides of a square around the cloistered courtyard included, he knew, Abbess Helewise's small room, and also, he surmised, the refectory and the reformatory. Stables and what looked like workshops and storage rooms had been on his right as he came in through the main gate, and, on his left, had been the porteress's lodge.

His eyes scanned the remaining buildings. Situated just inside the Abbey's rear wall, they now rose up to dominate the view in front of him. Both were built to the left of the church and close to it; indeed, one appeared to adjoin it. The other, slightly smaller building, was set apart, in the place where the side and rear walls met to form a corner.

From its position, he guessed that it must be the leper house. If so, then it was from there that the sealed passage led to the part of the church reserved for the exclusive use of the lepers and the sisters who cared for them. It was an area of the foundation which Josse fervently hoped he would not have to investigate.

Satisfied that he now had a mental map of the Abbey buildings, he let his thoughts return to the murder.

His mind reverberated all over again from the Abbess's new revelation. A rich cross, left at the scene – no, *planted* at the scene, for it had not belonged to the dead woman – surely could only amount to another attempt to confuse the facts? Make Gunnora's murder seem like a bungled theft, just as the murderer had tried to make it look like rape?

He could no longer ignore his strong conviction that, whoever had cut her throat, it certainly hadn't been riff-raff released from the local jail. Unless, that is, the jail had enclosed within its walls someone with a more sophisticated mind than your average poacher, pickpocket, sheep thief, or drunkard who had let his fists get the better of his common sense.

My job here is done, Josse reflected as he and the Abbess reached the convent walls. I could return now to Tonbridge, notify the local officials of my findings, and there would no longer be any question of King Richard's gesture of humanity having led to brutal death. They would surely accept, as I do, that there is far more to this crime than a casual, spur-of-the-moment assault that went too far.

But he knew he wasn't going to return to Tonbridge just yet. How much more thoroughly would his task be achieved, how much more praiseworthy it would be, if he were able to say not only who *didn't* do the deed, but who *did*.

Well, if he were going to go through with it – as everything in him was urging – then the next step was clear. Unpleasant – in fact, in view of the continuing heat, extremely unpleasant – but quite obvious.

'Abbess Helewise?'

Until he himself broke the silence, neither had spoken since they had left the spot where Gunnora had been found. He reflected that a nun made an admirable companion when you had things to run over in your mind. Especially – he turned to look at her – one whose wide brow and penetrating eyes spoke so clearly of intelligence.

'Yes?' she replied, acknowledging with a brief dip of her head his courteous gesture of standing back to allow her to go through the gate first.

'Abbess, I have to ask your permission for a task which I wish were not necessary.' He paused. Lord, was he right? *Was* it necessary? He wished, not for the first time, that he had more experience of murder. That this particular case were not his baptism into the art of investigation.

But, even if he was new to investigating brutal crimes, he had his common sense and his logic, both of which told him that what he was about to ask was essential. Before he could change his mind, he said, 'Madam, I have to see the body.'

She didn't answer straightaway, but he noticed that she seemed suddenly to be steering their steps towards the church. Above its door, he observed, was a particularly finely carved tympanum. 'It is two weeks, more or less, since she was found,' the Abbess remarked.

'Aye. I know.'

'And it is July, sir. An unusually hot July.'

'Aye.'

They stood together at the church door. She was watching him, a hand up to her eyes to shade them from the brilliant light. He returned her stare, resisting the temptation to hang his head as if in shame at being caught out in a salacious thought. He could not read her expression: it was is if her face were smoothed out. The smile which quirked her wide mouth and raised the well-shaped cheeks was absent, and it was only now that it wasn't there that he realised he was already recognising it as characteristic of her.

He was about to press his request, explain why he was making it, when she reached out and lifted the heavy latch. 'I will show you the way,' she said quietly.

He followed her down a short flight of steps into the church. She made her genuflection, which he copied, then walked up the aisle, past what appeared to be a totally enclosed side chapel – the lepers' chapel? – then, turning to her left some five paces in front of the altar, opened another, much smaller door. This, too, gave on to steps, but in this case not a wide, shallow flight carved of stone, but a narrow and steep little spiral made of wood.

The smell, which he had scarcely noticed in the church, had increased tenfold with the opening of the little door.

She made her careful way down the stairs. Over her shoulder, he saw the soft light of a candle. They emerged into a low crypt, its domed roof supported by massive stone pillars. He had the sudden sense of being buried deep in the earth, accompanied by an alarming recognition of the unbelievable weight of stone above him, pressing down on him. An atavistic dread shot through him, and he felt a slight prickling as the small hairs on the back of his neck and along his spine stood up.

'It is very cold down in the crypt, even now in high summer.' The Abbess's voice was cool, and her matter-of-fact tone brought him back to himself. 'We thought it best to lay her here, while we await her family's instructions as to her burial.'

There was no need for her to explain. He, too, would have found it hard to concentrate on his devotions with this silent, malodorous companion. Better – how much better, for his own purpose – that she had been put away in the cold of the crypt.

He swallowed, and took a step nearer to the coffin, on its simple bier. The coffin was made of fairly rough planks, butted and nailed together rather than carefully jointed. The lid was secured with six more nails. He looked around for some sort of implement with which to lever them out – fool, not to have thought of it before! – and was about to announce that he would have to go and find something when the Abbess silently pointed into a corner. Whoever had made the coffin had had wood left over, and had stacked it neatly under the stairs.

Josse selected a stout length of timber – presumably rejected as too thick – and, trying to control his strength so that both coffin and bier didn't end up being thrown over, banged its thicker end up under the edge of the coffin lid until he had made a wide enough gap to insert the other, thinner end. The Abbess, practical woman, perceived his difficulty and went to stand at the coffin's head, steadying it.

Now he could put his weight behind the effort. Leaning down on the end of the plank, he heaved as hard as he could. There was an ominous creak, and the plank began to bend; out of the corner of his eye he saw the Abbess take a firmer grip, as if she could predict his next move and was allowing for it. Placing his hands nearer the top of his lever, he took a breath, flexed his shoulder and arm muscles, and pushed down with all his might.

The coffin slewed sideways and all but fell, but the Abbess grabbed at it and saved it. And there was no need to see if he had been successful: the smell told them both that he had.

The Abbess had draped a fold of her wide sleeve across her face, and, taking hold of his arm, she pulled him away to the far side of the crypt. 'Let the noxious air dissipate for a few moments,' she said quietly.

It made sense. There seemed to be a good supply of air in the crypt, its slight draught making the candle flame dance. Standing there beside the Abbess, he looked at the coffin. The lid was a hand's breadth above the base on the side where he had been working; it would be easy, now, to tear it off.

When the smell had lessened – either that, he thought ruefully, or I'm getting used to it – he and Abbess Helewise walked back to the coffin, and he thrust the lid out of the way.

He hadn't really known what to expect. He had seen dead bodies before, many of them, seen the dreadful mutilations caused by warfare, seen bloated corpses that had lain too long on a sunny battlefield, seen half-putrid flesh crawling with maggots. He had been prepared for all of that.

The body of Gunnora, although clearly in the early stages of decomposition, was still relatively unchanged by death. The white skin of the hands and face, the only visible flesh, had a slight greenish tinge, and on her right hand, placed on top of the left, the main blood vessels were badly discoloured.

Someone had closed her eyelids. But the lower part of her face, still twisted into a rictus of horror, more than compensated for the absence of any expression there might have been in the dead eyes.

'She died hard,' he murmured.

'She did.' The Abbess, too, spoke softly. 'You will wish to see the death wound.'

'Aye.' Again, her undramatic tone was a help.

He watched as her swift hands folded back the veil and untied the barbette that bound the smooth forehead, revealing the ends of the wimple, neatly fastened on top of the short hair.

She lowered the wimple, laying it across the still chest.

And the great slash that killed Gunnora was revealed.

He felt a moment's faintness, and the hard stone beneath his feet seemed suddenly a perilously uncertain slope. He made himself relax. She is dead, he told himself firmly. Dead. And the best service I can do her now is to find her killer.

He leaned forward, bending close. The wound ran from ear to ear, a smooth, symmetrical cut that had severed the blood vessels and severely damaged the windpipe. It would, a detached part of his mind thought, be a matter of conjecture whether she died from loss of blood or asphyxia. He studied the ends of the cut. Interesting.

He had seen many men killed or injured by sword cuts, and it could usually be determined whether the attacker had used his left or his right hand, especially to anyone experienced in sword use. A cut was normally deeper at the initial point of incision, where it bore the full weight of the assault.

But this cut on the thin throat of Gunnora was as even, as perfect, as a quarter moon. Somebody had done it very carefully. Artistically, even. What an extraordinary thing to do.

It prompted him to look at her hands. He drew back the wide cuffs, trying to fold them as tidily as the Abbess had dealt with the veil and wimple; he might have ordered this violation of the dead girl's final peace, but at least he could show respect. He felt the Abbess's eyes on him, but she did not intervene. Feeling he had been awarded a good mark, he bent over Gunnora's hands and forearms.

There was a slight scratch on the left wrist, but it looked old; a scab had formed and partly fallen off, which he did not think would have happened had it been done at the time of death. The nails were bitten, and on the right forefinger a torn quick felt unpleasantly squelchy. Other than that, the hands were undamaged.

'Look, Abbess,' he said. 'Look at her hands.'

The Abbess did so. Then said, 'She did not put up a fight.'

'No, exactly. Had she struggled, tried to ward off the knife, her hands would show it.' He frowned, trying to work out what that meant. Either she was unconscious when the attack came – or asleep? – or . . . Or what?

Or she was assailed by more than one person.

He returned to the sleeves, pushing at them more urgently now, searching the upper arms . . . finding what he sought.

'Look.' He pointed. On the white flesh were small bruises, two on the right arm, four on the left. Without pausing to think if it was appropriate, he hurried round to stand behind the

Abbess, holding her arms. 'You see? She was held, like this, from the rear. Held hard enough for the attacker's fingers to make those bruises.'

'Held by one man, whilst another cut her throat,' the Abbess said, infinite pity in her voice. Standing so close to her, still holding her arms, he felt the slight sagging of her body. Then, as if they had simultaneously realised the unseemliness of their position, he stepped back and she moved forwards. His hands dropped to his sides, and he was about to apologise when she spoke.

'Do you wish to look at any more of the corpse?' she asked briskly. Corpse, he noticed. Perhaps it made it easier, to refer to Gunnora as a corpse.

'I think not. I am content to take the word of your infirmarer as to the contrived evidence of rape.' He sensed her relief.

He walked slowly round the coffin. There was something else he should check, he was sure. What? Absently he watched the Abbess as she rearranged the dead girl's clothing, placing the plain wooden crucifix under the crossed hands, smoothing the veil so that it lay in perfect folds . . .

Yes. That was it.

'May I look at her feet?'

The enquiry in the Abbess's eyes was not vocalised. Instead, she turned back the hem of the habit, revealing small feet in narrow leather shoes.

The soles felt cold, and, pushing with a finger, he detected moisture. Yes, she had been out in the middle of the night, hadn't she? Of course her shoes would be wet with dew. He inspected the feet, then the ankles, but the skin was clean.

'Would her body have been washed?' he asked.

'Naturally. The blood.'

'Aye, that. I meant her feet, her lower legs.'

The Abbess shrugged. 'I cannot say for sure. I imagine so.' Then, although he could sense her reluctance to have to ask, 'Why?'

'I'm wondering, Abbess, as I've been wondering all along, what a nun was doing out of her dormitory – out of her convent, even – in the middle of the night. I'm thinking, did she go far? She met her death close by, yes, but was she on her way out or on her way back? I ask about her feet and legs because, had she left the track, which she would have had to do had she gone further than the shrine, then she would have been walking through long grass. I would expect to have found the signs on her legs, on the hem of her garments. And her shoes would have been soaked through.'

The Abbess nodded quickly. 'Yes, yes, I see. You are right – the paths only extend to the shrine and the monks' house, and to the little pool that forms below the shrine. That track – the one, in fact, on which she was found – is smaller. It is not much used.'

That, then, was one question answered. Whatever mission had taken Gunnora out that night, she had not gone far. But, as seemed increasingly to be the case, one question answered posed more: had she completed what she had set out to do, or had she been killed on the way?

He watched as, again, the Abbess performed her rearranging task.

Then, coming to stand beside him, they both stood in silence, gazing at the dead girl.

He no longer had the feeling that there was more to be learned from her. It was time, finally, to leave her alone. He stepped forward, picked up the coffin lid and replaced it. Then, inserting the tips of the nails back into their holes, he used his baulk of timber to bang them down again.

He resumed his place beside the Abbess. Then, as if they had been waiting for some inaudible sign that they were dismissed, they turned and went back up the spiral staircase.

'I have been trying to arrange it that someone usually sits in vigil,' she said as they left the church, which, as it had been when they went in, was still conspicuously empty. 'But it has been so long, now. I sensed that my nuns were distressed by the task, that, by continuing to take their turn at sitting with poor

Gunnora, this dreadful event was kept in the forefront of their minds.' She gave a slight shrug. 'I no longer insist on it.'

'Wise, if I may be allowed to comment,' he said. 'Probably the feeling that she has been abandoned, that no one from her family has come for her, increases the poignancy.'

'It does indeed. My lord d'Acquin, it is strange, is it not, this failure in response? I sent word, of course, as soon as I could, and the family home is but a day's ride away at most. And I know my message was received, for the bearer reported back to me to that effect.'

'Did the bearer say how the tidings were greeted? With shock and distress, I'm sure, but—'

'He – it was one of the lay brothers – did say that the father appeared shocked, yes. But it was peculiar, he said, because the man seemed shocked before the brother had so much as got down from his horse.'

'He guessed, do you think? Surmised that a rider arriving on a hard-ridden horse from the Abbey where his daughter lives must be bringing bad news?'

'Perhaps.' She frowned. 'Yes, probably no more than that. But it's odd . . .'

He waited. 'Yes?'

Again, the shrug. 'The brother had the strong impression that the father hardly took in the news. He – the brother – took some pains to repeat his brief account of what had happened, this time in the presence of two of the household servants.'

'With no more response the second time?'

She gave a half smile, as if even she found it hard to believe what she was suggesting. 'That's the strangest thing of all. The father, so the lay brother says, seemed to brush him away. Gave the strong impression that he was preoccupied with something else, that this dire news of his daughter was a distraction.'

'A distraction,' Josse echoed. Yes, it was strange. 'You can trust the word of the lay brother? He is not the sort of man to embellish a tale so as to increase the drama?'

'Absolutely not.' She was vehement. 'Brother Saul is an

excellent man, reliable, trustworthy, and observant.' She glared at Josse, as if to say, why else do you imagine I chose him?

'Very well. Then let us ask ourselves why a father should treat news of a daughter's death – her murder, indeed – as if it were something of a nuisance, taking him away from more important matters.'

'Matters already causing distress,' she added.

'Aye. That too.'

They had moved right away from the church and were standing in the shade of the cloisters, and she, he was sure, was as relieved as he was to breathe in the clean, warm air. Now she made a move towards a doorway in the wing of the building on her left, gesturing with her hand.

'Let us reflect on that,' she said, 'while we make our way to the refectory for the midday meal.'

Chapter Six

The midday meal – more of the excellent bread, this time with a vegetable stew containing a few morsels of mutton – was taken in silence, other than the melodious voice of a nun reading from the Gospels. It was the parable of the talents, and, Josse decided, had a special meaning for him. The exhortation to use his talents, in the symbolic sense, was well-timed, and his shaky self-confidence was boosted as he reminded himself that, in-experienced as he was, he had wits.

And, as he ate his stew, he employed them.

He glanced around at the assembled company, trying not to make it obvious. He counted sixty-eight nuns sitting at the long main table, another seventeen sitting by themselves at a smaller table, separated from the main refectory by a screen. With the addition of the Abbess and the nun reading from the Gospels, that made eighty-seven. Plus, he reminded himself, the three sisters who chose to isolate themselves in the leper house. And, presumably, ten or a dozen sisters who were on duty in the hospital while the rest of the community ate their meal. Say, a hundred, roughly, in all.

Was one of them a killer?

Looking from face to face, he couldn't make himself believe it. Of the women he was able to study – for one or two kept their heads bent over the table, so that his view of them was cut off by their veils – not one showed any expression that was not calm and pleasant, not to say serene. There were women of all ages, from black-veiled fully professed nuns, in middle age or more, down to the obviously youthful, who wore the white veil of the novice or, in the case of one girl who looked scarcely out of her teen years, the plain black garb of the postulant. Was she, he wondered, the unsuitable Elvera, who had befriended the dead nun? Of all the women, he observed, she alone showed any signs of distress; there was a suggestion of redness around the eyes, and he caught her in the act of shooting him a rapid look; her eyes dropped the instant she noticed that he was studying her.

It heartened Josse that someone, at least, had been shedding tears for Gunnora.

By the time the meal ended and he stood to join the nuns in their prayers, he had made up his mind what the next step was.

Abbess Helewise seemed unsurprised when he announced, as they left the refectory, his intention of seeking out Gunnora's family, provided the Abbess was willing to divulge the whereabouts of their home.

'That I will,' she said. 'Follow me back to my room, and I will tell you where they live and how to get there. I think,' she added over her shoulder, 'that you are taking the logical next step.'

Once they were within the privacy of the Abbess's small room, he said, 'May I ask you a further question, Abbess?'

She inclined her head, which he took for an affirmative.

'The nuns sitting apart from the community just now, at the midday meal. I have not been able to work out why.'

She smiled briefly. 'And you are asking yourself if there is some lurid explanation? They are in disgrace for some heinous misdemeanour? Contaminated, perhaps, from nursing patients with the plague or the pox?'

'Neither of those things!' he protested, not entirely accurately.

'They are our virgin nuns,' she said quietly, all traces of amusement gone from her face. 'As in the abbey at Fontevraud, our community is divided, with separate accommodation according to how a sister opts to use her life in God. Most choose the easier life of the Madeleine Convent – many of us lived a full life in the world before entry here, and do not consider ourselves worthy of a life spent solely with God. But for those women who led an exemplary life in the world, who, even before taking the veil, lived quietly, modestly and in celibacy, there is the option of enclosure in the Virgin House, where they spend their days and much of their nights in contemplation and communion with the Lord.'

He was nodding earnestly, even while a part of him was thinking, what a life! 'And those sisters, the virgin nuns, do not join with you, even for meals?'

'No. The Rule considers it is best for them not to brush too closely with those who retain one foot in the world. They are segregated in chapel, also, and they live in separate accommodation; their small house is attached to the Lady Chapel.' Her eyes met his, and, anticipating his next question, she answered it. 'Gunnora would not have had any contact whatsoever with any of the virgin sisters. Assure yourself that none of them would even have known who she was.'

And so, she seemed to add silently, you can cross those seventeen women off your list of suspects.

He said gravely, 'I thank you, Abbess Helewise. I shall do precisely that.'

She said farewell to him in her room, wishing him a safe journey and God's speed. Then, with a pleasant sense of having earned her approbation, notwithstanding the more intrusive of his questions, he set off to find his horse.

A nun wearing a sacking apron over her habit was working in the stables, sleeves rolled back to display forearms any sailor would have been proud of. She was mucking out, and wielded a pitchfork with an easy rhythm that suggested long familiarity.

'I've fed your horse,' she said, as he greeted her and

announced he was about to leave. 'Rubbed him down and all. He'll not be thinking to work again this day, I reckon. You'll no doubt find him a deal frisky.' She grinned, showing gaps in her side teeth. 'I was about to turn him out with our lot, he'd have looked like a king alongside 'em.'

He looked out to the paddock she indicated, where a solid but amiable-looking cob had raised an enquiring head. There was a more delicately built but short-legged pony – surely on the small side for any but the slightest-built of the sisters? – and a mule. He saw what the sister had meant.

'Thank you for your care of him.' In any other stable, he'd have offered a coin or two, but it didn't seem appropriate in a convent. Instead he paid her a compliment: 'You run a sweet-smelling, well-tended stable, Sister—'

'Sister Martha,' she said. 'I thank you, sir knight.'

'Josse d'Acquin,' he supplied.

She grinned again. 'I know. I know, too, what you're here for and, as to where you're bound now, I can guess.' The smile faded and she moved closer to him, face intense. 'Find him, sir. I had no great love for Gunnora, God punish me for my lack of charity, but no creature ever deserved that fate.'

He met her honest blue eyes. 'I'll do my best, Sister Martha. You have my word.'

With an emphatic nod, as if to say, the word of a knight'll do for me, Sister Martha went back to her mucking out.

The lands of Gunnora's father lay some eighteen miles roughly to the south-east of Hawkenlye. Setting out the hour after noon, Josse would arrive at dusk. The estate was sufficiently close to the town of Newenden for him to put up there; it was his intention to view Gunnora's home this evening, gleaning what impression he could, and then retire to an inn. He would present himself to her family in the morning.

It ocurred to him on the road that it would better serve his purpose not to draw attention to himself. He stopped and dismounted, extracted a light and well-worn cloak from his pack, and, removing his embroidered tunic, stowed it away. He held the cloak at arm's length, studying it with a critical eye. Worn it might be, but it still looked suspiciously good quality. With a slight sigh, he threw it down on to the track and trod it into the dust. Then he shook it and put it on. He drew the hood over his head so that its edge shaded his face; the afternoon sun was strong.

Abbess Helewise's directions had been accurate, and he found his way to Winnowlands easily, only once having to ask for assistance. Odd, he thought, riding away from the small group of dwellings where he had consulted an old man laboriously winding up water from a well. The old boy seemed friendly enough as I rode into the yard – I even thought he was about to offer me water. But as soon as I mentioned Winnowlands, he changed.

Trying to put aside one possibly loopy old man's prejudice and maintain an open mind, Josse rode on.

The Winnowlands estates, he could see straightaway, were rich. The land here, on the edge of the escarpment that rose up to the north of the great marshland, was good, and put to a variety of uses. Herds of cows grazed in well-grassed meadows, and flocks of sheep fattened themselves on the sparser grass nearer the marshes. The land under the plough was well-tended and looked fertile, and the strips were neat and tidily fenced. There were several huddles of dwellings, and, inspecting one which was clearly visible from the road, Josse noted that the reed-thatch roofs looked sound. One or two small cultivated areas near to the dwellings were thick with cabbages, carrots and onions, and in one, someone was growing some tiny pink flowers. In a fenced-off run, a sow and her young rooted in the dirt.

The land, quite clearly, yielded a good living. This should have been a happy place.

Why, then, Josse wondered as he slowly rode on, was there such an air of despondency? The few people he had seen – and why were they so few? Where was everyone? – seemed hardly to be aware of the stranger in their midst. Wasn't that in itself strange? Josse had travelled countless miles, through all sorts of alien lands, and the one constant factor among all the different peoples he had encountered – especially the country people – was their curiosity. Well, you could understand it. They lived small lives, probably never went further away than the boundaries of the manor where they'd been born and where, in due course, they'd die. Saw exactly the same faces, year in, year out. A stranger was a rarity. Someone to be stared at, his possible provenance and purpose discussed and analysed for days, if not weeks, afterwards.

But these people working away on the Winnowlands acres seemed preoccupied. Dejected, Josse thought, would not be inaccurate. Was it – could it be – that they shared the family grief for a dead daughter? It was a possibility. But surely such an exaggerated response was unlikely; to grieve deeply, one had to have known the dead person well. And would any of these serfs working in the fields have known anything of Gunnora, other than a vague distant presence? Even more distant, for the last year of her life.

And, Josse thought as he rode on towards the manor house, hadn't Abbess Helewise said that her lay brother detected a deep misery in these people even before he gave them the news of Gunnora's murder?

No. Something else had happened here. Something so bad that it affected all the people whose security depended on the Winnowlands manor. And, whatever it was, it had predated Gunnora's death.

He drew rein on the top of a hillock that rose up on the other side of the road from the Winnowlands manor house, and, in the golden light of late afternoon, stared down at the place that had been Gunnora's home.

It was a solidly built construction, clearly the home of a wealthy family, and of generous proportions; stout stone steps led from the wall-enclosed courtyard up to the entrance, at first floor level, and there was space for a large hall. There was a solar at the western end, and what appeared to be a private chapel. Two turreted extensions suggested that the original building had been extended at some time, perhaps to make room for an increasing family. Beneath the living quarters was a wide under-croft; its narrow door stood ajar, and Josse could glimpse within the shadowy depths a profusion of stores.

As he watched, a man, clad in a leather jerkin over hose tucked into stout boots, appeared from behind the house. He called out a reply to some unseen presence within the house; it seemed to have been a demand for firewood, for he disappeared inside the undercroft and emerged with a basket of small logs.

A fire? When the day had been so hot?

A cooking fire, Josse decided. The person within wanted to get on with preparing the master's supper. But, as he watched, he noticed a billow of smoke issue from some aperture in the roof. Not the sort of smoke that comes from a well-established fire, such as might have been kept in all day for the purposes of cooking or water-heating; the smoke that comes when a fire is newly lit.

Someone, then, had ordered the man in the jerkin to light a fire. When the day was still so hot that Josse could feel the trickles of sweat running down his back, even sitting still.

He heard the sounds of an approaching horse, coming from his right. The man in the jerkin heard them too, and came slowly down the steps from the hall to await the new arrival. Josse quietly urged his horse to take a few paces back, so that he was hidden behind the bulge of the hillock; it did not seem wise, whichever way you looked at it, for Josse to be observed peering down at the goings-on in the Winnowlands household. Dismounting, he crawled forward so that he could peer down into the courtyard.

The newcomer was a young man, slim, well-dressed in the latest fashion. He had shortened his tunic to mid-thigh length, and the richly decorated hem was cut away into exaggerated slits at the side, revealing the muscles of the man's buttocks, clad in very tight hose. On his feet – and unsuitable, surely, for riding – he wore soft leather shoes with elongated points at the toe. His fair hair was very neatly cut, the fringe a dead-straight line above the wide forehead, except for where one careful curl had been arranged. He said something to the leather-jerkined man, who must, Josse thought, be some sort of senior house-servant, and the man shook his head. The young man leaned down off his horse, and, this time, spoke more loudly. Josse picked up a word or two: '. . . *must* see him . . . do insist . . . come all this way . . . no authority to bar the door against *me*!'

The older man's reply was also audible; even more so, since he was in fact shouting.

'I know very well what you're here for, and so does the Master! I tell you, young sir, he doesn't want to see you!'

'I *will* see him! It's my right!'

'You'll be admitted when the Master's good and ready, and not a moment sooner! Now you'd better be gone, Milon, afore the Master hears and comes out himself to send you packing!'

The younger man gave a short laugh, an unpleasant, mocking sound. 'That one? Come out here? Ha! It'll be the first time in a long while if he does, Will, and you know it!'

'I'll not admit you, Milon, so there's no use you hanging around.' The man in the jerkin – Will – now advanced towards the youngster, and even from a distance Josse could see the menace in his face. 'Be gone! You'll be told, when there's aught for you to know.'

Milon turned his horse with a savage jerk at the reins. Glaring at Will, he had his parting shot: 'I'll be back, you dirty peasant! Just you wait!'

Will stood looking after him as he spurred his horse into a furious gallop and, raising clouds of dust, set off back the way he had come. Then, the heavy face full of disgust, he spat out a heavy gobule of phlegm in the direction the young man had taken. There could not, Josse thought, have been a more eloquent valediction.

Josse waited until Will had gone back inside, gave him a few minutes in case he came out again – somehow he didn't fancy having to explain himself to Will right there and then – and, after a good interval, mounted, rode down off his hillock and set off for Newenden and his bed for the night.

He returned the next morning. He had found lodgings in an acceptable inn, eaten a good supper, even been provided with hot water to remove the dust and sweat of the journey. Now he was dressed in his best, as befitted an emissary from the Abbess of Hawkenlye Abbey; he and Helewise had agreed that this would be his role, and that, as his reason for calling on Gunnora's father, he would say that the Abbey urgently needed to know what were his wishes concerning his daughter's body.

He rode up to the manor house, and was about to call out to advertise his presence when the man, Will, came out from the undercroft.

'Sir?' he said, looking up at Josse from beneath a hand shading his eyes from the sun.

'Josse d'Acquin,' Josse said. 'I come from Hawkenlye, with matters of a personal nature to discuss with your master of Winnowlands. May I see him, please?'

Will went on staring at him. Then, slowly, shook his head. But it was not in rejection of Josse's request; it appeared to be more in distress at the whole situation. 'Aye,' he said on a sigh. 'Bad business. I've tried to say to him, gently, mind, that he should make up his mind, send word. Can't be pleasant for them at the Abbey, left with a body they can neither send away nor bury. Wouldn't like it, myself.' He had summed up the dilemma with admirable brevity. 'But, sir, it ain't as easy as that. He won't listen to me, won't listen to nobody. He's—' He broke off, and scratched his head as if perplexed at how to describe his master's condition.

'Disturbed? Wrong in his mind?' Josse suggested, hoping he wouldn't offend the man by plain speaking.

But the man, far from taking offence, seized on Josse's words with apparent relief. 'Aye. Wrong in his mind. Aye, sir, that he is. Wrong in his body an' all, but that he's been these many years. Worse now, of course. Much, much worse.' Sadly he resumed his head shaking. 'But this here, this wrong in his head thing, this is what I find so hard to deal with, sir. I mean, I can't *tell* him what to do, now, can I? Not me in my position. But then someone ought to. It ain't right. None of it.'

This time the rueful head shaking went on for some time. Josse said gently, 'May I dismount?' And instantly Will looked up at him, dismay on the blunt features.

'I'm sorry, sir, that I am! Of course, of course, here, let me help.' He leapt to take Josse's horse's bridle, and Josse swung down out of the saddle. 'I'll put him here for you, in this nice patch of shade,' – efficient man that he was, he acted as he spoke – 'and take off that saddle. Like some water, eh, my fine fellow?' He patted the horse's neck affectionately. 'Bet you would!'

The horse secured, Will returned to Josse. As if he had been turning it over in his mind in those few moments, now he seemed to have reached a decision. 'You come in with me and see the master, sir, if you will,' he said firmly. 'Can't do no harm. Nothing can make him any worse than he is, not now. Nor any better, seemingly.' The features drooped briefly. 'A good man, he was, sir, in his way,' he said earnestly. 'Don't let how he's fetched up deceive you. He has his faults, like all of us, but he was never all bad.'

With this ambiguous introduction echoing in his head, Josse followed Will up into the hall and went forward to meet the lord of Winnowlands.

Gunnora's father, it was immediately apparent, was dying. He was lying on a bed as close to the great fireplace as he could be placed, despite the fact that, in the sun-warmed hall, the fire hadn't yet been lit. He barely stirred as Will quietly spoke to him – 'Sir Alard? Be you awake?' and announced Josse, other than to turn his head towards them. He wore a fur-trimmed gown of heavy wool, over which a rug had been arranged. At his neck could be seen the collar of a linen shift, quite clean; dying he might be, but those who were looking after him were tending him devotedly.

His face was pale grey, without so much as the suggestion of colour. The flesh had all but gone, making the strong nose the more prominent. The eyes were dark, made more so now by the fact of lying deep within their sockets. In the dimness of the hall, as Josse's eyes adjusted from the brilliance outside, he could, he thought, be looking at a skull.

'What do you want, Josse d'Acquin?' Alard of Winnowlands asked, in a voice that cracked on the words.

'I come from Hawkenlye, Sir Alard. From the Abbess Helewise, who requires of you to know what are your wishes regarding the body of your late daughter, Gunnora.'

'My late daughter Gunnora,' Alard echoed. Astoundingly, the words were infused with bitter, mocking irony. 'My late daughter.' There was a pause. Then he said, this time quietly and expressionlessly, 'With Gunnora, do what you please. Bury her with the nuns. She wished to be with them in life, let her stay with them in death.'

'Thank you, sir,' Josse said. 'Abbess Helewise and the sisters will be relieved to have your decision.' He hesitated. 'Sir, may I—'

'Get out.' The words, said in the same toneless way, at first failed to register. Then, as Josse stayed where he was, Alard raised himself slightly, fixed Josse with those burning black eyes and yelled, '*Get out!*'

Josse had scarcely begun to move when the coughing began. At first quiet, it grew so swiftly to its violent, prolonged climax that Will only just had time to thrust a square of linen to Alard's lips before the blood spurted out. The linen, washed and smoothed, was soon covered with fresh stains to lie alongside the old. Josse watched, transfixed and helpless, while the master of Winnowlands coughed away some more of what remained of his lungs.

Will joined him outside some time later.

'It's a pity you had to witness that,' he said, coming to stand beside where Josse leaned against the sunny front of the house.

There was a scent of lavender from bushes growing against the undercroft; Josse had been breathing in the good, clean smell.

'Aye,' Josse said. 'Has he long been like that?'

'The sickness grew slowly in him,' Will replied. 'At first no more than a cough that persisted, gradually growing till he was troubled constantly. He began to grow weak, didn't want to eat. Then, last winter, he began to cough up blood.'

'Ah.' And that, Josse knew, invariably meant life would not go on much longer.

'He'd have gone afore now,' Will said, 'only he's so strong. Used to be, anyhow. There was plenty of him to waste away, if you take my meaning.'

'Aye.' Josse had seen the same in other men.

'And, besides, he can't go yet.' Will paused, glancing sideways at Josse as if wondering how many more family affairs to reveal to this stranger.

'Oh, no?' Josse tried to sound casual, disinterested.

Will's quick smile indicated he wasn't taken in. But, nevertheless, he went ahead. 'No. He can't die, not afore he's decided.'

'Decided?'

'He's not got long for this world, as well he knows, what with the priest and the physician either side of him with their long faces and all that telling him so. Prepare your soul, priest says, make a good confession, arrange your earthly affairs so as you have credit in heaven. But it ain't as easy as that, is it, sir?'

'No,' Josse agreed. It seemed sensible not to lead Will off at a tangent by asking, what isn't?

'And there's the living to consider, too, along of the matter of credit in heaven, ain't there? The living as has their needs, too.'

'Quite.'

'See, it all looked so straightforward, year or so back,' Will said, leaning confidingly close to Josse.

'Before Gunnora entered the convent?' Josse guessed. The timing was right, anyway.

'Aye, that. But that weren't the start of it.' Will was shaking his head again. 'Sir, I tell you straight, I'm glad I'm a simple man. I've my little house, my woman, and that's that. My house ain't mine to leave to nobody, and as for the rest, what I own I wear on my back, mostly.'

'Yes, I see.' Josse did. Began to see, at last, where this was leading. It all began to fit together.

'There was the two of them,' Will began suddenly. 'Gunnora, she was the eldest, and there was Dillian. Lovely lass, Dillian, but she was his second-born. Gunnora had to come first, that's only right and proper, so she it was Sir Alard offered for the match. But, sir, she wouldn't have him! Wouldn't marry him, and all the reasoning, all the threats and the punishments in the world, wouldn't make her change her mind. So Sir Alard, he says, go on, then, go to your nunnery! But you're no more daughter of mine! And *then* it's Dillian's turn, because, sir, you can't say you've overlooked an elder sister, now, can you, not when you've offered it to her and she's said, no, thankee just the same, I'm going to be a nun?'

'No, indeed.'

'So Dillian, *she* marries my Lord Brice instead.' Abruptly Will stopped, face working with some deep emotion. After a moment he recovered sufficiently to say, 'I'm sorry, sir, that I am, only it's such a recent pain, see. I still thinks as how she's going to come riding up the track like she used to, calling out, laughing, playing her little tricks, only she didn't, of course, all that stopped, when she married him.' He shook his head sadly. 'Naturally, they all say it was an accident. She fell off the horse, that's for sure, and I know there's witnesses to say so, good, honest souls who mean no harm, who are just telling the truth. But why did she get up on that great beast and gallop off like that? That's what I'd like to know! And I know him, sir, I know that Brice. I tell you, I don't blame Miss Gunnora for refusing him. I only wish my lovely Dillian had had the wisdom to do the same, but, there you are.' He gave a deep, gusty sigh. 'The ways of women always were a mystery, weren't they? Always will be, too, I reckon.'

There seemed nothing to add to that remark, with which

Josse was tempted to agree. Respectful of Will's evident sorrow, Josse let the silence continue for some time. There was no need, anyway, for hurry. Not now, when he had guessed what had happened. Knew, or so he thought, what had caused the abiding misery of Winnowlands.

Not the death of an elder daughter, an unappealing woman whose departure into a convent hadn't really dismayed anyone, but the death of her sister. *My lovely Dillian,* with her laughter and her tricks.

'So he lost them both?' he prompted eventually.

'Hm?' Will seemed to have forgotten Josse was there. 'Aye. One after the other, not a sennight between them.' Another deep sigh. 'No more daughters. No female heir, securely married to a good man.' He raised his head and met Josse's eyes. 'And the master's every breath threatening to be his last. What's to become of us all, sir? That's what I'd like to know!'

'Aye,' Josse said absently. His brain was working hard, and, despite the depressing circumstances, there was an elation in him, at having surmised correctly.

He did a swift résumé of Sir Alard's dilemma. Both daughters dead, one immediately after the other. No more children, and this Dillian, apparently, had herself borne no child. And a son-in-law who, according to Will, was held by popular opinion to have been at best a poor husband, at worst responsible for his young wife's death. The sort of man, surely, to whom a father-in-law would scarcely leave his undoubted wealth.

No wonder the peasants of the manor seemed so dismal and dejected. There was, in Josse's experience, nothing more guaranteed to lower the spirits than uncertainty about the future.

And, with the succession of Winnowlands undecided and threatening to remain so, how much more uncertain could the future of everyone on this particular estate be?

Chapter Seven

Will, preoccupied with his own worries, barely raised his head at Josse's casual request as to where he might find the Lord Brice. He gave brief instructions – which proved to be easy to follow and totally accurate – and, as if as an afterthought, mentioned that Josse was unlikely to find the master at home since, so it was rumoured, Brice of Rotherbridge had gone to Canterbury. 'You'll likely find his brother, though.' This with a sniff which could have been interpreted as disparaging. 'The young Lord Olivar's usually around.' Will shot Josse a knowing look. 'Keeping an eye on things, like.'

Suspecting he wasn't going to learn any more – indeed, Will had turned and was heading back to whatever task he was working on down in the undercroft – Josse set off to search out either, or both, of the brothers Rotherbridge.

The Rotherbridge manor adjoined the Winnowlands estate on the east and on the south. Brice had his share of ridge-top pasture and arable land, but the majority of his acres were on the marsh-lands; he must own enough sheep, Josse mused, to make him a man of considerable means. English wool was obtaining a fine reputation in the markets of France and the Low Countries; there were fortunes to be made, and, from the look of the newly extended manor house, Brice of Rotherbridge was busy making his.

No wonder, Josse thought as he rode up the track to the house, Alard wanted an alliance with this man. Not only are they neighbours – and Alard may well have cast an occasional covetous eye on Brice's acres of sheep pasture – but Brice is the sort of husband a father would welcome for his daughter. As regards his money and his position, anyway. Would it have weighed with Alard, that other aspects of Brice might make him less desirable? Would he have known about them, even, other than as servants' gossip?

Yes. He'd have known. Gunnora would have told him. Wouldn't she? Surely, during one of those protracted arguments between furious, determined father and stubborn daughter, she would have said something on the lines of, I'm not marrying him, he's a brute.

Or perhaps she hadn't. For Dillian had needed no persuasion to marry the man.

There was a tale there, Josse reflected as he rode into the shady yard of Rotherbridge manor house. And, hopefully, he'd find someone to tell it to him.

'Hello?' he called, still sitting his horse. 'My Lord Brice? My Lord Olivar?'

There was no reply for some moments, although he thought he heard sounds of movement within. 'Hello?' he called again.

'I'm coming, I'm coming!' shouted a female voice, suddenly loud in the still warmth. 'Can't be doing two things at once, and that fool of a boy'll ruin it if I don't tell him exactly what to do, you'd think he'd have more wits, but there you are, some are born stupid and stupid they remain. Now, sir, what can I do for you?'

She had emerged from the house talking, and the out-pourings had continued as she made her way over to Josse. She was getting on in years, stout, and walked with a limp that threw her with a jerk over to her right at each step. She wore a plain brown gown, and over it a clean white apron, on which she was wiping work-worn hands.

Hoping fervently that her flow of words indicated a character disposed to hob-nobbing with strangers, Josse said, 'I have come in search of Brice of Rotherbridge.' Improvising, he added, 'To pay my condolences on the death of his wife.'

The leathery face, which had been screwed up into a deep grimace of interested enquiry as she stared up at him, instantly slumped into lines of sorrow. 'Aye, aye,' the woman murmured. Then she sighed deeply, and repeated, 'Aye.'

Josse waited. Would a gentle prompt be in order? 'I have come from Winnowlands,' he began, 'and I—'

'That poor old man!' the woman exclaimed. 'First Dillian, then Gunnora! If this double tragedy doesn't tip him over into his grave, I'd like to know what would. How is he, sir?'

'Not well. He—'

'No, he wouldn't be. Nor will any be among them what has the misfortune to depend on him, neither. The master isn't here,' she said, abruptly changing to the practical. 'He's gone to Canterbury, sir.'

No explanation followed – indeed, Josse thought, why should it? – so he repeated, with a delicate note of enquiry, 'Canterbury?'

'Aye. To bare his soul before the good Brothers, do an honest penance, take his punishment and say Mass for her, God rest her soul.'

'Amen,' Josse said. What, he wondered, mind seething, had Brice to do penance for? But it wouldn't do to ask – wasn't it likely that he'd get more confidences from this old soul if he pretended he was already in the know? 'He'll rest more easy in himself after that, I dare say.'

She gave him a swift look, as if assessing how much of the background he really knew and how much he was guessing. After a fairly uncomfortable pause – the deep-set brown eyes were disturbingly penetrating – she appeared to accept him at face value. 'Well, I dare say,' she agreed grudgingly. 'No knowing how these things affect a man, that's what I say.' Another long, considering look, under which Josse did his best to make his expression bland and faintly earnest. The picture, he hoped, of a distressed family friend come to pay his respects.

It must have convinced her. Turning back towards the house, she yelled, 'Ossie? Get yourself out here, lad!' Too soon for him to have been anywhere but eavesdropping behind the door, a boy of about fourteen appeared, gangly, slightly spotty, hanks of greasy hair hanging limp over the low forehead, the epitome of young adolescence. 'Take the gentleman's horse,' the woman ordered, 'see to it' – it! she obviously didn't concern herself overmuch with such equine matters such as gender – 'and then get you back to the stove. Don't you *dare* let it stick, or it'll be you as cleans my pan!'

'No, Mathild.' The boy flashed a quick grin at Josse – he had, Josse observed, a broken and discoloured front tooth, which must surely soon start giving the boy agonies, if it wasn't doing so already – and Josse dismounted and gave the boy the reins.

Then, with a jerk of her head as if to say, this way, Mathild led Josse into the cool hall of Rotherbridge Manor.

'You'll take some ale, sir?' she offered, going to where a covered pewter jug stood ready on a long side table. A hospitable house, this.

'Aye, thank you.'

She filled a mug, and watched as he drank. 'Thirsty day,' she remarked. 'You've come far?'

She was probing, he decided. 'I put up last night at Newenden.'

'Hm. Found a place to lay your head that didn't make your skin crawl, did you?' Then, before he had a chance to answer, 'You knew her well, my lady Dillian?'

'I didn't know her at all,' he replied honestly. 'It was Gunnora I knew.' That was not so honest. In fact, it wasn't honest at all.

'Gunnora.' Mathild nodded slowly. 'Went in a convent, she did.'

'Aye, Hawkenlye Abbey. I know the Abbess.' That, anyway, was truthful. 'My mission here is primarily to discuss with Sir Alard the disposal of the poor girl's body.'

'Aye, and he'll have told you, do what you please,' Mathild said with devastating accuracy.

'More or less,' Josse agreed. Then, taking a step in the dark, 'A shame, that they never made it up before she died.'

'Aye, aye.' He'd got it right. 'No one should die with bad blood between them and their kin, sir, should they?'

'No,' he agreed gravely.

'Not that it was entirely his fault, mind. She were a difficult girl, Gunnora. Wouldn't have liked the care of her, I wouldn't. Now Dillian, she were different.' The creased face took on a softer expression.

Mathild, Josse thought, was at the stage of mourning when there is a great need to talk endlessly about the deceased, singing their praises as if that might weigh with the delicate business of the judgement of their soul. Like an ongoing prayer for those in purgatory.

But it was not to discuss Dillian that he had come. Not entirely, anyway.

When Mathild paused for breath – she didn't seem to need to do so all that often – he interjected mildly, 'Gunnora was – let me see – two years older?'

'Four.' Mathild took the bait. 'But you'd have said more, I reckon. Old in her ways, she was. Mind, she had responsibility put on her young, what with her mother dying like that.'

'Aye,' Josse said, nodding as if he knew all about it. 'Never easy, for a young girl to lose her mother.'

'That it isn't.' Mathild leaned forward confidingly. 'She was an odd child, though, even before it happened. And she never let him spoil her like he did her sister. Blamed him and his wealth for her mother's death, I shouldn't wonder. Stands to reason, really. The Lady Margaret shouldn't have had another child, but, there you are, a man wants a son to inherit, and that's an end to it. Except it wasn't a son, it was Dillian.' She sighed deeply. 'Dillian never blamed him, but then she was so little when she lost her mother, under a year old, she can't have any memory of the lady Margaret except what others told her. But in Gunnora, it came out in her rejection of all he had to give. And that, of course, is why she wouldn't have Sir Brice. For one thing, it was her father planning for her again – she'd never have that – and, for another, it would have been more of the same. She'd have gone from being a rich man's daughter to being a rich man's wife. And it was *that* which she reckoned saw off her dear mother.'

Yes. The reasoning was sound. It would be, Josse thought, in this observant old woman. 'Poor Gunnora,' he murmured.

'Poor?' Mathild put her head on one side as if considering. 'Aye, to die at a murderer's hand. But if she'd married Lord Brice, sir, she might have died like her sister did. As it was, Dillian died in her place.'

And that, Josse thought, looking at the resentment in the old face, was, to Mathild's mind, unforgivable.

He said, 'How did Dillian die?'

If Mathild was surprised that he didn't know, it was not apparent. 'They'd been arguing again, her and Brice,' she said quietly. 'They were always at it. Well, it was him started it.' She shot Josse a quick look, as if to assess how he would react to hearing a servant criticise her master. He smiled encouragingly. 'I hate to say it,' she plunged on, obviously not about to let that put her off, 'but she wasn't the same girl as what she was when she married him. He's a tough man, the master, likes his own way. Used to being obeyed, he is, and, being that much older than Dillian, he thought all he had to do was say jump, and she'd jump. Didn't allow for her spirit, he didn't. She went along with him to begin with – I do reckon, sir, that she loved him, or least-ways thought she did, which amounts to the same result – and she tried hard to please him. But there wasn't any *give* in him – all the pleasing and the accommodating was one way. And, soon as she started standing up to him, that was that.' Again, the sigh. 'It was a shock, when she first realised what he was like. Shocked him and all, when she changed. The shouting began, then he started to knock her about. Many's the time I treated her cuts and bruises, poor lass. And' – she cast a quick glance around as if to ensure they really were alone – 'he used to force her. You know.' Josse was all too afraid he did. 'Wanted a child, he did. A son. And her, poor Dillian, well, even if she'd have liked a child, she didn't like what brings a child into being, not with him, anyway. That was what they were fighting about that morning. Ran out of the bedchamber in her wrap, she did, hair all over the place, marks of his fingers on her poor pale cheeks where he'd slapped her, and she was crying out, "I'm not staying here with you! I *hate* you!" Flew down the steps to the yard, she did, and, as evil chance would have it, the first horse she sees is the master's, still standing there from when he came in from his early morning ride – he liked to ride early, sir, then come in and eat, then go up to Dillian.'

'I see.'

'So she pulls the master's horse across to the mounting block, throws her bare leg over its back, picks up the reins and gives it a kick in the belly with her sharp little heels. Well, it had just been standing there minding its own business, looking forward to a bite to eat, I dare say, when suddenly this howling little thing starts mauling it about, and it doesn't like it. It throws up its head, tries to buck a bit, then sets off out through the gates and away. She managed to stay on till it jumped the ditch down there, sir. Then she fell off.'

The echoes of Mathild's sad voice died. Josse could picture the scene, see that small figure in her wrap, bare legs trying to cling on to a horse far too big and strong for her.

'Did she – was it quick?' he asked. It seemed important to know that Dillian hadn't suffered.

'Aye. On the instant, they say. Broke her neck. They brought her poor body home on a hurdle. Laid her just here, by the fireplace.'

Josse looked to where Mathild was indicating. 'And Brice? How did he react?'

'Angry, to begin with. Yelling about her foolishness. Then, when it dawned on him she was dead, remorse. He's not a bad man, sir,' she said earnestly, repeating, did she but know it, what Will had said about Alard. 'Hasty, like all of his family, and thinking more of his own needs than anyone else's, but, there, show me a man that's different.' Josse could have showed her quite a few, but wisely held his peace. 'Still, he's sorry enough now. He's taken the blame on himself, says he shouldn't have been so rough with her, and that if he hadn't, if he'd kept his hands to himself and been kinder, she'd never have rushed out like that and she'd be alive now. That's why he's gone to Canterbury. Stands to reason, someone like him, a man of action, full of energy, won't feel he's washed the stain of sin out of his soul till someone beats it out. He'll be under the lash right now, I shouldn't wonder. And those monks lay it on with a strong right arm.' She didn't look as if that were anything to be sorry about; quite the contrary.

She noticed Josse's empty mug, and, reaching for the jug, poured him some more ale. 'Thank you,' he said. Then, after a sip, 'Is the Lord Olivar here? Perhaps I could give my message to him.'

'You could, aye, if he were. But he's not. He's gone to Canterbury too.'

'Has he also got a death on his conscience?' Josse said lightly, and Mathild smiled in response.

'Nay. He's gone to keep his brother company. Make sure he doesn't go too far in this penance thing. Leastways, that's what he'd like us all to think.' She winked at Josse. 'Fact is, our young Lord Olivar doesn't pass up an opportunity to go to the city. Hot-blooded, he is, if you take my meaning.' Another wink. Josse thought he knew exactly what she meant.

'I see.' He drank some more of the ale. It was a good brew, and cool from standing in the hall. He let the conversation run through his mind. He had learned a great deal, but was there more he could elicit from this willing informant?

Possibly there was.

'So, with both Gunnora and Dillian dead, Sir Alard has no heir,' he ventured. 'Will he leave his estate to Brice, do you think?'

She shook her head vehemently. 'No, not he. Blood's thicker than water, and, anyhow, he must have heard the rumours. People talk, you know, sir, and it was common knowledge hereabouts that Brice was too ready with his fists when it came to his wife. Sir Alard loved her, in his way. No, I reckon it'll all go to Elanor and that worthless new husband of hers.'

'Ah.' Elanor? Josse held back the enquiry; surely Mathild wouldn't disappoint now?

She didn't. 'Surrounded by women, Sir Alard,' she said, with a rueful smile. 'Two daughters, two sisters, only one of them's dead. And the surviving one bred girls, like her brother. Only the one, in her case, and, to make a bad matter worse, the girl's just gone and married a man like Milon d'Arcy. And her silly mother let her! I ask you!'

Milon. Milon? Yes! Josse saw again the young man with his kiss-curl and his skin-tight hose. So he was married to Alard's niece! That made it quite clear what he'd gone to see Alard about. No wonder Will had shown him the door.

Josse thought he might complete his visits to Gunnora's family by paying a call on the cousin and her husband. Although he couldn't immediately see any likely benefit, other than that it would widen his knowledge of Gunnora's circumstances. He was just wondering how to find out where this Elanor and Milon could be found when Mathild spoke.

'He's fond of Elanor, Sir Alard is,' she said. 'Well, it's hard not to be, she's a lively little thing. Bright, full of fun.'

'More like Dillian than Gunnora.' It seemed a safe comment.

'Aye, though she hasn't the kindness of Dillian. There's a ruthless streak lies underneath the laughter and the lightheartedness, of that I'm sure. She's always had an eye on the main chance, that one – made sure she was around when Sir Alard was dishing out largesse. Why, he'd quite got into the way of treating her like one of his daughters when it came to presents. When he had those crosses made for his own girls, he didn't hesitate to order one for Elanor as well. And now she stands to inherit the lot.' Mathild shook her head, as if such sudden and unexpected good fortune were quite incomprehensible. 'Well, good luck to her, I say. No doubt that foolish young flower she's married to will run through it all in double-quick time.' She gave a sudden loud laugh.

'Perhaps she needs some advice,' Josse said, seeing his opening. 'I have experienced a similar situation within my own family,' he improvised, 'and possibly I might be of some help?'

Mathild gave him a very long look. Then she said neutrally, 'Possibly you could, sir. Only Elanor's from home. Been away a month or more. Staying with kin of her husband's, they do say, down Hastings way.'

'Oh.'

He sensed her suspicion. Was she regretting having been so forthcoming? Did she think he was plotting, by some devious means, to get a share of Alard of Winnowland's fortune? He couldn't be sure. But it seemed an opportune moment to remind her gently of why he had come, and where he had come from.

He stood up, placing his empty mug down on the side table. 'I must be going,' he said. 'I am sorry to have missed Sir Brice. Thank you for the ale, Mathild – it has refreshed me for my long ride back to Hawkenlye Abbey. The Abbess will be anxious for the tidings I take her.'

It did the trick. Mathild's expression cleared, and she jumped up from the bench she had been perched on to see him to the door.

The boy, Ossie, had secured Josse's horse in the corner of the yard. Noticing the mounting block, Josse had a sudden vision of Dillian, throwing herself on to her husband's horse and racing off to her death.

Riding away from the house, feeling Mathild's eyes on his back, it was a considerable relief to leave Rotherbridge Manor behind.

Chapter Eight

Josse got back to Hawkenlye Abbey in the late afternoon. He hadn't hurried; for one thing, it was too hot, and, for another, he had a great deal to think about.

There was no one around when he rode up to the gates, which were closed. But then, hearing the sounds of a horse's hooves, a lay brother appeared from within the stable, and hurried across to undo the stout chain. He had apparently recognised Josse – which was useful if unexpected, since Josse didn't recognise him – and he took Josse's horse as Josse dismounted, volunteering the information that the sisters were at their devotions.

Josse's heart sank. He was tired, hungry, and thirsty, and, for the last five miles at least, had been looking forward to sitting with the Abbess in her cool and peaceful little room, expounding at length on the subject of the family background of the late Gunnora of Winnowlands, while Abbess Helewise, after plying him with a mug of some cold and delicious wine and a chunk of bread, listened with rapt attention.

Well, it always had seemed somewhat unlikely an image. But a man could dream.

With time on his hands, Josse decided that this might be his chance to go down into the vale and have a look at the holy spring.

*

He followed the path which he and Abbess Helewise had taken the day before. The sun was still hot enough to suppress animal and insect activity in the long grass on either side of the track, although, when he paused to listen, he could hear a soft, distant humming, as if a thousand bees were busy somewhere out of sight in the shade.

This time, he stayed on the main path, and, after only a few minutes, was standing outside the small and fairly basic dwelling where the monks lived. The wattle-and-daub house, low and quite small, was in deep shade beneath its thatched roof. A nearby trio of chestnut trees spread their branches over it, increasing the gloom. As in the Abbey above, there was nobody about; presumably the monks were at prayer with the sisters.

Curiosity getting the better of him, Josse peered in through the open door. The floor of the room was beaten earth, and on it stood a roughly made table with benches along both sides. A hanging divided off the sleeping quarters, but, for the daytime, it had been tied back. The quarters themselves were further divided, presumably so that the professed monks slept slightly apart from the lay brothers. Both monks and lay brothers, Josse observed, slept on thin straw pallets, and the neatly folded covers looked as if they would provide scant warmth and absolutely no softness. Even now, in the middle of a hot summer, the room felt damp and smelt slightly of mould. Underlying the mould was another, even more unpleasant smell. Either the monks had not situated their necessarium far enough from their sleeping quarters, or the warmth of the day was heightening the stench of the dung mixed in with the mud of the walls.

It must, Josse thought, backing out of the room, be even worse in winter. Particularly for any monk who had the misfortune to suffer from that crippling curse of damp-engendered pain in the joints. And, down in this grassy, shaded vale with the water source so close, the air would never feel dry.

He headed on towards the shrine, and the simply made,

lean-to shelter that adjoined it. Within the shelter he could make out benches, a small hearth, at present swept out and empty, and a wooden shelf bearing roughly fashioned earthenware cups and jugs. There were more of the straw pallets, but these ones were rolled up and tied neatly, pushed out of the way underneath one of the benches. Pilgrims to Hawkenlye, Josse observed, were cared for adequately, but with not the smallest touch of luxury. Well, those who came as supplicants, with sincere and devout hearts, doubtless expected no more. Would not the healing powers of the sacred water be gift enough?

Another lay brother came out from behind the lean-to shelter on hearing Josse approach, broom in hand, cuffs rolled back, feet bare and long brown robe hitched up. Again, he appeared to know who Josse was; at any rate, he neither asked him to state his business nor assumed him to be a pilgrim in need of the miracle water. Instead, with a vaguely approving nod, he simply said, 'You'll be wanting to look inside Our Lady's shrine. Go ahead, sir, you'll have the place to yourself,' before turning back to the obviously dirty task of sweeping out whatever detritus had accumulated behind the shelter.

Josse went on down the well-worn path to the shrine. Although he didn't know what he was looking for, he had the strong feeling that he must be alert, all senses aware.

He stood for a moment outside the little building, staring up at the tall wooden cross on the roof, noticing how the shrine had been made. The spring, it seemed, issued out of a small and steep-sided depression in the ground, and the shrine was scarcely more than a roof and two walls, the remaining walls being formed by the natural rocky outcrops that bordered the spring. The walls had been economically made, again, of wattle and daub, but, unlike the monks' quarters, this time fortified with pillars of stone, and a wooden door with a solid-looking lintel stood partly open.

Josse pushed it further open, and stepped into the moist coolness of the shrine.

The only light came through the door, and, since he was standing in the doorway, he was blocking most of it out. He waited until his eyes adjusted to the dimness, then took a couple of paces forward. The ground beneath his feet was of the same beaten earth as the monks' house, and the rock walls appeared to have been untouched; the result was that there was a great sense of naturalness about the shrine, a pleasing effect that seemed to say, this is the Holy Virgin's place, we do but tend it.

The water seeped up out of a crevice right at the back of the shrine, where the two rock walls met. Over the countless years that it had welled up out of the ground, it had formed for itself a pool; the soft sound of running water was soporific, relaxing, and for a brief moment Josse was tempted to lean against the wall and rest.

No. He had work to do.

He moved forward again, and noticed a short flight of steps going down to the edge of the pool. They had been hewn out of the rock, and were wet with condensation. They were, he found out as he started his descent, extremely slippery. He put out a steadying hand to the rock wall beside him, and had a fleeting sense of fellowship with the countless other visitors who, momentarily unsteady just like him, had grasped at the same hand-hold.

He stopped on the third step from the bottom, and looked up at the statue of the Virgin.

The only man-made element in the shrine, someone had done his best to make sure that it was a good one. Carved of some dark wood, indeed it was. The Virgin stood above the spring, her feet at eye level and her outstretched hands palm-upwards, as if to say, come, drink of my healing waters. Her slim, graceful silhouette was elegantly draped in a hooded robe, and she inclined her head forward, a distant but welcoming smile on her lips. Above her head was a halo, a perfect circle, generously proportioned as if to emphasise her holiness.

As Josse stared at her, he noticed that the platform on which she stood had been cleverly designed to echo the shape of the halo, and had a gently reflective surface; it looked, he observed, as if, staring down into the waters of the pool, the

Holy Mother could see her own halo-encircled face smiling back at her.

It was a most original and effective concept. Descending the last couple of steps, Josse had a closer look. The platform had been let into the rock, out of which it jutted some four or five hands' span; to support the weight of the wooden statue, it had been braced underneath, although this was not apparent from above. It was made of the same dark wood as the statue, but the upper surface had been faced with a skin of silver. The Virgin's delicate bare feet made a pleasing contrast with the bright metal; Josse found himself staring at her toes, and, without any great surprise, discovered he was smiling.

It was a powerful place, this shrine, he decided, returning back up the stone steps. Easy to see how it had moved men to reverence, easy to believe that the Holy Mother had wished this new and important centre of healing to come into being. Moved by it himself, he stopped at the top of the steps, turned once more to face the Virgin, and, dropping to his knees, began to pray.

Helewise found herself suffering from an uncharacteristic inability to concentrate during the late afternoon devotions. It was not, in fact, that she couldn't force her brain to focus, but that it wouldn't focus on her prayers. With a determined effort of will, ruthlessly she put the many disturbing matters clamouring for her attention to the back of her mind and made herself listen to the singing of the choir nuns.

Leaving the church afterwards, she felt uplifted; as if it were a divine reward for her efforts, she sensed that suddenly her mind was sharper. As she crossed towards the archway into the cloisters, Brother Michael appeared from the stables and informed her that Josse d'Acquin had returned, and had gone down to the vale to visit the shrine.

Thanking him, she walked slowly to a shady spot on the western side of the cloister, and, sinking down to perch on the stone bench that ran along inside the wall, swiftly she began to order her thoughts.

Josse would have information to impart to her, that was certain. Word from Gunnora's father, if nothing else. But there *would* be more; Josse d'Acquin was not, she had already decided, the sort of man to be satisfied with what people elected to tell him, not when there was even the remotest possibility of winkling out more for himself.

And I, she thought, what have I to tell him?

Free now to return to the matters that had been demanding her attention in church, she put them in order of importance.

And uppermost in her mind was the postulant, Elvera. Who, in the days since Gunnora's death, had changed. At first almost imperceptible, the speed of the change had suddenly accelerated, until, in the space of the last twenty-four hours, the young girl seemed like a different person.

I could have understood it, Helewise thought, had the alteration happened as soon as we learned of Gunnora's death. After all, they obviously liked one another, and what would have been more understandable than that Elvera would have been struck both by grief and by the horror of her friend's slaughter? Although Elvera did not appear to be the sort of girl who needed someone to lean on – Helewise would have said rather the opposite – one couldn't always tell, and possibly the strangeness of Elvera's new life within the Abbey's walls had made her act out of character, affecting her with an unusual feeling of being at sea, in need of the stabilising influence of a sister who was more settled, more secure in the religious life.

Except that, were that the case, then Elvera would surely have latched on to one of the sisters who exhibited such an air of security. A girl of her intelligence – and, it was clear, Elvera did possess considerable intelligence – would not have chosen Gunnora.

Pulling her thoughts back from that intriguing diversion, Helewise returned to the question of Elvera's changed behaviour.

No. For a week – over a week – following the murder, she

had been much the same. Horrified, as they all were, but, had Helewise had to make an assessment, she would have said that, then, it was more a matter of Elvera's reaction being less than one would have expected, not more. The laughter had been suppressed, but Helewise had had the strong impression that this was for form's sake; nobody had so much as smiled in the dreadful days after Gunnora's death.

It wasn't like that now. Now, Elvera was pale and distracted, and the smooth young brow wore a frown. It was almost, Helewise reflected, as if the reality of what had happened had only now got through to her.

Was that it? Was it simply a case of delayed shock? Helewise had seen such phenomena, following both physical injury and bereavement.

Slowly Helewise shook her head. That wasn't the answer, she was quite sure, tempting though it was to accept it and pursue the matter no further. No. Something had happened to upset Elvera, something that had occurred since Gunnora's death.

Twenty-four hours since Elvera had been stricken. Twenty-four hours since Josse d'Acquin had blown into their lives and, as suddenly, gone off again. And it was common knowledge within the Abbey what he had come for and where he had gone.

The coincidence was too strong to be dismissed; the conclusion was, quite obviously, that something about Josse or, more likely, about his mission to Gunnora's family, had unsettled Elvera.

Why should either be a cause for distress? And in Elvera, of all people! The youngest of the sisterhood, the most recently arrived, the only person who could have been called, even in the loosest of terms, a friend of Gunnora. Helewise shrugged off an unaccountable sense of foreboding; I am being needlessly dramatic, she told herself, allowing my imagination to run away with the thought of a mystery, an intrigue, when, in all probability, what Elvera is suffering from is no more than reaction to what was, after all, a truly horrific event. And, naturally, a certain apprehension, since a girl as bright as she is must have worked out that, sooner or later, she would be summoned to speak to the man who has come to investigate Gunnora's death.

Yes, Josse said he wanted to talk to the girl, Helewise remembered. Said, when I remarked that she probably wouldn't last much longer in the Abbey, 'Don't let her go till I've spoken to her.' There wasn't the occasion before he left for Winnowlands, but there's plenty of time now.

Getting to her feet, Helewise left the cloister and went across to the Abbey's rear gate. Going on along the track until she could see down into the valley, she noticed a familiar figure just beginning on the walk back up to the Abbey.

Smiling to herself, she retraced her footsteps. On the way back to her room, she beckoned to one of the novices.

'Sister Anne?'

Sister Anne bobbed a rather graceless curtsey. 'Yes, Abbess?'

'Would you please find the postulant Elvera for me – I believe she may be with Sister Beata in the herb garden. When you find her, ask her to come to see me.'

'Who?'

Sister Anne, Helewise reminded herself resignedly, was not the brightest of women. 'Elvera, Sister Anne.' Chastising herself for her momentary irritation, she made herself smile and added, 'If you would be so kind.'

Sister Anne managed to look both interested and faintly shocked. A summons from the Abbess was – or could be – a serious matter. And for a postulant to be sent for! What could she have *done*? Helewise could imagine the lurid possibilities racing through Sister Anne's mind.

There was enough gossip and speculation rampant in the Abbey already; with a quelling look, Helewise said, 'It is not a matter to interest anyone save Elvera and me, Sister Anne. Now, off you go.'

'No, Abbess,' Sister Anne only seemed slightly contrite. 'Sorry, Abbess.'

Helewise watched her hurry away, white veil flapping, large feet slipping about in the solid wooden clogs: Sister Anne's particular way of serving God in the Hawkenlye community was in the vegetable patch. Ah, well, Helewise thought, producing a large, tasty cabbage was just as important and, no doubt, as pleasing to the Lord, as spending most of the day in fruitless speculation over the motives of some innocent postulant.

Dismissing both Sister Anne's cabbages and her own rueful thoughts from her mind, she turned and made for her room. Josse, she was sure, would look for her there; it would be interesting to observe Elvera's reaction when they came face to face.

Chapter Nine

Helewise, sitting behind her oak table, had only been waiting for a few moments when Josse arrived. She inclined her head in response to his greeting, then, even before she could invite him to sit down, he announced that he'd seen Gunnora's father and had been given permission for Gunnora to be buried at Hawkenlye.

'Thank God,' Helewise murmured fervently. Her mind already turning to the details of the service and where Gunnora might be laid to rest, she was distracted by an awareness that Josse had more to tell her.

'I am sorry,' she said, giving him a swift smile. 'What other news do you bring?'

He told her.

'Her sister dead, too, and by such ill chance!' she exclaimed. She couldn't recall if she had been aware that Gunnora had had a sister. The business of her admission to the convent had been conducted by her father and her aunt. The father, she remembered, had, although weak with exhaustion after the long ride, still managed to summon the energy to give both his sister and his daughter severe and almost brutal reprimands during the course of the brief visit. She said, 'How is Sir Alard?'

'Dying,' Josse said starkly. 'He is wasting away with the lung rot. He cannot, I fear, have long.'

'And, with both daughters dead, there is no one to whom he may leave his wealth.' She should not, she admonished herself, have gone straight to the practical matters; she should have said a few words about the poor sick man, whose sufferings were now so greatly increased by bereavement. Should have made a moment for a brief, compassionate prayer.

But Josse didn't seem to have noticed. 'I was going to ask you,' he was saying, 'was there any question of Sir Alard bequeathing money to the Abbey? There was a dowry, I presume, but I wondered if possibly he intended to ensure favour in Heaven by a gift?'

'He provided Gunnora's dowry, yes, although one had the sense he did so grudgingly.' She recalled the scene, enacted right here in her room. Sir Alard had looked seriously ill a year ago, so much so that Helewise had thought him unwise to have undertaken the journey. Not that he was the sort of man to whom you could say such a thing, even had she been given the chance; Sir Alard had made his laborious way into the room, supported by Gunnora's aunt and by a heavy stick, flung a small bag of coin on the table, wished Helewise and her nuns well of Gunnora, and stumped out again. 'But there has never been any mention of a bequest.' She thought for a moment. 'I would consider it highly unlikely. Especially since his daughter's death has removed her from our community.'

'Not the man for a magnanimous gesture?' Josse suggested.

She hesitated, not wanting to speak ill of a dying man. But Josse was after the truth. And, besides, she did not think he would think the less of her for her plain speaking. 'That was my impression.'

'Hm.' Josse was frowning. Aware that, sooner or later, he would tell her what he was thinking, she waited. Presently he said, 'It looks as if the estate and the money will go to a niece. She's got a new husband, a fashionable young fellow who seems all too eager to get his hands on his uncle-by-marriage's fortune.'

'You met them?'

'No. The niece, I was told, is staying with her husband's family somewhere near Hastings. I saw him, though. The husband.' He laughed briefly. 'Can't say I was impressed.'

'A little uncaring, wouldn't you consider,' Helewise said

thoughtfully, 'for a niece who stands to inherit her uncle's estates not to be present when he is dying?'

'I do indeed,' Josse replied, with some heat. 'The least she could do, I'd have thought, is to show some respect, even if she couldn't manage genuine tears of regret.'

Helewise was about to go on to ask Josse what overall impression he had formed of Gunnora's family and circumstances, when she recalled the present, more pressing, matter. 'I don't wish to interrupt, but I have summoned Elvera here to meet you.'

Momentarily he looked blank, then said, 'Aye! The young postulant, friend of Gunnora's.'

'You expressed a wish to speak to her.'

'Aye, I did.' He flashed her a grin. 'Thank you, Abbess.'

'I must tell you, before she arrives, that she has been behaving oddly.'

'Oddly?'

'Distracted, pale, eyes heavy as if she does not sleep well.'

'Aye, I remarked myself on her reddened eyes.' Did you, indeed, Helewise thought. I must never, for an instant, forget how observant you are, Josse d'Acquin. 'Grief for her friend, do you think?' he was asking.

'Perhaps. I have told myself that is most likely.'

'But you have not convinced yourself.' Again, the smile. 'Why not, Abbess?'

'Because her distress only started when you arrived, Sir Josse.'

He met her eyes, and she saw that he was thinking along the same lines. 'So, not the murder that grieves her, but its investigation,' he said softly.

'Indeed.'

Before either of them could comment, there came the sound of approaching footsteps, quickly followed by a tap on the door.

'Come in,' Helewise said.

Sister Anne put her head round the door. 'Here's Elvera,' she said, standing aside and ushering in her charge. 'Go on, girl, she won't eat you!'

Josse, Helewise noticed, had pushed his chair back so that he was hidden by the opened door. It would appear, to Sister Anne and, more crucially, to Elvera, that Helewise was alone.

Elvera took a step into the room, and Sister Anne followed.

'Thank you, Sister Anne,' Helewise said.

'Oh! But . . .'

While she was thinking up an excuse for staying, Helewise added, 'I'm sure you have duties requiring your attention.'

Sister Anne gave Elvera a last glance, then turned and left, closing the door behind her with exaggerated care.

Elvera stood facing Helewise, who studied the white face and the tense body for a few moments. Yes, there was definitely something amiss with the girl. Could it be that she was ill? In pain? Then wouldn't she have said so?

There was only one way to find out.

Still holding Elvera's eyes, Helewise said, 'Here is someone who wishes to meet you, Elvera. I present Josse d'Acquin, who comes from our new king's presence with his grace's express orders to investigate the murder of Gunnora.'

Elvera's first reaction was to shut her eyes tight and shake her head, as if, perhaps, she hoped that by denying Josse's presence she could make it not so. As Helewise watched, slowly her eyes opened again and she turned to face him.

She does not lack courage, Helewise thought. Then she said, 'Elvera, as Gunnora's friend, you may be able to help Sir Josse by telling him anything that occurs to you about how she was during the last days of her life. If, for example, she seemed worried about anything. If she confided in you any secret anxieties.'

'Any secret hopes,' Josse put in. He was, Helewise observed, looking kindly at the girl. 'Don't be alarmed, Elvera. I realise you must be very upset to lose a good friend in this way, but—'

'She wasn't my friend!' Elvera burst out. She was clutching at the cloth of her black robe, where it hung loosely over the rounded breasts. The drab black headdress, which would have made almost any other girl or woman look plain, was not enough to remove the lively appeal of Elvera's face, even in her present state. 'I hardly knew her! I'd only *been* here a week when she died! We weren't close at *all*!'

'No, all right, Elvera.' It wasn't all right, but Helewise didn't think they'd get anything useful out of the girl if she were not swiftly brought back from the brink of panic. 'Just as a fellow member of the community, then, can you help in any way?'

'Why are you asking *me*?' the girl flashed back. 'They're already gossiping about me, all those old nuns, saying isn't it strange, Gunnora and me being so close, anyone'd think we already knew each other before! Goodness, their eyes were out on stalks when Sister Anne came galumphing over her cabbage patch to fetch me just now!' She paused for breath, then added, her voice unsteady and beads of sweat on her white face, 'None of *them* gets sent for to be asked horrible questions by the king's investigator!'

Then Helewise knew exactly what was ailing Elvera. She was terrified.

But, terrified or not, a postulant did not speak to her Abbess in that way.

'Elvera, you forget yourself,' Helewise said coldly. 'It is not for you to question my actions. You have undertaken to be obedient.'

'I—' Some inner battle was going on inside Elvera. It was apparent that she longed to hurl back some pert denial, but something stopped her. Lowering her eyes, she straightened her expression and said demurely, 'Yes, Abbess.'

Her whole demeanour was so clearly false that it was almost amusing.

Getting up from his seat, Josse moved round to stand beside Helewise, facing Elvera across the table. 'Friend or not,' he said mildly, 'it was noticed by several people that you and Gunnora got on quite well. That you laughed together. That sometimes she sought you out, and—'

'She didn't!'

'Elvera, we *know* she did,' Helewise put in gently. 'You

sought each other out. That is a fact. It's quite senseless to go on denying things which more than one other person noticed and remarked on.'

'Well, it wasn't my fault if she came to look for me,' Elvera said triumphantly. 'Was it?'

'No,' Josse acknowledged. 'I suppose not.'

'She hadn't made any friends all the time she'd been here,' Elvera went on, with the air of one who has seen a way out and is making all speed to set off down it. 'Lonely, she was. She latched on to me because . . . because . . .' A sudden fierce frown disturbed the young face, then, as quickly, cleared. 'Because I was new!' she finished.

'You were new,' Helewise echoed.

'Yes! New and not set against her like everyone else!'

'You must not malign your sisters in this way,' Helewise said. 'Nobody was set against Gunnora. Her self-absorption was her own choice.' Dear God but I'm judging her, she thought. And, what's worse, expressing my judgement in front of this disturbed child.

As if understanding why she had suddenly stopped speaking, Josse said, 'Elvera, look on it this way. Gunnora believed you to be her friend, enjoyed your company, your light-heartedness. Perhaps it would comfort you to think that you might have made her last days happy, and—'

'*No!*'

The single word seemed to emerge from Elvera as if its expression gave her agony. As Helewise and Josse watched, she shut her eyes again. This time, two tears appeared from under the lids and slid down the pale cheeks.

Josse seemed to be at a loss as to how to continue. Helewise didn't feel any more confident, but, in her own room and in her own abbey, it was up to her to do something.

'Elvera, I understand your pain but you must tell us anything that might help,' she said gently. 'Take a moment to think back over that last day. You and Gunnora were heard laughing together outside the infirmary, and Sister Euphemia—'

'She came thundering out of her hospital and gave us a right telling-off,' Elvera said sulkily. 'Especially Gunnora, since she was senior to me. But she had a go at me, too. Sister Euphemia, I mean. She told me I was a child, that I had to grow up.'

'Never mind that now,' Helewise put in. 'Did you see any more of Gunnora that day?'

'Of course. In the refectory, during the Holy Offices, here and there around the Abbey.'

'I meant did you see her alone?' Surely the girl realised that!

'No.' Elvera raised her head and looked Helewise straight in the eye. Her face looked strangely smug. 'You told her we mustn't. Didn't you?'

'Not that day!' Helewise exclaimed. Elvera must know that, too. Oh, the interview seemed to be going round in circles! 'We respect your feelings, Elvera, and we know what you're going through, but—'

'You don't.' Elvera spoke so softly that Helewise hardly heard. 'You can't.'

'We want to help,' Josse put in. 'We must find her killer, Elvera, and he must be tried and punished for his crime.'

Josse, Helewise was well aware, was trying to reassure the girl. Encourage her to unite her efforts with his and find the murderer.

But, when once again Elvera raised her head, she looked neither reassured nor encouraged. She looked suddenly ten years older.

She said dully, 'I know.'

Then, without waiting for permission, she turned and quietly let herself out of the room.

Helewise sat staring at the closed door. Beside her she sensed Josse start to move; returning to his chair, he said, 'What did you make of that?'

'She's afraid.'

'Indeed she is.'

'She knows a great deal more than she has told us.'

'She hasn't told us anything!'

Helewise felt his frustration. 'I am sorry, Sir Josse. She was, as you imply, singularly unhelpful.'

'She's bright, that one,' he said musingly. 'Not as bright as she believes she is, but not the sort to be pushed into revealing her secrets just because someone in authority orders her to.'

Helewise said mildly, 'I did my best.'

He smiled. 'Aye. And I thank you, Abbess.' The heavy brows came down again. 'Why does she deny the friendship? Do you believe this convenient explanation, that all the overtures were made by Gunnora, and Elvera just went along with it?'

'Not for a moment. For one thing, it didn't happen like that – I saw with my own eyes that, if anything, Elvera was the instigator. For another, Gunnora wasn't the sort of woman to woo others for their favours.'

'Hm. Why lie, then?'

'She was horrified when she saw you hiding behind the door,' Helewise remarked.

'Many people react that way.' He grinned. 'I was comely when I was young, they used to say.'

Absurdly – and most inappropriately – she had to quell a desire to laugh. Pulling herself together, she said, 'Did you observe her reaction when you suggested she had provided some happiness for Gunnora in her last days? And, later, how she looked when you spoke of Gunnora's killer?'

He nodded. 'Aye. Go on.'

She had the feeling he already knew what she was about to say, but went ahead anyway. 'I think, Sir Josse, that our little Elvera is carrying a burden of guilt.'

Still nodding, he said, 'A singularly heavy one.'

Between Compline and Matins, when most of the sisters were deep in the first dreamless sleep that comes from a busy day and a clear conscience, somebody was abroad.

As Gunnora had done the night she died, somebody crept along the dormitory and descended the steps, careful to avoid the third stair. Made her way in the shadows to the rear gate, slid back the bolts, emerged on to the track.

The slim figure pushed back her short, ugly veil, and the springy hair, not yet confined by wimple and barbette, caught the soft moonlight. The girl breathed in deeply, striding over the short grass as if glad to be free, to be outside the confines of the convent wall and, for a short time, out of sight of the watching, gossiping nuns.

There was nothing tentative about the way she walked; an observer would have gained the impression she had done this before, and, indeed, would have been right. For anyone within the Abbey who wanted a private meeting with an outsider, going out secretly by night was the only way to achieve it. And she wanted such meetings. Oh, she did! Wanted them, needed them, for more than one reason.

Nearing the meeting place, well hidden in the undergrowth beside the path, she broke into a run. Let him be there! He *must* be, it is the day of the week that he always waits!

She left the path and made her way into the bushes. Called his name softly, waited for an answer.

Nothing.

Called again, went deeper into the shrubbery.

Then, as she stood still to listen, heard a footfall.

Turned, a smile of relief and love on her face.

And, as he approached, moved forward into his arms.

The Second Death

Chapter Ten

Josse had been offered accommodation in the shelter down in the vale, where pilgrims coming to the shrine were put up. Just as he had suspected, it was not particularly comfortable, but the floor was swept and the straw filling of his palliasse was reasonably fresh.

Whether or not it was because rumours had spread about the recent murder, at present there were no visitors to the shrine. Few, if any, pilgrims were arriving during the long, warm summer days to take the miracle waters; certainly, none were asking to be accommodated overnight.

Josse was inclined to be impatient with a man – or a woman – who would let a surely unreasonable, superstitious fear stand between them and a possible cure for whatever sickness or trouble ailed them. Why, the greatest fool in the kingdom could see, couldn't he, that this was no random crime of violence? That, whoever had slaughtered Gunnora, he had somehow been involved in her secretive, complicated life?

No. He corrected himself. Of course they couldn't see it. For Josse's speculations had been shared with no one but the abbess, and she, he was quite sure, hadn't been passing them on.

No. As far as the outside world was concerned, this murder remained what it had been from the start. A random crime committed by a released prisoner.

Mentally putting spurs to himself, Josse vowed to increase his efforts and prove, once and for all, otherwise.

Settling down as best he could in his solitary discomfort, he closed his eyes and made himself relax.

He did not sleep well. Disturbed by dreams of violence and by the conviction that there were living things within the straw, things, moreover, determined to feast off his blood, it was a relief when the faint grey of dawn lightened the eastern sky.

He got up and, scratching, went outside and walked the short distance to the latrine, hidden behind a paling fence. He held his breath as he relieved himself. It appeared to be some time since the trench had been dug, and the contents now neared ground level. Then he crossed to where a trough of water stood against the wall to the rear of the shelter. Plunging his head into it, he scrubbed at his short-cropped hair and splashed the back of his neck. It served to bring him to full wakefulness, even if he didn't feel a great deal cleaner. On his wrists, he noticed, were several rough circles of small red bites, which, he was sure, hadn't been there when he went to bed.

I'm getting soft, he decided as he stood staring out at the scene before him, the details gradually clarifying as daylight brightened. Shaking the drops of water out of his ears, he thought, fleas, lice, a hard pallet and the constant stench of shit, what should they matter to a former soldier? I'm too used to the comforts of court, to the pleasure of cleanliness. To the sweet perfumes of the ladies of Aquitaine. I must accustom myself to different standards here.

Outside the narrow world of the convent, the English, Josse had been discovering, stank.

His thoughts wound to a halt as his eyes focused on an object on the path. The smaller path, the one that led to the pool.

The path where Gunnora had been found.

Not pausing to raise the alarm, he was off, running as fast as he could. Although, even then, some deep awareness within him was telling him it was too late for haste.

She was lying face-down, and her head and shoulders were under the water. Grabbing her by the tops of her arms, he dragged her backwards, then, turning her on to her back, he put his cheek right by the partly open mouth.

He could feel not a whisper of breath.

Her face was dead white, the lips blueish. Her tongue, protruding slightly, looked swollen. Rolling her over on to her front, he pressed down with his hands and leaned his weight on her back, at the level of the lungs: he had seen a man saved that way once, seen how the pressure squeezed the water from the body, brought the victim back from the brink so that he coughed out the muck in his throat and drew a life-restoring breath . . .

But that man had been under water for a matter of minutes. And this girl, this poor girl, had, Josse was forced to recognise, been immersed for hours.

She was quite dead.

He sat back on his heels, staring down at her. He felt tears running down his face, and brushed them away.

Her hair, he noticed absently, had been reddish. Curly, springy. It would have been sad when the day came to clip it short for the donning of barbette and wimple. He hadn't noticed it yesterday . . . No. Of course not. Yesterday she had been wearing the short black veil of the postulant.

He took off his tunic and draped it over her head and the upper part of her body. Then, bare-chested, he went to find Abbess Helewise to tell her that Elvera had drowned.

If the Abbess were surprised at being summoned by a half-naked man before Prime, she gave no sign. Very shortly after Josse had located one of the sisters on night duty in the hospital, and told her the brief details of his urgent mission, Helewise had appeared, gliding down the steps from the dormitory, perfectly dressed, bringing with her a faint scent of lavender.

She, Josse thought absently, was indeed the exception to the general rule. She was as sweet-smelling as an Aquitaine gentle-woman.

'Good day, Sir Josse,' she greeted him. 'It was you who found her, Sister Beata tells me?'

'Aye, lady.'

'Drowned.'

'Aye. Drowned.'

She was having the same dreadful thought; he could read it in her eyes. She glanced over her shoulder, but Sister Beata had gone back to the hospital. Drowned postulants, her attitude seemed to say, were not her business, not while she had the sick and the suffering in her charge.

'Do you think she died at her own hand?' Helewise asked quietly.

He shrugged. 'I don't know. It's possible.'

She was nodding slowly. 'We both noticed her state of mind yesterday,' she said, in the same quiet, controlled tone. But he noticed the agitated hands, the strong fingers pulling at each other. As if she realised, she folded her hands and hid them away inside her sleeves. 'I should have stayed with her, comforted her,' she went on. 'If she took her own life, I am to blame.'

He wanted to shake her. Tell her that, ultimately, every man and woman on God's earth is responsible for themselves. That, if a soul is intent on self-destruction, that is their choice.

He said simply, '*If* she took her own life, Abbess, it was because it had gone so terribly awry that she considered it no longer worth the living. And that, you must agree, is not something for which you must blame yourself.'

She didn't answer for some time. Then, after a faint sigh, she said, 'We had better arrange for her body to be brought up to the Abbey.'

'Not just yet.' He heard the urgency in his voice. 'I only had the briefest look at her. Let us return together. There may be things we can learn.'

She gazed at him. She seemed hardly to hear, and he wondered if she were in shock. Then abruptly she gave herself a shake, and said, 'Of course. Lead the way.'

She made a detour from the track to go to the lay brothers' quarters, and he heard her telling one of them about this latest death. 'Come along in a little while,' she said, 'and bring something on which to carry her.'

The lay brother glanced at Josse, made some remark, and disappeared inside the shelter, to emerge with a brown robe in his hands. He nodded towards Josse.

The Abbess, returning to him, handed him the robe. 'With Brother Saul's compliments,' she said.

'I am sorry to appear before you like this,' Josse said belatedly, putting on the robe. 'My tunic covers her face.'

The Abbess nodded.

Then, silently, they went on to Elvera.

It was Abbess Helewise who noticed the marks on Elvera's throat, purely because, out of delicacy, Josse had left it to her to unfasten the neck of the robe and expose the soft, creamy flesh.

Josse had been inspecting the girl's hands – the right, which had been in the water, was dead white and crinkled, but the left had been on dry land, and there was something about it he wanted to show the Abbess – when he suddenly noticed Helewise's stillness.

'What?' he asked. 'What is it?'

Helewise pointed.

Elvera had a long neck, slim, graceful. At the front, neatly, side by side, were two clear thumb marks. And descending down the soft skin behind each ear were two rows of finger marks.

As Josse watched, Helewise put her own hand over the marks. Whoever had done this had hands considerably larger than hers.

'She was throttled,' Josse said quietly. 'I would think, by a man.'

Helewise was stroking the bruised neck, tenderly, as if trying to assuage the pain of the wounds. 'Throttled,' she repeated. Then, looking up, she met Josse's eyes. 'God help me, but I am so very glad. I was so afraid that she had killed herself,' she said, speaking rapidly.

He understood. Knew, too, even from his brief experience of her, that, by and by, she would realise what she had just said.

He did not have to wait long. With a sort of gasp, she stopped her ministrations, put both hands to her face and said from behind them, 'What have I said? Oh, dear God, I'm sorry!'

He watched her anguish, aching with sympathy. He did not know what to do; on balance, it seemed best to do nothing. Pretend he hadn't noticed. He gave a brief rueful smile; that would be impossible.

After some moments, he said, 'Abbess, I don't want to intrude, but Brother Saul . . .'

She removed her hands from her face. She was ashen, and the anguish in her eyes made his heart ache for her. She said, very quietly, 'Thank you for the reminder.' With a visible effort, she pulled herself together. She bent over Elvera's body, and, as if she were tucking the covers around a sleeping child, rearranged Josse's tunic over the girl's head. Then, standing up, she turned to look up the path towards the shrine. 'Brother Saul is on his way,' she said, in what sounded very like her normal tone.

Josse looked too. 'Aye.' Then, suddenly remembering the mass of footprints at the place where Gunnora had been found, obscuring any trace a fleeing killer might have left, he hurried along the track and spoke briefly to Saul. Then, very aware of both Saul's and the Abbess's eyes on him, he began to walk slowly along the path in the other direction.

The short grass on the path was dry, the earth hard-baked, and there was little chance he'd find anything. But then he saw a disturbance in the longer grass between the path and the pond; it looked as if someone's foot had missed the path and slipped sideways into the softer gound at the edge of the water.

Hardly daring to hope, he knelt down and went forward on all fours.

Very gently, he parted the long grass. And saw, quite clearly, the marks of running feet. Whoever it was had taken three . . . four . . . five paces on the softer ground. Perhaps he had been looking back over his shoulder at what he had left behind him, and not noticed that he was no longer running on the path. But he had certainly been running, there was no doubt of that. The prints were of the front part of the foot, and the toes had dug deep into the soft ground as if he had been pushing himself as hard as he could.

Josse stared down at the footprints.

And, as he did so, pieces of the puzzle started to fit together.

He got up and walked back to the Abbess, beckoning to Brother Saul; it was safe for him to advance now. For any number of people to churn up the ground, as long as nobody obscured those tell-tale prints on the margin of the pond. Not, at least, until Josse had found some way to make a cast of them.

Helewise walked up the slope to the Abbey behind Josse and Brother Saul, neither of whom seemed to find their sad burden very heavy. They had lain her on a hurdle – was it, Helewise wondered absently, the one on which Gunnora had been carried? – and both Saul, at the head, and Josse, at the feet, seemed slumped in sorrow.

They entered inside the walls. Brother Saul turned to her. 'To the infirmary, Abbess?'

She nodded. 'Yes. Wait, Saul, I'll ask Sister Euphemia where we should put her.'

She walked ahead, and Sister Euphemia came out to meet her. With a brisk nod – Euphemia, Helewise was well aware, always coped with grief by an ostentatious display of efficiency – she indicated a little side ward, nothing more than a curtained-off recess. 'In here, please,' she said.

It was where she had laid out Gunnora.

The men carried Elvera's body inside, and Helewise watched as they placed it on the narrow cot. They were turning to go when Helewise, removing Josse's tunic from the corpse, silently returned it to him. For a moment he stared at her, and she could not read what was in his face. Then, with his usual brief bow of reverence, he was gone.

I do not deserve reverence, Helewise thought. Not this morning.

Guilt was still strong in her. She had a fierce need to put herself to some disagreeable task, force herself, in charity, to do something she hated.

Taking a deep breath, she said to Sister Euphemia, 'It is not fair that you alone should bear the burden of the laying-out of a second young victim, Euphemia. If you will permit it, I will assist you.'

Sister Euphemia's round eyes reflected her astonishment. 'But, Abbess, you—' Abruptly she stopped. She was too well-schooled to question her superior, even though, as Helewise well knew, she must be perfectly aware of Helewise's squeamishness. 'Very well,' she said instead. 'First thing is to get the poor lass's habit off her – it's wet almost as far as the waist. We'll put her in a dry one for burial.'

Helewise made her reluctant hands get to work, unfastening the black gown, peeling it off the poor cold body as Euphemia propped the dead girl up. The bruises on the girl's neck were livid now, showing up more clearly than they had done down by the water. As the garment came clear of the breasts, Euphemia made a small exclamation.

'What is it?' Helewise asked.

Euphemia didn't answer. Instead she took the neck of the robe in both hands and, more swiftly than Helewise had been doing, pulled it right down to the girl's thighs. Then she unfastened the undergarments and removed them too.

Then she put her hand on the girl's belly, low down, just above the pubic bone. Frowning, she paused for a moment, her hand exploring the area. Then she said to Helewise, 'Abbess, I must make an internal examination. I'm sorry, but it's necessary.'

Helewise had opened her mouth to protest. But then she closed it again, and gave a quick nod.

She couldn't bring herself to watch.

After a short time, Euphemia said, 'You can open your eyes. I'm done.'

Helewise did so. She noted with relief that Euphemia had

covered Elvera from shoulders to thighs with a piece of sheeting. Reaching beneath it, Euphemia stripped the dead girl's clothes right off her body.

Then, without looking at Helewise, said, 'She was pregnant. About three months gone, I'd say at a guess, maybe a little more. I thought she was when I saw her breasts – that darkening of the nipples is a fairly reliable sign, young girls usually have rosy pink ones, specially redheads like her. But when I felt her belly, I knew. I can feel the enlarged womb.'

Helewise, shocked to her core, stood staring at Euphemia in utter silence.

Mistaking this, Euphemia said, 'I'm quite sure, Abbess. There's no doubt about it.'

'I wasn't doubting you.' Helewise had difficulty speaking with a suddenly dry mouth. 'Three months gone, you said.'

'Perhaps more. The womb's just peeping above the pubic bone.'

Helewise nodded absently. A couple of weeks here or there didn't really make a lot of difference. The crucial fact – from Helewise's viewpoint, at least – was that Elvera had been pregnant before she entered the convent. By at least two months.

'Did she – would she have known?' she asked.

'Oh, yes.' Euphemia nodded for emphasis. 'She couldn't *not* have done, unless she was a total innocent, which somehow I doubt.' She gave the body on the cot an affectionate look. 'Little chatterbox, she was, and many's the time I've had to reprove her for her light-hearted ways, even in the short time she's been with us. But I'd not have said she was the sheltered sort of lass who didn't know the facts of life. She'd have missed her courses, a couple or three times, her breasts would have been tender, she'd have needed to pass her water more than usual. She'd have been sick a few times, likely as not, and sometimes found herself suddenly bone-achingly tired.'

Helewise could well recall the symptoms of early pregnancy. 'Quite so.' Her brain was working hard, trying to remember the full details of the background Elvera had related on her admission to her postulancy.

A background, Helewise now realised, which was total fiction. For, although some aspects would not come readily to mind, the one thing she did remember – because Elvera had emphasised it by at least one repetition – was that she was not interested in men and could never envisage herself having children.

Both of which statements, in the light of this new and alarming discovery, were complete falsehoods.

Chapter Eleven

Josse, impatient to speak to the Abbess, knew that, out of respect, he must not disturb her in her laying-out of the dead. A task which, he had seen only too plainly, was not in the least to her liking. He understood why she was doing it. Understood her guilt. For didn't he, who had been scratching his flea bites and restlessly sleeping not a hundred paces from where Elvera had been found, also feel the same burning emotion?

To occupy the time, he returned to the shelter in the vale and changed back into his tunic. Giving the robe back to Brother Saul, he thanked him and asked where he might find something with which to make a cast.

'A cast,' Saul repeated doubtfully.

Josse explained. Saul's face brightened, and, with a touch on Josse's sleeve, he said, 'Follow me.'

He led the way to a small shed attached to the back of the shelter. In it was an assortment of cracked vessels, benches awaiting mending, objects left behind by visitors. And candles. Tall, votive candles. And, in a bin on the floor, dozens and dozens of candle stubs.

'Brother Saul, you're brilliant!' Josse said. Picking up the bin, he was about to head off down the path when, again, Saul touched his sleeve. This time, without speaking but with a faint smile, he handed Josse a flint.

*

It was no easy task, Josse discovered, to make a satisfactory cast. It proved to be the very devil of a job acquiring enough molten wax to fill even the front half of a footprint, and, in the end, he'd had to light a small fire on the dry mud of the path. But at least he was done, and, having thoroughly stamped out his fire and returned the unused candle stumps in their bin to the little shed, he went up to the Abbey to report to Abbess Helewise. She had by now left the infirmary and, according to Sister Euphemia, would be found in her room. Carrying his carefully wrapped cast, he went to find her.

She was sitting at her table, hands folded before her and resting on the well-polished wood. There was no sign, now, of the pallid, stricken woman who had knelt by the dead girl and buried her face in her hands. She looked as she always did. Calm, controlled, slightly aloof. And as if, whatever the day threw at her, she would always remain so. But Josse, who had seen her in her distress, knew better. And found himself liking her the more for having seen her fallibility.

'So, Abbess, you and Sister Euphemia have prepared Elvera for burial,' he said, responding to her invitation to sit. He was, he found, tired out, for all that the day had scarcely begun.

'We have. Sister Euphemia entirely supports the notion that she was killed by manual strangulation.' The words were uttered tonelessly.

Josse hesitated. Should he say what was uppermost in his mind? He met her eyes. He thought she read his thought; abruptly she turned her head and fixed her glance on something over to her left. Hard to say what, he thought, when, following her gaze, he discovered that all there was to see was an unadorned stone wall.

It needs saying, though, he told himself. Even if the Abbess is reluctant to speak of such matters. 'She did not kill herself,' he said, his voice low. 'Abbess, there is no question of our actions having driven her to her death. Any, anyway, we had to speak to her, we had no choice. She was close to Gunnora, and we still have—'

'How can you say that?' she hissed back. 'That we did not

drive her to her death? Very well, she didn't put her head under the water and drown herself, that I accept! But would she, do you think, have left the safety of the convent in the middle of the night, venturing out into the dangers of a lonely place in darkness, had we not forced her to?'

'It was not we who forced her!' His voice had risen. 'Abbess, ask yourself this! Were she innocent, with a clear conscience, why in God's holy name would our gentle questioning have upset her so? And it *was* gentle, you know that as well as I do. Neither of us bullied the poor child.'

'But we – I – knew her to be disturbed already! I should have prevented the interview! Then she would have stayed safe in the dormitory, and this second killer would have been robbed of his victim!'

He leapt to his feet. '*Second* killer? No! Abbess, that's not the way of it! Two nuns from the same community, brutally murdered within weeks of each other, and you tell me there is no connection?'

'A connection, yes, of course. But I do not believe they were murdered by the same hand.' She looked doubtful, as if her own conclusion were surprising her.

'But—' He couldn't believe it. Swallowing his angry frustration, he said, 'Can you explain?'

'I doubt it,' she murmured. Then, with a visible effort, 'Sir Josse, consider the methods. Gunnora was held from behind while a second assailant slit her throat. Very neatly, very tidily. Then she was laid on the ground, her skirts were arranged around her waist and her legs and arms placed symmetrically. Her own blood was smeared on her loins, to confuse the crime with that of rape. Elvera, on the other hand, was strangled. By someone's bare hands. We have both seen his finger and thumb prints, we know he used no other weapon.' Her brows went up suddenly, as if something had just occurred to her. 'Perhaps,' she added tentatively, 'that – the fact that he had brought with him no weapon – implies there was no premeditation.'

'He killed her in a fit of passionate fury?' Josse mused. 'Aye, perhaps, but that's no reason to suspect he was not the same man who killed Gunnora. Surely, Abbess, he *has* to be?' How to convince her to abandon this irrational line of reasoning! 'Elvera, let us surmise, was somehow involved in Gunnora's death, which seems likely because you and I both observed her distress when I came to start asking questions. She went out to meet her fellow conspirator, and poured out to him her terror and her fear at having been interviewed by the king's investigator. "It's all very well for you," I can imagine her saying, "you're out here where nobody knows of your presence. *You're* not having to face the gossips and the accusing comments, not having to brace yourself to answer questions from people who seem to know far more about this business than you'd like!" And, in her hysteria, perhaps she says she can't go on. "*You* killed her," she says, "yet it's I who am having to go through all this!"' Warming to his imagined scene, he leaned forward, and the small stool creaked ominously. He ignored it.

'She tells him she's got to confess,' he went on eagerly, 'tells him that anything, any sort of retribution, is better than this dreadful suspense. She's crying, getting noisy, and he fears that any minute someone will hear. "Hush!" he says. She takes no notice. "*Be quiet!*" he says, and grabs at her. She struggles, opens her mouth to scream, and he grasps her round the throat. Before he knows what's happening, she's dead. Slips out of his arms, falls on the path, her head in the water. He now has two deaths on his hands. Aghast, it's his turn to panic. He runs away, pausing only for a quick look over his shoulder. Then he's off, back to wherever it is he's been using as his retreat.'

She waited to see if he was going to say any more. When he didn't, she drew a deep breath, held it a moment, then said, 'Plausible, yes. But what evidence have you to support it?'

'One, the marks on her neck. The neatness of those bruises, as if he placed his hands with the same eye for a tidy pattern that he used to arrange Gunnora's body.' She was looking sceptical, so he hurried on. 'Two, I found his footprints.' He removed the piece of cloth from his wax cast, and placed it carefully on the table.

She studied it. 'It's the toe of a shoe,' she observed.

'I found it in a row of half a dozen or so, widely spaced.'

She nodded. 'Hence your conclusion of someone running away.'

'Aye. And—' No. Too soon for that. He must present his facts as he had discovered them. 'Abbess, Elvera presented herself here at Hawkenlye as an unmarried virgin, I imagine?'

The Abbess's eyes widened, as if the question surprised her. 'Yes, although – Yes. Why?'

'Because she wasn't. Well, as to her not being a virgin, I only surmise. But I know she was married. Her left hand bore a distinct indentation at the base of the third finger. Until very recently, she had worn a wedding ring.'

He had expected amazement. None came. Instead, she said slowly, 'Married. One question answered, and, yet again, many more raised.'

'You suspected?'

She lifted her eyes to his. 'She was pregnant,' she said. 'Some three months, Sister Euphemia says. I had, naturally, been speculating on the circumstances of this conception, and why, indeed, she should choose the strange course of entering a convent, assuming she knew herself to be with child. At least, now, I know that it was her husband who fathered her child. Although that is scarcely any help when we have absolutely no idea of his identity.'

He said quietly, 'But we have.' And, when her eyebrows went up in enquiry, touched his wax cast.

'How can you know?' she murmured.

He traced the elongated point at the front of the print. 'Not know, perhaps, but make a very likely guess. Because I have seen someone wearing shoes like this. They are common, I dare say, in fashionable circles in London, but, hereabouts, people do not dress in the court style.'

'No,' she acknowledged. But she was frowning, as if she did not entirely agree with him. 'Assuming this print was made by the shoe you saw, then who do you think made it?'

'His name is Milon d'Arcy,' he said. 'And I further conjecture that I also know the identity of the girl lying dead in your infirmary. I believe she was his wife. Elanor, niece to Alard of Winnowlands. Gunnora's cousin.'

'Oh, but this is too much!' the Abbess cried. 'A set of footprints – not even entire prints! – and a finger which, you claim, recently wore a wedding ring, and you present to me the identity of both murderer and victim! Sir Josse, much as I would like to believe you, I can't!'

Then, he thought, I must make you.

How?

He said, 'Abbess, may I have your permission to look at Elvera's possessions? Will you come with me now to her cubicle in the dormitory?'

'A nun has few possessions,' Helewise said. 'What, pray, do you hope to find?'

Two things, he could have said. But he did not. Instead he said evasively, 'Anything that might help.'

She watched him for a long moment. Then said, 'Very well.'

Elvera's bed had been half-way along the dormitory. Again, the neatly folded covers, the thin hangings pushed back and secured. And, as the Abbess had said, little evidence of personal belongings.

He bent down and looked beneath the plank-like bed. Nothing, not even much dust; the nuns kept their quarters clean. He stood up, running a hand beneath the thin palliasse. Again, nothing. It was beginning to look as if she'd hidden them somewhere else, but she must have—

His hand encountered a small package. Something hard, wrapped in a square of linen.

He withdrew it, put it on the bed. Unfolded the linen. And there, glinting faintly in the morning light, was a wedding ring and a jewelled cross.

Back in Helewise's room, they compared Elvera's cross with Gunnora's, and with the one that had been found by her body.

The three were virtually identical, but for the fact that the rubies in both Gunnora's own cross and the one found beside her were larger than those in Elvera's. As was only to be expected, Josse thought, when Gunnora was Alard of Winnowland's daughter and Elvera – Elanor – but his niece.

'Your postulant Elvera gave you a false name and a fictitious identity,' he said to Helewise, who was holding Elvera's cross in her hands. 'She was in truth Elanor, wife to Milon. Her uncle gave her a cross, as well, when he presented his daughters with theirs.'

In his head he heard the echo of Mathild's words. *He's fond of Elanor, Sir Alard is. Well, it's hard not to be. She's a lively little thing. Bright, full of fun.* Who, he wondered, his mind running off at a tangent, would have the sorry task of telling the dying man that, having lost both daughters, now his pretty and vivacious niece was dead, too?

Dear Lord, not me, he prayed silently. Please, of thy mercy, not me.

Helewise had put down the cross and was picking up the wedding ring, trying it on her own third finger. 'Too small for me,' she remarked. 'Should we try it on the dead girl's hand, do you think?'

'If you like,' he said. 'Although I feel there is little point.'

She replaced the ring beside the three crosses, folding the linen around them once more. 'Gunnora's,' she said, pointing, 'and Elvera's. Elanor's, I should say. And this?' She pointed to the one that had been left next to Gunnora.

'It can only have belonged to her sister, Dillian,' Josse said. 'Although God alone knows how it ended up where it did.'

Helewise was watching him. The intent grey eyes were disconcerting. 'God knows, yes,' she said neutrally. 'It is up to us to find out.'

He was trying to think, to put all these new facts racing through his brain into some sort of order. Some order that began to make sense.

After some time, he said, 'Gunnora's father is dying. He has two daughters, one who has entered a convent, and who, presumably, has forfeited her right to inheriting any of his undoubted wealth. Her sister, Dillian, married to the suitor chosen by Alard as eminently suitable for one of his girls, looks set to get the lot, but then she dies. She leaves no child, and her husband, it appears, is not without involvement in her death, albeit indirect. So who can Alard leave his fortune to? Gunnora is the obvious candidate – she is, now, all he has left. But what of the niece, who, so we understand, was always treated generously by her uncle? Given a cross only a little smaller than those given to his own girls?'

Warming to his theme, he leaned his hands on Helewise's table, putting his face closer to hers. 'What if, Abbess, this niece understood herself to be in line to inherit, only to have her young fashion-conscious husband discover, on one of his visits to check up on how near to death is his uncle-by-marriage, that the uncle is thinking of changing his will? Of reinstating the daughter who rejected him and gave herself to God? What would such a greedy and unscrupulous young man do?'

'You are only conjecturing that he is greedy and unscrupulous,' she pointed out.

'Aye, maybe. But would he not have the greatest motive in the world for disposing of Gunnora? So that his wife, the niece Elanor, would then inherit?'

'Perhaps.'

'Abbess, there are two basic motives for murder, lust and the hunger for money. Nobody, it seems, lusted after Gunnora – you said yourself she was not bothered by the rule of chastity. In addition, we know that she was not raped, indeed, that she had never—' He paused, trying to think of a delicate way of saying it. 'That she had never tasted of the fruits of love.' He was aware of a very swift twitch of the Abbess's lips, quickly suppressed. 'She died a virgin,' he said firmly. 'So, with the lust motive removed, that only leaves money.'

'You oversimplify!' the Abbess cried. 'And, however plausible your reasoning on the surface, what of the details?'

'Such as?' he demanded.

'Such as, how did he persuade Gunnora to leave the convent

that night? And why did she not recognise Elvera as her cousin Elanor?'

'Who says she didn't?' he countered. 'Elvera herself, in this very room, complained that the nuns kept saying she and Gunnora got on so well together that you'd almost think they'd met before. That was hardly surprising – they had.'

'Then why did not Gunnora reveal that Elvera was married?' Helewise demanded.

'Oh.' Why indeed. Then he heard Mathild's words: *that worthless new husband of hers*. And – although this was hardly incontestable proof – Elvera had only been three months pregnant. A passionate young husband, bedding his new wife nightly, impregnating her soon after the marriage? He said triumphantly, 'Because Gunnora didn't know. Elvera and Milon were married *after* she entered the convent. And Elvera had taken off her wedding ring.'

Helewise nodded slowly. Then, suddenly: 'How did you know about the cross?'

'It had to be hidden somewhere. She wasn't wearing it when she died.'

She gave a brief sound of exasperation. 'How did you know she *had* a cross?'

'If she really was Elanor, she had to have one. And I knew she had – I saw it.'

'You did?'

'Well, no, not exactly. I guessed. Remember when we spoke to her? She was grasping at the cloth of her gown – like this.' He demonstrated. 'I thought then it was just a nervous gesture. Only afterwards did it occur to me she might be clinging to her own personal talisman, hidden under her robe.'

Helewise's expression was distant, as if she were thinking hard. 'You make a good case, sir knight,' she said eventually. 'But, again, I ask for your proof. Oh, not of Elvera's identity – we must, I think, accept that you are right.'

'We can check,' he said eagerly. 'I can return to my informant at Sir Brice's manor and ask after Elanor. Go to Milon's house, to the relatives where, so I was told, she is staying.'

'And what if you find her safe and well?'

'Then I will have to accept that I am wrong.'

'You are not wrong,' she said quietly. 'You will not, I fear, find any Elanor. She is Elvera, and she lies dead in my infirmary.' She frowned. 'But those established facts alone will not prove who killed my nuns, Sir Josse. And I do not know where we can go from here to find that proof.'

'I will find Milon,' he said simply. 'I will go, now, to his house. If he is not there' – he was almost certain that the young man would be anywhere but at home – 'then I shall search elsewhere.'

She gave him a quizzical look. 'England is a big country,' she remarked. 'With many lonely and desolate places where a fugitive may run and hide.'

'He has not run away yet,' Josse said.

And, before she could ask him how he could be so sure, he bowed, retreated from the room and set off to find his horse.

Chapter Twelve

On his way to Rotherbridge, Josse had decided, he would pay a call on Sir Alard. He needed to seek the old man's confirmation that he had indeed given jewelled crosses to his daughters and to his niece. It was probably unnecessary, he thought as he neared the Winnowlands estates, but he felt he should not ignore any proof that was reasonably easy to obtain. Not if he were going to make a convincing case to back up all his theorising.

But he arrived back at Winnowlands to discover that Sir Alard had died the previous day. While Josse had been making his slow, hot journey back to Hawkenlye Abbey, Alard of Winnowlands had finally lost his long battle with death.

Josse knew. Even before he was told, he knew. There was a difference about the place. Sir Alard's estates had not been a cheerful environment before, but, whereas previously the few of the peasantry that Josse had seen had looked merely dull-eyed and dejected, now he saw signs of more dramatic distress. Outside one hovel, a man had sat doing nothing but gaze down at his large hands, hanging idle between his knees, as if his situation were so dreadful that everything pertaining to normal life had suddenly come to a halt. From within another, better-kept dwelling, Josse heard the sounds of a woman weeping, so violently that he suspected she was close to hysteria.

Under the usual customs of inheritance, it would have been a case of 'the king is dead, long live the king!', as the new lord took over from his father; few, if any, major changes would be anticipated to alter the lot of those who depended for their very lives on the manor. But here, where there *was* no new lord . . .

Will, who came out into the yard on hearing Josse's approach, broke the news.

'He's dead,' he said flatly. Not even specifying of whom he spoke. 'Last evening, it was. Afore supper, and he had a nice bit of pie to look forward to.' Sudden tears glistened in the man's eyes, swiftly blinked away. Josse, who had observed before how it was so often the little poignancies that undermined the recently bereaved, murmured sympathetically. 'He began to cough, and the blood just flowed.' Will went on. 'Didn't stop. Master, he sort of choked, couldn't draw breath. Well, stands to reason, nothing left to draw it into, like, with his chest all rotten.' He gave a sniff, wiped the back of his hand across his nose, and said softly, 'I held him, till he was gone. Propped him up, like I always did, till he couldn't breathe no more. Then I held his hand. After a bit, I knew he were dead. I let him be, overnight. Tucked him up, settled him down, with the fire well-stoked and a candle burning. Then, this morning, I sent word. Priest's been,' he added, in a matter-of-fact tone.

Josse nodded. Will himself, he noted, looked in a bad way. Haggard, his skin yellow and unhealthy looking, he had the appearance of a man who has spent far too long at his master's sick bed, drawn in far too many breaths of contaminated air. Praying that this loyal servant should not himself succumb to the wasting sickness, Josse got down from his horse and, rather awkwardly, patted the sorrowing man on the shoulder.

'I'm sure you did all you could to make his passing as comfortable as it could be,' he said, hoping to console. 'No man could have been better tended, Will, of that I'm certain.'

'I didn't do it for what I could get out of him, no matter what they say!' Will burst out surprisingly. 'Did it for his sake,' he added more quietly. 'For old times' sake. We go back a long way, Master and me.'

'Aye, Will.' Trying to sound as if he were merely making polite conversation, Josse added, 'Leave you a bit, did he? That's a nice reward, for all your loyalty.'

Will shot him a swift assessing glance. 'Left me a tidy sum, thank you, sir,' he said stiffly, and Josse sensed the unspoken comment, if it's any business of yours. 'Priest, he was here first thing this morning, like I was telling you, along of that sister of the master's. They'd got hold of the will, and they read it out.'

'Really?' Josse pretended to be busy pulling a tangle out of his horse's mane.

'Aye. All to the niece, saving a few small sums here and there, just like they suspected. The lass's mother were right pleased, I can tell you.'

'And the young Lord Milon d'Arcy? How did he react?'

Another suspicious look. Too late, Josse realised he shouldn't have referred to the youth by name. 'Fancy you remembering what he's called,' Will said, with a casual inflection that didn't fool Josse for an instant. 'Well, sir knight, he didn't react at all, seeing as how he wasn't here.'

'No? Wasn't that a surprise, when he'd seemed so eager to know of his wife's uncle's intentions?'

Will shrugged. 'Maybe. The girl's mother was here fast enough, though, like I said. Reckon she'll have passed on the good tidings by now.'

Josse doubted that. But then he had the advantage over Will, who could have no way of knowing that Elvera was dead and Milon – if Josse was right about him – was still lurking somewhere on the edges of the forest near to Hawkenlye.

'I must go,' he said to Will. 'My commiserations on the death of your master, Will.' He fixed his eyes on Will's; those last words, at least, were sincerely meant.

'I thank you, sir,' Will responded.

'I am going to pay another call at Rotherbridge,' Josse added as he turned his horse. 'Perhaps this time I shall find Sir Brice at home. Good day, Will.'

'Sir.'

He felt Will's heavy-lidded eyes on him as he rode out of the yard. It was not a comfortable feeling.

*

On the way to Rotherbridge Manor, Josse spotted a horse and rider, stopped down by a stretch of the River Rother where the water flowed fast and shallow over a stony bed. The horse was a good one, and the man's elegant tunic and soft leather boots indicated he was a person of substance. He was bareheaded, and the dark hair had a streak of white running from the left temple, petering out behind the ear. Josse was just thinking that this particular bend in the river would be a good place for salmon when he heard the sound of sobbing.

The man, who was standing beside his horse, had his face buried against the horse's neck, the fingers of his strong hands entwined in its mane. His whole attitude spoke eloquently of despair, and his shoulders were heaving with the extremity of his grief. Face hidden, he did not see Josse, up on the road.

Josse felt guilty, as if he had deliberately set out to spy on another's distress. The man had chosen a secluded spot; it was, surely, an unlikely piece of bad luck that someone had come along the lonely track to disturb his privacy.

Not wanting to subject the unknown man to the awkwardness of knowing himself observed, Josse made haste to pass before the man should look up.

As before, it was Mathild who came out of the house at Rotherbridge to meet him.

'Master's back, but he ain't in,' she said.

'Oh? Are you expecting him to return soon?'

'Could be.' She gave him her same assessing squint. 'He's gone out for a ride. Wants to be alone, he says. He's missing her, see. The mistress. He's done his penance, like a good Christian should, but seems it's not been enough.' She gave a great gusty sigh. 'He'll no doubt get over it, but likely it's going to take some time.'

The grieving man by the river. Yes, Josse thought. It must have been Brice.

Poor man.

'I seek the whereabouts of Milon d'Arcy,' he said.

'Aye, like you did before, the last time you were by,' she remarked. She seemed in no particular hurry to divulge the information.

But Josse had his story ready this time. 'I come from Winnowlands,' he said, 'where—'

'He's gone at last,' she interrupted him. 'God rest his soul.'

'Amen,' Josse said. News travels fast hereabouts, he thought. 'How did you know?'

She shrugged. 'Will's woman told Ossie's mother last night. Said Will were right upset, wouldn't leave the old man's body by itself.' She shot Josse a sharp look. 'Reckon he'll have a deal more to be upset about soon, him and all the rest of the Winnowlands folk. Told you, did they? What's to happen?'

'Will told me of Sir Alard's bequest to his niece, aye, and how the girl's mother was there to hear the terms of the will.'

Mathild seemed to have overcome her reservations, and was now positively eager to talk; gossiping about the death and the will of a neighbour were, apparently, more entertaining than listening to Josse explaining himself. 'Like I said, it'll upset them, all right,' she said, nodding in affirmation.

'The estate going to Sir Alard's niece, you mean?'

'Not her, so much, she's not a bad lass. Flighty, overfond of her own comfort and a mite too ready to clamber over others to get what she wants, but then, that's not uncommon, now, is it?'

'No,' Josse acknowledged.

'No, it's that Milon d'Arcy who'll cause all the trouble,' Mathild predicted grimly. 'Nobbut a lot of air between his ears, that one, no thought but for the newest fashion, the best wine, the most delicate of dishes.' She shook her head, thoroughly enjoying herself. 'Can you see him having the sense to run a great place like Winnowlands? He'll have neither the knowledge nor the wits to ask the advice of those what has. It'll be ruin, for the lot of them.' She looked up at Josse, the shrewd eyes narrowed. 'Mark my words, sir, the Winnowlands folk are quite right to be worried.'

'Aye,' Josse said. 'Poor Will.'

'Still,' she went on, her expression lifting, 'look on the bright side, that's what I say! Young Elanor, now, she'll be a happy girl when they tell her. What a piece of news to break to a pretty young thing, eh?'

'She is still from home?' he asked casually.

'Fas as I know she is. They live over the next hill, her and my little lordship Milon – tidy place, small but elegant, mind, other side of the bridge – but I hear tell there's none of the family there now. She'll still be with her new Hastings kin, I reckon. And him, well, maybe he's gone to join her there.'

'And the kinfolk, they live . . . ?'

She told him, giving the information in such an abbreviated form that he was obliged to ask her to elaborate. She was, quite clearly, impatient to get back to her theme of how wonderful it must be for a lass not yet twenty to inherit a fortune, why, if it had been her, what she could have done with it when *she* was twenty! Goodness, she'd have had jewels, fine gowns, someone to cook and scrub for her, and she wouldn't have spent her life running round after other people, *that* was for sure.

'No, indeed,' Josse murmured, although he doubted if she was listening. Breaking away as quickly as he could, which was not in fact quickly at all, he was moving off towards the gateway when suddenly she ceased her daydreaming and called after him, 'Will you tell them, sir knight?'

'Tell them what?' he asked, although he knew what her answer would be.

She tutted briefly. 'About the fortune, of course! And about the poor old man's death,' she added, trying, and failing, to adopt a suitably mournful expression.

He hesitated. Then said, 'Oh, no. I don't think that would be suitable at all. It's hardly my place, as a stranger to the family, to break such tidings.'

She was looking at him strangely. Wondering – fearing – that she was about to ask why, if he was a stranger, he was involving himself to such an extent in family matters, he forestalled her. Calling out a swift farewell, he spurred his horse and set off to find the house of Elvera's – Elanor's – relations-in-law.

*

She was not there.

Whoever had concocted this story of her prolonged visit to her husband's kin clearly had not anticipated that anyone would actually go checking up. The servant who came out to greet Josse announced, after his initial denial, that he'd go in and ask the mistress, since it was possible she'd arranged a visit and omitted to tell the staff; he returned not only with the mistress, but also with the master and three or four other members of the household. Milon's kin, Josse noticed absently, came from a different mould than Milon; it was hard to believe that the stolid and sensibly dressed family in front of him had produced the dainty, yellow-haired youth.

Not only was Elanor not there, but nobody knew of any proposed visit. The master and the mistress, frowning at each other in perplexity, said so repeatedly. As far as they were aware, Elanor d'Arcy was contentedly at home with her husband, and planning on staying there.

Feeling both slightly foolish – quite a few of the household were looking at Josse as if he were next door to an idiot – and also unpleasantly guilty – it was not a good feeling, listening to them speaking happily of Elanor as if she were still alive when he knew full well she was dead – he said he regretted that he must have made a mistake. He apologised for having disturbed them all and took his leave. Then he hurried away and set off on the long road back to Hawkenlye.

He got back as twilight deepened into night. Hot, dirty, ravenously hungry and weary to his very bones, he was good for nothing but food and sleep. Brother Saul, tending him efficiently and with the consideration not to ask him any questions, reported briefly on the day's events at Hawkenlye since Josse had left that morning.

'The little lassie's lying in the crypt, where they put Sister Gunnora,' he said as he brought Josse a wooden platter heaped with steaming, fragrant stew. 'The Abbess has been sitting with her all day.'

Josse heard the concern in his voice. 'She is taking this hard,' he remarked.

Brother Saul shook his head sadly. 'As do we all, sir. As do we all.' He stood frowning in the direction of the shrine. 'This whole sorry business has made folks disinclined to come for the waters, too. And that's not right. Those in distress have need of the cure, and now these terrible deaths are frightening them away.'

It was, Josse thought, an aspect of the murders which ranked high with Brother Saul. He studied him, noting the kind, honest face set now in lines of distress. 'We'll find the man who is responsible, Saul,' he said softly, 'and bring him to justice. That I promise you.'

Saul turned to look at him, and, briefly, a smile softened the features. 'Yes, sir. I know you will.' Josse was just feeling the beginning of a warm glow of pleasure at the man's faith in him when, to gild the moment, Saul added, 'So does the Abbess.'

Josse slept for ten hours, and awoke feeling thoroughly refreshed. His mind must have been working while he was asleep; he returned to consciousness knowing exactly what he must do next.

Brother Saul gave him a bite of breakfast, and then he set off the short distance down the path to the area where the two dead nuns had been found. He stood first in the one place, then the other, turning slowly in a full circle, studying the immediate surroundings. Then, making up his mind, he began a very thorough inspection of the undergrowth beside the track.

He had reasoned that, since it appeared that Milon had made at least two and probably more nocturnal visits to the little valley, the young man must have had a hiding place. Perhaps not many people would be abroad down there at night – in fact, Josse thought, probably none – but, nevertheless, it seemed unlikely that anyone with nefarious intentions would have the confidence to stand about in the open.

He walked very slowly along the path, staring intently at every yard of undergrowth, eyes searching for the smallest sign of passing feet. There was nothing. Nothing! Sick with disappointment, he was about to turn back when, only a little distance from where the shrubbery began to thin out, he saw it.

You would, he thought, have had to be looking out for it. Clever young man, to forge your way through at a place where the greenery was most resilient. But not quite clever enough to check that you really had left no mark.

Pushing his way through the thick foliage, Josse was careful to avoid the two small half-broken branches which were the only sign of Milon's passage. It might be necessary to show them as proof of his theory.

Once off the path, the young man had been less cautious, and Josse followed his tracks more easily. After going for some fifteen paces, he found himself in a tiny clearing, in the midst of the undergrowth. The short grass had been trodden flat, and someone had made a crude shelter out of broken branches; presumably one of Milon's night-time vigils had been spent in the rain.

Something caught his eye; a small object, half-hidden under dead leaves. Kneeling down, he uncovered it. It was the two halves of an oyster shell, placed together; lifting up the top one, he saw inside a tiny pearl.

He had seen something like it before. Searching his memory, he had a sudden image of his old nurse, saying her prayers after the marriage of Josse's younger brother. She had, he knew, been praying for the newlywed couple's fertility, and when she had finished, she placed a single pearl in an oyster shell. It had worked; Josse's sister-in-law's firstborn son had come into the world eleven months later, swiftly followed by two girls and another boy.

They met here often, those other two young newlyweds, he now thought. Crept in here in the darkness, hand in hand, lay down on the bare ground, made love. Which one, he wondered, brought this object here? Milon, anxious for a child to inherit the fortune he was expecting, or Elanor, passionately in love with her new husband, wanting so badly to please him with a pregnancy?

As with Josse's sister-in-law, the charm had worked.

Suddenly very sad, he put the oyster shell back in its hiding place. The little clearing was full of their spirit, those two young people, and, for the first time, he felt a distinct distaste for what he had to do.

But, if my reasoning is right, Milon killed her, he reminded himself. And both of them were greedy and envious enough to plot the murder of Gunnora.

Resolving firmly to keep his compassion for those who deserved it, he made his way out to the track.

He found himself a quiet spot on the bank of the pond, some fifty paces from where he had discovered the secret hiding place, and sat down to think. He was full of a strong conviction that Milon was still near at hand; he had to be, for he had urgent business at the Abbey.

Only one thing, as far as Josse could deduce, linked Milon definitely with the murder of Elanor, and hence with that of Gunnora. And that object – although Milon could not know it – now lay safely in Abbess Helewise's cabinet. Where did the young man imagine it was? It must have been a terrible moment, when he discovered it was not on his wife's body; fleetingly Josse wondered why not. Why, when he was fairly sure she had been wearing it beneath her robe when he had interviewed her the day before she died, had she removed it before setting out that night? Wrapped it up carefully with her wedding ring, hidden it beneath her palliasse? It seemed a strange thing to do.

Never mind that, now.

Milon, then, would have found the cross missing. Would realise she must have left it in the convent, would guess, probably, that she'd have hidden it in the one place a nun could look upon as her own. Her cubicle in the dormitory.

He *had* to come back for it! Surely he did! And quickly, before Elanor's bed was allocated to another new postulant who might discover what was hidden there. I'd waste not a moment in searching for it, Josse thought, if I were in his place. It reveals the true identity of the postulant Elvera, and, once it is known that she is Elanor d'Arcy, then Milon is automatically involved.

His mind returned to the other two crosses, belonging to Gunnora and Dillian. Milon, he thought, must somehow have got hold of Dillian's cross. Had it perhaps been left to her aunt, Milon's mother-in-law, on Dillian's death? Likely, since the woman was Dillian's only surviving female relation other than Elanor, who already had her own cross. Well, however he had got his hands on it, he had known what to do with it. Leave it by Gunnora's body, as if dropped by a panicking, fleeing thief, so that those who found her would think she had been killed during a robbery.

But they hadn't thought that. Because Abbess Helewise had known it couldn't be Gunnora's own cross, which was then, and still was, securely in her care.

His mind was becoming fudged. I need to do something, he decided, something positive and, hopefully, useful, to fill the day ahead.

He decided, after brief thought, to go down to Tonbridge. It was possible he might hear word of Milon, if he asked a few questions; the lad wasn't easy to overlook, with his fancy clothes and haircut. It seemed unlikely that he would risk putting up at an inn in the town, but, on the other hand, he had to eat. And there were precious few places selling food in the Wealden Forest.

I will ride down to Tonbridge, Josse thought, and treat myself to a decent dinner and a few mugs of Goody Anne's excellent ale.

Then tonight, when it begins to get dark, I shall return here and wait for Milon.

Chapter Thirteen

Tonbridge was full of people; it was, Josse realised, market day.

All activity in the little town centred around the church today. Glancing up at it, Josse observed that, some time in the fairly recent past, it had been enlarged; more evidence, he reflected, on the growing fortunes of the town. On three sides, the church was surrounded by stalls, as if the merchants and stallholders were crouching under the sandstone walls for protection. There was the sound of chatter and laughter as people bartered with the stallholders and gossiped with one another; the occasion was as much for the exchange of news as for the purchase of new goods and chattels.

Were they, Josse wondered, talking about the murders up at the Abbey?

Of course they were. He did not fool himself for a moment that this wouldn't be the chief topic of conversation. And whatever was said here stood a good chance of being repeated in more influential circles up in London.

Promising himself that he would lay a thoroughly satisfying solution before the King as soon as he possibly could, Josse pushed on through the market.

Many of the stalls sold local produce, including, on the outer fringes, livestock; there were also craftsmen's stalls, where, had Josse wished to, he could have bought himself a new belt or a nicely turned wooden milking stool. In addition, and reflecting the proximity of the town to the main trade route from Hastings and Winchelsea up to London, there were a handful of stalls selling more exotic wares. Fine linen, spices, some brilliant pieces of jewellery which, Josse was sure, would lose their shine before the month was out . . .

Catching a waft of some spicy smell that instantly transported him back to the Languedoc, resolutely he turned his back on the delights of the market and elbowed his way through the throng back towards the bridge.

The inn, too, was busy, and Goody Anne was doing a robust trade in food and drink.

She greeted Josse as if he were a regular customer who had inexplicably been absent for months.

'There you are!' she exclaimed. 'How are you, now? Well, I trust? A mug of ale this warm day? There! That's the idea!'

Josse wondered if she had greeted her regulars with such affectionate enthusiasm when she had still plied her former trade. If so, then he wasn't in the least surprised she had made enough money to set herself up in the inn.

'I'm well, thank you, Mistress,' he said when he could get a word in. 'Grateful for your good ale, and hungry enough for ten men.'

'What will you take?' She was pouring ale for another customer as she spoke. 'I've choice in plenty today, being as how it's market day.'

'Aye, I noticed.' He looked at the platters of neighbouring customers; carp in some sort of sauce, eels, mutton stew, hare, what appeared to be a sort of game pie . . . The pie seemed to be going down particularly well. 'A portion of your pie, please.'

She loaded a platter, deftly cutting a hunk of bread and balancing it on top of the pie crust, then put the meal down in front of him with a thump. 'Eat up,' she said, eyeing his body, 'a man with a fine, big frame like yours needs a good helping of food regular.' She put her head on one side, giving him a considering glance. 'Not to mention his other appetites.'

Was it his imagination, or did she raise an enquiring eyebrow?

Well, even if she had done, and even if he'd felt like a quick roll with her, there wasn't time. She was still looking at him; whatever sort of toll her former profession had demanded, it hadn't affected her too adversely. Her skin was still good, and she had most of her teeth. And she really did have beautiful breasts . . .

It was, Josse reflected as, with an almost imperceptible shake of his head, he turned his attention to the delicious pie, just as well he was here on important business.

When Anne had gone – with a swirl of her hips which seemed to say, you don't know what you're missing! – Josse glanced round to see if any of the men he had met the other day were about. He thought he saw Matthew, and, finishing his food, went over to speak to him.

It was indeed Matthew. 'Morning, stranger,' he greeted Josse. 'Come to make your purchases at market? Or are you come to sell your birds?' He smiled as he spoke; Josse was not dressed as a chicken farmer.

'Come to search for someone,' Josse said. What harm could it do to ask one or two people if they'd seen Milon? Even if word got back to him that Josse was on his trail, it could hardly come as a surprise. If, that was, Josse was right about his guilt.

And Josse entertained no doubts about *that*.

'Oh, aye?' Matthew said.

'A young man, hardly more than a lad, really. Slim, fashionably dressed, yellow hair cut in a fringe, with a curl on his forehead?'

Matthew muttered something on the lines of, 'Sounds like a right pretty boy.' Then, his brow creased in concentration, he said, 'That's familiar, that is. Reckon I did see a lad looking like that, but it was a while ago.'

'Did you?'

'Aah. I did that. I remember, I watched him ride by – it were over Castle Hill way, going up towards the ridge there.'

The Castle Hill ridge, Josse thought. That lies between

Tonbridge and Hawkenlye. If Matthew's memory was serving him truly, then this was news indeed.

'Of course, I've only given you a fairly vague description,' he said, trying to sound casual. 'There are probably dozens of young men that answer it. People from London, visiting the castle, merchants on the road, passing through.'

'This lad I'm thinking of weren't no merchant, nor no guest up at the castle,' Matthew said decisively.

'How can you be so sure?'

'Because he weren't anywhere near the castle, nor the market neither.' Matthew sighed, as if to say, isn't it obvious? 'Like I said, he were up there towards the ridge. Well, he was the first time I saw him. Second time, he were skulking around the back of the baker's house. Hungry, I reckoned he was.'

'You saw him twice.'

'Aye.' Matthew swirled the last half inch of ale around in the bottom of his mug. 'Thirsty work, this remembering,' he observed.

Josse caught the tap boy's eye. When Matthew had taken the top off the refill, he said, 'Turns out quite a few folk noticed him. Your pretty lad. We all had a good laugh.' He gave a reminiscent chuckle.

Josse couldn't for the life of him guess what they had found so funny. 'At what?'

'Them shoes!' Matthew laughed again. 'He'd have had to thread those daft toes through the stirrups like a good-wife threading her needle!'

Trying to keep the excitement out of his voice, Josse said, 'How long ago was all this?'

The frown returned. 'Ah. Now that'd be asking. Weren't last market day, nor the one afore it. Or were it?' Josse waited. 'It were a fortnight ago,' Matthew announced decisively. 'Give or take.'

'Give or take how much?'

'Ah. Hmm. Day or so?'

There seemed little point in trying to pin him down any more precisely. In any case, Josse thought, I have the information I need. Milon d'Arcy was in the vicinity at the time of Gunnora's death.

'I suppose you'd recognise the fellow if you saw him again?' Josse asked casually. It might be important to have a witness to Milon's presence in Tonbridge.

'That'd depend,' Matthew said.

'On what?'

Wearing a self-righteous expression suggesting that he didn't want to be accused of handling the truth carelessly, he said, 'Well, it was more the hairstyle I remarked on, like, than the face. And the shoes, like I said. And the tunic, come to that. Fair bum-freezer, were that tunic.' He grinned. 'See, if the young laddie came back in the same tackle, I'd know him again. But, there again, if he wore a hood and an old cloak, reckon he could stand me my ale all night and I wouldn't recognise him. See what I'm getting at?' he finished earnestly, as if desperate to prove his integrity. 'I mean, ain't easy, with strangers.'

'No, indeed.' Matthew had a point, Josse had to concede. 'Well, thank you for your time, Matthew.' Discreetly he laid a couple of coins on the table. 'In case your thirst isn't quite assuaged,' he remarked.

'Aye, aye, always a chance of that.' A grubby hand shot out like a rat from a midden and the coins disappeared. 'Thankee kindly, sir.'

Assured that he had done as much as he could to ensure Matthew's future co-operation, should it prove necessary, Josse settled his bill and left.

He returned to the market, pushing his way around the stalls for a while, but could see nobody who looked remotely like Milon, even disguised in a hood and cloak. Giving it up, and glad to turn his back on the heaving, shoving crowds, he headed back for Hawkenlye.

He paused at the top of the ridge. The day was hot, with the sun shining strongly from a clear blue sky, and there had been little shade on the long trudge up from the vale. Letting his horse find his own way to a cool patch of grass beneath an oak tree, Josse relaxed in the saddle and sat looking back the way he had come.

From the high ground, the contours of the land showed up clearly. Visibility was good that afternoon, and, far away to the north, Josse could make out the line of the downs. His eye followed the roughly west to east course of the River Medway, down in the bottom of the valley, and he focused for a few moments on the great castle and the bridge over which it loomed. The township of Tonbridge, for all that it had seemed crowded and busy when he was down in it, appeared, from up here, small and insignificant, its whole existence brought about merely because it was the place where the river was crossed by the main road.

All around the town, in a clearly defined area within the encircling woodland, were the agricultural demesnes; now, at the height of summer, the rich alluvial land was heavy with ripening crops of corn, fruit and hops.

No wonder, Josse thought, pulling his horse's head up and turning him back on to the track, the market was so well attended.

He still had time to kill. The track to Hawkenlye looped around a great bulge of the Wealden Forest. Making up his mind suddenly, he found a spot where the undergrowth was thin – a badger run, perhaps, or a deer path – and took a detour in beneath the trees.

Even on a bright July afternoon, the place was cool and dark. Josse could readily appreciate how it had come by its sinister reputation; riding through the steadily thickening trees and the rampant undergrowth as he went deeper in, he had to fight the urge to keep looking over his shoulder.

Oak predominated, interspersed with birch and beech. Some of the giant oaks must, Josse reckoned, be centuries old. Massive in girth, their upper branches high up above merged to form a thick canopy which entirely blotted out the sunlight. Many of them were thickly wreathed with ivy, which trailed down to ground level to merge with bramble, hazel, holly and thorn in an all but impenetrable thicket.

In places, he came across evidence of better-defined tracks through the forest, some of which, judging from the height of the banks on either side, were possibly as ancient as the old oaks. Were they the vestiges of roads made by the Romans, built straight, built true, built to last? Or were they what remained of the old iron ways, made by men before history began? Men who knew the forest like a brother, understood its nature and penetrated to its very heart, men who worshipped the oak as a god, in whose name they carried out unspeakable violence.

And who, according to some, still did . . .

Already apprehensive, it was not, Josse told himself, the best moment to let his imagination run free.

Coming to a clearing, he drew rein and sat staring about him. For the first time since he had left the sunshine of the world outside, there was evidence of human occupation. Not much, to be sure, just a huddle of mean-looking huts, simply constructed, scarcely more than a pole frame draped with a covering of branches and turves. Shelter enough, perhaps, to keep out the rain. There was evidence that charcoal-burning had been going on, although not, apparently, for some time; the patches of ground where fires had been set were no longer totally bare, but covered with small green tendrils as nature began to reclaim her own.

Josse dismounted and, tethering his horse, approached the largest of the huts. Bending his head, he went inside. There had been a small fire in there; putting his hand over it, Josse detected faint warmth. On a raised bank at one side was a mattress of bracken. Freshly cut.

It could have been anyone, Josse reflected as he remounted. All manner of fugitives and itinerants would know of these old huts, and it must be a common occurrence for someone to come and lie up here for a few days, while the heat died down and they planned their next move.

It didn't *have* to be Milon.

But, as he set off back to the outside world – which, he had to admit, had rarely seemed so attractive a prospect – Josse couldn't help being quite certain that it was.

He told Abbess Helewise what he had in mind. He saw her instinctive reaction before she could dissimulate: she didn't want him to do it.

'Don't worry,' he said quietly. Was it impertinent to assume she *was* worrying? 'I can cope with Master Milon. And he may well not turn up!' He tried to laugh.

'He's a murderer,' Helewise said, equally quietly; it was as if neither of them wanted to speak aloud of such matters in the sanctity of the convent. 'He has killed, if you are right. And, having done so once, he will not, I think, find it so difficult to do so again.'

He was surprised at her perspicacity, at a nun having the experience to understand the mind of a murderer. 'Indeed, Abbess, it has often been observed that murder is easy after the first time.' Suddenly he realised what they were saying. 'But we speak of only one killing, whereas there have been two, surely!'

'Two deaths, yes.' She glanced at him. 'But we do not yet know if both victims died by the same hand.'

We do! he wanted to shout. He restrained the impulse. 'Whether he killed them both or not, Abbess, I am determined on this,' he said instead.

'I know.' She smiled faintly. 'I can see. But, Sir Josse, will you at least let me send some of the lay brothers to wait with you?'

'No.' The reply was automatic: Josse liked to work alone. 'Thoughtful of you, Abbess, but the paramount need will be for silence. Any warning that he is expected and he will take to his heels.'

She tutted briefly. 'I do not propose a band of gossiping, fidgeting old monks complaining about their aching bones and moaning at having been dragged from their sleep, although it might do some of them good to make the sacrifice. No. I propose only that you enlist the aid of Brother Saul, and perhaps one other lay brother selected by him. He knows who is sound, have no doubt.'

'I'm sure he does.' Josse was impressed by Brother Saul. 'But—' He had been on the point of refusing when it occurred to him that the Abbess was talking sense. Milon, terrified at being exposed as the killer of Gunnora, hadn't hesitated to kill again. Even though the person he'd had to dispose of to ensure his safety had been his own wife. Under the circumstances, would it hurt to have Saul at his side in his vigil?

No. In fact Josse welcomed the idea.

'Thank you, Abbess,' he said. 'May we ask Brother Saul if he is willing?'

She was, he thought, about to make further mention of a second brother. But, as if knowing she had won from Josse all the concessions he was prepared to give, she merely nodded and said, 'I will send word to Brother Saul. And now, Sir Josse, I have ordered food for you. At least I can ensure that you begin your night's work on a full stomach.'

Milon d'Arcy, product of a comfortable home, indulged by his mother over her other, worthier sons, was living a nightmare.

It was not the fear of the great, sinister Wealden Forest where he had hidden away that threatened to unhinge him – or so he was managing to convince himself – nor the fugitive's need to survive on his wits; a loaf of bread stolen here, a fat roast chicken off the spit there, an apple scrumped while nobody was looking that proved only to be half-bad, these were, for Milon, minor triumphs that it quite pleased him to think about.

He was, he had reassured himself not a few times, proving to be pretty good at looking after himself.

Sometimes he would forget. For a whole morning, once, he had been happy. Lying on his stomach over a stream on the fringe of the forest, staring down into the clear, cool water and trying to catch tiny, slippery, silver fish in his fingers, he had thought himself back in the life that used to be his. Had, when he stood up and brushed off the fine tunic – now damp, stained and showing distinct signs of wear – been on the point of thinking cheerfully ahead to what might be on the table for the midday meal.

To remember, at that particular moment, had been cruelly painful.

His mind increasingly shied away from the pain. He was, he knew, finding it easier and easier *not* to remember. To go on living in that pleasant land where it was always nearly dinner time and Elanor was waiting for him.

Elanor.

Red hair, strong, unruly, full of life. Just like her. Lusty and passionate, her ardour matching his own so that, when all the family and friends had said what a good match it was, how suited the young couple were one to another, he and she had turned their faces aside and sniggered.

That – their mutual physical hunger – they had discovered immediately. But there were other compatibilities, which had taken a little longer to surface. Such as their shared, strong sense of what was owing to them. Which, if not handed to them on a plate, they would stretch out their hands and grab.

What a clever brain she had, his Elanor! What an excellent accomplice! What *fun* they'd had together! Until—

No.

His mind closed down on that. Refused to let him go on.

When that happened, he would go back to his stream, and get down to something useful such as cleaning and sharpening his knife. Or he would creep into his hiding place. But there, very often, he would have to endure another attack of the terrors.

Because, one night, not long after he had first come there, a night of clear skies and brilliant moonlight, he had seen a man. *Thought* he'd seen a man, he kept having to correct himself. A man in a long white robe who bore a sickle-shaped knife in his hand. A man who *spoke to the trees*.

Cowering right at the back of his pitiful shelter, shaking, sick with fear, Milon had watched as the man, chanting in a soft, hypnotic monotone, circled the clearing.

As, at last, the man approached the huddle of huts, Milon had closed his eyes and, terror turning his bowels liquid, covered his head with his arms.

When, after what seemed like an eternity, he gathered what little remained of his courage and looked up, the man had gone.

It was a dream, he told himself, then and on many occasions since. Nothing but a dream.

But, sometimes when he was very tired and very low, when the moonlight came filtering down through the branches black against the night sky, he thought he saw the man again.

And, each time, the terrors took a little longer to overcome.

So far, he was winning. By concentrating his mind on the past, where it was sunny and people were kind to him, he could make the horror go away. And, after a while, the door to the pleasant land would open again.

Sometimes he would sit up with a start and ask himself what he was doing there. It was quite nice, yes, a bit of an adventure to be off on his own in his camp, but why not go home? Why not return to Elanor, waiting in their bed for him with her white breasts and her smooth rounded hips, as ready for lovemaking as he was, wetting her lips, legs languidly apart, arms out to . . .

But, of course, she wasn't waiting. Not in bed, not anywhere.

And he couldn't go home. There was something he had to do, something important.

By concentrating *very* hard, he could make himself remember what it was.

But it was getting more and more difficult each time. Today, lying by his stream, the few rays of sunshine that managed to penetrate the trees warm on his back, he could hardly concentrate at all. The water was so cool, so pretty, rushing along over the stream-bed and . . .

Think!

No.

Yes! THINK!

Reluctantly, moaning aloud, he thought. And, when he did manage to remember, wished that he had not.

But act he must, before the whispering darkness, and the magical, dream-like pleasant place that was his escape from it, became his only reality.

He must do it now.

Tonight.

Then he could go home, and Elanor would let him back into her bed.

Josse and Brother Saul had been hiding in the undergrowth for what seemed like most of the night when Milon came.

It was Josse's turn on watch. Seeing the slight figure coming carefully along the path by the pond, at first Josse had thought he was seeing things. It wouldn't have been the first time, in those long hours. But this was no trick of the light: it was Milon.

He moved well, Josse thought detachedly, smoothly, silently, using all available cover, keeping to the deepest shadows. And he had chosen a cloudy night. Josse was surprised by the young man's skill; he looked such a shallow, feckless fool, with his pointed shoes and his fancy clothes. With a part of his mind, Josse wondered what sort of desperate need had led to the development of these survival skills. Skills that included the dreadful final resort of murder, when someone had got in his way.

He stepped silently back to the little clearing and beckoned to Saul, who had been lying on the ground. Not sleeping, or he wasn't when Josse summoned him. He got to his feet, eyebrows raised. Josse nodded, pointing in the direction of the path. He moved back to the edge of the undergrowth, and sensed Saul quietly following after him.

They stood side by side on the edge of the path, in the deep shade of a vast oak tree.

And Milon, using that same tree to provide his next patch of shadow, walked right into them.

As Josse's arms closed around him, he let out a shriek of terror. Struggling with him – he was trying to reach down to his belt, where, no doubt, he had a knife – Josse spared him a moment's pity. To be creeping along like that, already afraid, and have someone grab you! No wonder the youth's heart was hammering so hard, hard enough for Josse to detect it.

Saul must have been able to see Milon's weapon, for, with a sudden gasp, he shot out his hand. Josse was aware of the two of them, Milon and Saul, wrestling grimly, grunting with effort, and then Saul was holding something up in the air.

It was a knife.

The blade was long and quite broad, tapering to an evil point. It was double-sided, and — as Saul tested it on the hairs of his forearm — quite obviously honed to a vicious sharpness.

Josse was in no doubt that he was staring at the weapon that had slit Gunnora's throat. His moment of pity for the youth vanished as if it had never been.

'Milon d'Arcy, if I'm not mistaken,' he said grimly, twisting the youth's arms behind his back and taking a firm grip on his wrists. 'And just what are you up to, creeping along here in the dead of night?'

'You've no right to apprehend me in this way!' Milon cried, his voice thin with fear. 'I'm on my way back to my camp, I've done no harm!'

'Done no harm?' Josse was momentarily so angry that he gave the boy's wrists a savage jerk, causing him to cry out. Brother Saul muttered, 'Easy, now!' and Josse relaxed his hold slightly. 'Where is this camp?' he demanded.

'Up in the forest,' Milon said. 'Where the charcoal burners go.'

'Aye, I know it. And what are *you* doing there?'

'I have come to these parts to see a friend,' Milon said with surprising dignity. He had clearly recovered some of his courage. 'And you, whoever you are' — he tried to twist round to look at Josse — 'have no right to prevent me!'

'I have every right,' Josse said. 'Brother Saul and I are here at the express wishes of the Abbess of Hawkenlye Abbey. Another quarter of a mile, my fine young man, and you'll be climbing up to her convent walls.'

'I will?' The attempt at innocence did not convince.

'Aye. As well you know.' Josse hesitated, but only for an instant. Then said, 'Hard, was it, seeing a beautiful young bride go inside those walls pretending she wanted to take the veil?'

Still clutching at Milon, he was close enough to feel the momentary tension. But Milon was a better actor than Josse would have given him credit for; he said mildly, 'A bride – *my* bride – taking the veil? I think you are mistaken, sir. *My* bride would not do anything so foolish, certainly not now that she *is* my bride.' The sexual innuendo was unmissable. Gaining confidence, Milon added, 'And if, sir, you are aware of who I am, then it is possible you have been looking for me in my own home, where, I am perfectly sure, you will have been told that my wife stays with kin of mine, near—'

'Near Hastings. Aye, that's what they said.'

Milon gave an exaggerated sigh, as if to say, well, then! 'In that case, might I be allowed to continue on my way?'

'I went to your kin at Hastings,' Josse said tonelessly. 'They knew of no visit. Elanor d'Arcy was neither with them nor expected there.'

'You went to the wrong place!' Milon cried. 'Fool!' He had begun to struggle again. 'Go back, sir! I'll tell you the *right* place, then you can go and check! She'll be there, my little Elanor, sitting in the sun of the courtyard, waiting on my return, lovely as a summer day, she is, you know, a fairer bride no man ever had.' Twisting round, he put his face closer to Josse's. 'And in our bed when the lamps are blown out, sir, well, if I say I've had not a full night's sleep since the day my Elanor and I were wed, I'm sure you won't need any further detail to make your own pictures!'

Was the man raving? Josse felt strangely uneasy, as if he were in the presence of madness as well as evil. 'Stop that, Milon,' he ordered. 'It will do you no good. Your wife Elanor d'Arcy came to the convent as a postulant, assuming a false identity and calling herself Elvera. She met up with her cousin Gunnora, who, once Dillian was dead, stood between her and the inheritance of Alard of Winnowland's fortune.'

'No!' Milon protested. 'Oh, *no!*'

'Between the pair of you,' Josse continued relentlessly, 'Gunnora's brutal death was planned and executed. When I arrived, Elanor took fright and, fearing she would give you away, you strangled her.' Holding Milon in his grip, so close to a man who had ruthlessly done away with two defenceless women, suddenly Josse's temper boiled over. Shaking Milon like a terrier with a rat, he shouted, 'You bastard! You foul, murdering bastard!'

Screaming with the agony of having both arms twisted up behind his back, Milon wriggled like a hooked fish and wrenched himself out of Josse's grip. Turning a furious face on him, he screeched, '*Don't call me that!*'

Then he collapsed, weeping, on to the ground.

Chapter Fourteen

For some moments Josse and Brother Saul stood staring down at him in stunned silence. Then Saul said, 'I suppose we'd better get him up to the Abbey, sir. There's nowhere down here in the valley where we can secure a prisoner.'

A prisoner. Aye, Josse thought, that's what he is, from now on. And, once he has been tried and found guilty, his imprisonment will only have one end.

'Let's get him to his feet,' he said, and he and Saul each took hold of one of Milon's arms. As they dragged him up, Josse heard the thin, fine cloth of the young man's shirt start to tear. Again, Josse felt the painful mixture of emotions surge through him; so proud, Milon had been, of his appearance, so careful of his fashionable clothes. And now look at him. In the pale pre-dawn light, he was revealed as a sorry figure, dirty, stinking, the daringly cut tunic stuck with burrs and covered in grass stains, the shirt with a sleeve all but ripped out . . .

Cross with himself – the youth was a double murderer! – once again Josse found that he was having to fight down his compassion.

And, with Milon as silent and unresisting as if he were walking in his sleep, they made their way up to the Abbey.

Dawn was breaking when they closed the door on Milon. Saul had suggested putting him in an end chamber of the undercroft beneath the infirmary, which was empty but which had a stout lock.

The young man kept up his silence until they were descending the steps into the undercroft. Then, as the dank darkness wrapped itself around them, he started to emit a thin, high screaming. An awful sound: Josse felt the hairs on the back of his neck start to prickle.

'A light, Brother Saul,' he commanded gruffly. 'We cannot pen him down here in the pitch dark like an animal.' Saul fetched a flare and lit it, sticking it in a bracket on the wall of the passage.

But the door to Milon's cell had only a small grille, up at eye level. Little of the warm, comforting light would penetrate inside to him.

'Is it clean?' Josse asked as Saul turned the heavy key on the boy.

Saul said, with a slight suggestion of reproof, 'It is indeed, sir. Abbess Helewise, she does not allow slack housekeeping, not anywhere within the Abbey.'

Josse touched his arm in mute apology, both for having suggested the cell might be dirty, and for the underlying accusation that Brother Saul would have put a prisoner in there if it had been.

Prisoner.

The word kept reverberating in his head.

'If you have no further use for me, sir,' Saul said as they left the undercroft, trying unsuccessfully to suppress a yawn, 'might I be allowed to go and catch a few hours' sleep?'

'Eh?' His voice brought Josse back from the disquieting paths where his mind had been walking. 'Aye, Brother Saul. And my thanks for your company and your help this long night.'

Saul bowed his head. 'I'll not say it was a pleasure, sir, but you're welcome none the less.' He paused, and Josse was certain he had more to say. Then: 'He is guilty, Sir Josse? Without any shadow of a doubt?'

'It's not for me to judge him, Saul,' Josse said gently. 'He will go to trial. But me, I have no doubts.'

Brother Saul nodded. He said dolefully, 'It's as I feared. He will hang.'

'He almost certainly killed two young women, Saul! Nuns, who had done him no wrong except prevent him getting a fortune!'

'I know that, sir,' Saul said with dignity. 'It's just that . . .'

He didn't finish. Sighing, as if all this were far beyond his comprehension, he lifted a hand in valediction and set off back to the shelter in the vale.

And Josse, after a moment's indecision, went into the cloister and sat down to wait for the Abbess.

It would be, he was well aware, a long wait. But then he had nothing better to do.

Helewise saw him as she went to her room after Prime.

He was slumped in a corner, wedged in the angle formed by the junction of two walls. He looked hideously uncomfortable, but, notwithstanding that, he was fast asleep.

His craggy face was pale, and there were deep lines running from the sides of his nose to the corners of his mouth. The heavy brows were drawn down as if, even asleep, he was troubled and frowning. Poor man, she thought. What a night he has had.

Word had been brought to her of Milon d'Arcy's arrest as she went into church for the Holy Office. Brother Saul had spoken to Brother Firmin, who had taken the tidings straight to the Abbess.

It had taken most of her reserves of self-control to proceed with her devotions, when everything left in her that was worldly – and there was quite a lot – was telling her to go straight to the undercroft and start demanding some answers from the murderer.

Now, though, she was glad she had made herself go to pray. The dignity, power and atmosphere of the Abbey church was always most moving, for her, in the early morning, and the solace and strength she derived then was the greatest. And, perhaps because of that, it was at the first service of the daylight hours that she felt closest to the Lord. It was, she often thought, as if God, too, was enjoying the innocence of the world as another new day began. Was, perhaps, like the Abbess – if the comparison were not sacrilegious – revelling in the purity of the morning, before the concerns of those who peopled their two domains, God's so vast, her own so small, had a chance to sully it.

Feeling uplifted, strong from having come fresh from communion with the Lord, she crossed the cloister, approached Josse and gently touched his shoulder.

He shot into wakefulness, hand going to where, no doubt, he usually carried a sword, eyes glaring up at her.

Seeing who it was, he relaxed.

'Good morning, Abbess.'

'Good morning, Sir Josse.'

'They'll have told you.' It was a statement, not a question.

'Indeed. You and Brother Saul did well. And my congratulations on the accuracy of your prediction. You said Milon would come back for the cross. And he did.'

'We don't know for certain that's what he came for.' Josse was stretching in a huge yawn as he spoke, remembering only half-way through it to cover his mouth with his hand. 'Sorry, Abbess.'

'It's all right. When do we speak to him?'

Josse got to his feet, scratching at a day's growth of beard. 'Now?'

She had been unaware she'd been holding her breath. Overwhelmingly relieved – she didn't think she could have borne delay – she said, 'Very well.'

She sensed a new tension in him as they went down the steps to the undercroft. She was about to speak, but just then she became aware of the noise.

Was it what had disturbed Josse? She would not have been surprised if it was. It was a dreadful noise, like that of an animal in a snare, containing both pain and, predominantly, despair.

As if he, too, felt the need of light in this suddenly terrible place, Josse took a flare out of its bracket on the wall and held it in his left hand as he unlocked the door of the makeshift prison, carrying it in with him as he and Helewise advanced into the cell.

She saw him immediately, for all that he was cowering right in the far corner. As the light from the flare fell on him, his face relaxed into a smile. But only for a moment; seeing who stood beside her, he gave a low moan, and slumped back against the wall as if he were trying to bury himself.

Glancing over her shoulder, Helewise noticed that Josse had positioned himself with his back to the closed door of the cell, his stance appearing to defy the prisoner to challenge him. His face, in the light of the flare, was stern; she was, she reflected briefly, now seeing the man of action, the King's agent, making quite sure a murder suspect didn't make a break for freedom.

The young man whom she knew must be Milon d'Arcy was now sitting with his legs drawn up to his chest, head dropped on to his knees. Stepping forward, Josse said, with a gentleness which greatly surprised her, 'Milon, get up. The Abbess Helewise is here, and you must show her respect.'

Slowly the youth did as he was told. For the first time, Helewise was face to face with the husband of the late postulant, Elanor d'Arcy, known in this community as Elvera.

She hadn't known what to expect. But it certainly wasn't this thin, white-faced young man, whose fine bright clothes were muddied and torn, and whose eyes bore an expression which, although she couldn't yet read it, struck a chill in her.

And who, quite obviously, had been crying.

Not knowing of any better way to begin, she said, 'Did you kill your wife, Milon?'

She heard a brief exclamation from behind her – Josse, apparently, did not approve of her straightforward interrogation methods – but, after a tense moment, slowly Milon nodded.

'And why was that?' she continued, in the same quiet tone.

'I didn't mean to,' he whispered. He sobbed, sniffed, and wiped his wet nose on his sleeve. Raising his eyes to Helewise, the pupils wide in the dim light, he said urgently, 'She came to me, you see, that night, down in our secret place. Just like she always did on a Wednesday. I used to wait for her, on those nights, in the bed I'd made for us deep in the undergrowth. We'd lie together till the very first glimmer of light, then she'd run back to her dormitory and pretend to be asleep when the summons came for Matins.'

'Prime,' Helewise corrected automatically.

'Was it?' Incongruously, in that dread place, he gave a sudden swift smile. 'She said it was Matins.'

'Well, she was very new to convent life.' Dear God, but this was difficult! 'So, she came to you that night, Milon. And you – you spent some time together.'

'We made love,' Milon said. 'We made love a lot, ever since we were wed.' An echo of the smile again. 'Before that, once, although we never told anyone. Many, many times, once we were man and wife and we were allowed to. She was pregnant.' There was a distinct note of pride in his voice. 'Did you know that, Abbess?'

Helewise nodded. 'Yes, Milon. I knew.'

'It was wonderful, wasn't it,' he hurried on eagerly, 'for her to be with child so soon after our marriage? Of course, she didn't tell Gunnora. Didn't even tell her we were wed. So, apart from me, there was nobody she could chat to about how happy she is, how excited.' He frowned. 'That was sad. She needed to tell people, Elanor did. She always needs to share it when something good happens to her. That's why it's – why it was so hard for her being in the Abbey.' He looked around him, as if suddenly remembering where he was. 'Being here,' he added, in a whisper.

Helewise wondered if Josse, too, had noticed Milon's confusion of past and present. Turning to look quickly at him, she saw that his deep frown of disapproval had lifted slightly. And that, mingled with the outrage and the anger, was pity.

Yes, she thought. He has noticed. And, like me, he is torn between condemning this youth for what he has done and pitying him for the frailness of his mental state.

But now was no time to allow compassion to overrule justice.

'The child – your and Elanor's child – would have been rich, wouldn't he?' she pressed on. 'Or she, of course. Born into wealth.'

Milon was nodding again. 'Yes! Yes! He'd have had a silver spoon, all right! That was why, you see.' He looked eagerly from Helewise to Josse, as if inviting their understanding. 'We were thinking of ourselves at first, I can't deny it, thinking how unfair it was, that, with Dillian gone, the old fool was thinking of changing his will and leaving the lot to Gunnora after all. And she didn't want it!' He opened his hands wide as if to say, just imagine! 'That was the stupid thing! She hated wealth, and everything to do with it! That's why she had to come in here – it was all part of her plan. She was going to—'

Just then Josse interrupted. 'And you couldn't bear the thought of your uncle-in-law's wealth ending up in Hawkenlye Abbey, could you? So you killed her.'

'*No!*' The denial came out with such deep anguish that Helewise began to sense she had been right all along.

'There's no point keeping on saying no when we—' Josse began furiously.

But Helewise said, 'Sir Josse, if you please?' and, with an obvious effort, he stopped.

She turned back to Milon. 'So Elanor posed as the postulant Elvera, entered the convent and met up with her cousin. How did she explain herself?'

Milon smiled. 'She told Gunnora it was for a bet. That I'd bet her a gold coin she couldn't fool everyone into believing she really wanted to be a nun, and she'd claimed she could, and, what's more, she'd show me. Of course, she said it wouldn't be for very long, that, soon, she'd pretend she'd changed her mind and go again. Before they threatened to cut her hair off, that's for sure!'

The sound of his laughter – bright, happy, as if he hadn't a care in the world – was, Helewise thought, almost as dreadful as that moaning had been.

And then, looking confidingly into her eyes, he added, 'She's got lovely hair, hasn't she?'

Fortunately for Helewise, who was, just at that moment, incapable of continuing, Josse took up the questioning.

'And Gunnora believed in this stupid prank?' He sounded incredulous. 'But didn't it strike her as deeply irreverent, when she herself was about to take the first of her final vows?'

But she wasn't, Helewise thought. And she was beginning to understand why. She sighed. 'Yes,' she said, 'Gunnora swallowed the story. She believed everything Elanor told her. Didn't she, Milon?'

'Yes.' He was grinning. 'She went along with it. She actually thought it was as funny as Elanor did.'

'But all the time Elanor's presence here had a much darker purpose,' Josse said. 'All along, you and your wife were planning to kill Gunnora.'

'I keep telling you, it wasn't like that!' Milon cried. 'We just wanted to make a friend of her, wanted her to like us, so that when she got her father's money, she'd pass it on to us and not give it to the Abbey.'

'You felt that your need was the greater?' Helewise said, with some irony.

He turned to her. 'No.' His expression was aggrieved. 'It wasn't because of that.'

'What, then?' Josse demanded.

Again, Milon looked at both of his questioners in turn. Meeting the tormented, shadowed eyes, Helewise was reminded of a wild animal cornered by hounds.

But then, finding from some unsuspected reserve a vestige of pride, Milon sat up and straightened his shoulders. Raising his chin, he said with quiet dignity, 'Because I'm his son.'

There was utter silence in the cold little room. Then Josse repeated, 'His son.'

Helewise's mind had leapt to one crucial thing. Silly, really, she thought, when so much else is at stake. 'Your marriage wasn't legal, if Sir Alard was indeed your father,' she said. 'A union between first cousins is within the prohibited degree.'

Milon dropped his eyes. 'I know. But Elanor didn't – I didn't want to upset her, when we loved each other so much. Getting married was the only way, you see – we'd never have been allowed to be together unless we were wed. So I never told her who I really was.'

'But surely Sir Alard would have done!' Josse protested. 'Great God in heaven, he should have been more responsible than to let such a union go ahead, no matter how much the pair of you wanted it!'

Milon waited until the blustering had finished – Josse must be beside himself, Helewise thought absently, to blaspheme like that, although the provocation was understandable – and then said, 'Alard couldn't have told her, since he didn't know himself.'

'Then how can *you* be so sure?' Helewise asked gently.

'My mother told me,' Milon said. 'When she was dying, I was the one she wanted to be with her.' He gave a brief ironic smile. 'That didn't go down at all well with my brothers, but then they've always been jealous of me. I was different, you see. I looked different, for one thing, and I always had my mother's favour. Even when they all ganged up on me, she'd look after me.' He sighed. Then, as if recalling himself to the present, went on, 'She didn't have long to live, they were all saying that, so I did as she asked and went up to her room.' His nose wrinkled. 'It smelt. *She* smelt. I didn't like it there, I wanted to go back to Elanor. But then my mother said I had to go and find my father, and when I said, all right, I'll fetch him, she grabbed my arm and said she didn't mean *him*, she meant my real father.'

'That must have come as a great shock to you,' Helewise said tonelessly.

'It did, oh, it did!' Milon agreed. 'Of course, though, once it had sunk in, I realised. I saw how it explained a lot of what had been happening, all through my childhood. Then I got interested, and I asked her to tell me about him. My father.'

Helewise pictured the scene. The dying woman, anxious to impart a long-held secret to her favourite son. And the son, listening not out of love but because he was 'interested'.

'She said, "Go and find him, and get your inheritance off him,"' Milon was saying. 'She was very bitter, you know. She always had been, but I didn't know why till then. From what she said – and she said a lot, believe me, for a woman who was meant to be dying – I gathered that she had imagined it would mean a bit of comfort for her, having a child by a rich man, even if she wasn't married to him. And when the child turned out to be a son, well, that made it even more important, given that the man only had daughters. But it didn't work out that way. She never even managed to tell him about me – he sent her letters back unopened. Didn't want his wife, the Lady Margaret, knowing he'd had sex with another woman, that's what she reckoned. She – my mother – couldn't pursue it, she said, because, if she made too much fuss, she'd risk her husband finding out. And she only slept with Alard the once!'

What a tale, Helewise thought. Dear Lord, what a tale of greed and dishonour.

But it was not all told yet.

'So your mother ordered that you try to obtain what she felt you were entitled to?' she prompted. 'Having told you where to go, she left it up to you to announce yourself? To convince Sir Alard that you were his son?'

'Yes.' Milon smiled faintly. 'Daunting, wasn't it? I mean, if, as my mother said, he only bedded her the once, would he even remember? I thought it was unlikely. And, if I told him and he refused to believe it, what then? I'd have blown my chances, and, no doubt, he'd have thrown me out and told his damned manservant to make sure I never darkened his door again. I had no *proof*, you see!'

'Indeed I do,' Helewise murmured.

'The alternative – my plan to marry Elanor – was the best I could come up with,' he went on. 'It was her or nothing, I reckoned. Gunnora wouldn't have looked at another man, and Dillian was smitten with Brice. So I went in search of my father's niece.' He paused, and the silence continued for some time.

Then he said, 'But I fell in love with her, you see. It wasn't about the money any longer, or not just the money.' His eyes met Helewise's. 'I truly loved her.'

That, apparently, was too much for Josse. 'Loved her enough to put your hands round her throat and choke the life out of her!' he burst out. 'Fine kind of love *that* is!'

It could have been that Josse didn't see that Milon was weeping. But Helewise did. 'Can you tell us what happened, Milon?' she asked gently. 'The night Elanor died?'

He raised his wet face to look at her. 'We'd been making love, like I said. Carefully, because of her being pregnant. But it was as good as it always is. Then, afterwards, she was telling me about him. That Sir Josse.' It was as if he'd forgotten Josse was in the room. 'She was frightened of him, frightened of the questions about Gunnora, and she wanted me to let her come away with me there and then. But I said no, it'd only make things look even worse if she did, the only way was to sweat it out and keep denying everything. So she said she couldn't, that she was tired, and sick, and needed me, and I got angry with her because we were *there* then, we'd all but done it, my father was on the very point of death and very soon it'd be over, she'd inherit and we could go away and live happily ever after!'

Happily ever after, Helewise thought. Just like a fairy tale. Appropriate, when this man and his wife were a pair of children. 'You got angry,' she repeated. 'Lost your temper with her.'

'It was frightening, her saying she wanted to tell him everything! I mean, how would it look? He'd never have believed I didn't kill her, none of you would!'

'But you did kill her,' Josse said coldly. 'You throttled her.'

Milon gave a sigh of exasperation. 'Yes, I know! I didn't intend to, my temper got the better of me. I was just trying to stop her crying so loudly. But I didn't mean Elanor. I'm not *talking* about Elanor.'

Helewise felt a small — a very small — song of triumph. I knew it! she thought. Knew it! She wondered what Josse was thinking.

'Elanor,' Milon was murmuring, smiling and humming to himself. 'She's my wife, you know,' he said to the room at large.

'My loving, clever, pretty wife. She's going to have my baby. I'm going to go home to her, very soon now, and she's going to take me into her bed and make me warm again. She's going to light all the candles, and drive the dark and the shadow men away.'

Helewise made herself block it out.

Had Josse realised? she wondered. Did he know, before an answer was demanded of Milon, what it would be?

'Milon?' she said softly. 'Milon, listen to me. If you weren't talking about Elanor, what *did* you mean?'

'I meant' – Milon spoke as if to a dim child – 'that I didn't kill Gunnora.'

Helewise stepped back then, and Josse took up the questioning. I have no heart for this, she thought as she listened, this brutal hurling of words at someone who is already broken. Besides, I know that, even if Sir Josse carries on till Christmas, Milon will not vary his story.

Because he is telling the truth. We have to look elsewhere for the killer of Gunnora.

'You ask us to believe,' Josse was saying, with heavy sarcasm, 'that, although you admit that you and Elanor cooked up a plot to separate Gunnora from her inheritance, yet you are innocent of her murder? When we *know* you were in the immediate vicinity at the time of her death, and she was killed only yards from your secret hiding place? With the marks on her arms where Elanor held her, and the slit in her throat which *you* made with that great knife of yours? Milon, give us credit for more sense!'

'It's true!' Milon cried for the fourth time. 'She was dead when we found her!'

'You're telling us that you and your wife – her own cousins, damn it! – *found* her, lying with her throat cut, yet did nothing for her?'

'She was dead! What *could* we do?'

'You could have run for help! Gone searching for the

brothers at the shrine, come up to the Abbey and alerted the Abbess! Covered the poor lass up! Anything!'

'But you'd have thought we killed her,' Milon protested.

Suddenly Helewise had a mental image of Gunnora's body, as they had found her. The skirts, so neatly folded. Without thinking, she said, 'Elanor arranged her. She tidied Gunnora's skirts, just as a nun is taught to fold her bedding, and then smeared the blood on her thighs. Didn't she?'

Milon turned to her. He seemed to have gone a degree more ashen. His eyes held some sort of appeal; he said, 'Yes, Abbess. She felt bad about it. We both did. But she said if we made it look like Gunnora had been raped, then even if anyone *did* start to think we'd killed her, they'd soon stop again, because we'd just have wanted her money. If she'd been raped and *then* killed, it couldn't have been us.'

Helewise nodded thoughtfully. 'Thank you, Milon. I understand.'

Josse was shaking his head in disbelief. 'Elanor did that?' he said incredulously. 'Gunnora's own cousin? Turned back the poor woman's skirts and spread her own blood on her? Dear God, what sort of a girl was she?'

'A desperate one,' Helewise murmured. Who, remembering the instruction she was being given in convent life — always fold your bedcovers like this, fold back, fold back again, just so — had, in some gesture of appeasement, tried to be neat in the arrangement of her dead cousin's habit.

'What of the cross?' Josse demanded. 'It wasn't Gunnora's own, and it wasn't Elanor's; hers was smaller. Did you drop it by her body?'

'Yes.'

'You brought it with you? Where on earth did you get hold of it?'

'I didn't bring it! It *was* Gunnora's! It must have been, she was wearing it — she had it round her neck. Elanor said she'd have it, since the rubies were better than the ones in her cross, but I wouldn't let her. Well, she realised, soon as I said, that it'd be a daft thing to do, it'd lead people straight to us if Elanor was seen with Gunnora's cross. So we just dropped it.' He sniffed. 'That's what I came back for. Elanor's cross. She didn't have it on her when I – She didn't have it that night, or, if she did, I couldn't find it. I was going to have another look down near our secret place, then follow the path she'd have taken down from the dormitory, searching all the way. Not that I had much hope of finding it *there*. I was going to come into the Abbey and try to get into the dormitory, then have a look in her bed.' He seemed to slump suddenly. 'I had to get it,' he said wearily. 'You'd have known who she was, if you'd got your hands on her cross. And then you'd have come straight for me.'

Josse turned away from him then, paced back to the door of the little room and stood, arms folded, shoulder leaning against the wall, staring down at the dusty floor.

Helewise watched Milon. He seemed surprised at the sudden cessation of the questions. Looking from Helewise to Josse and back again, he said, 'What will happen to me?'

Helewise glanced at Josse, but he did not seem about to answer. So she said, 'You will remain here until the sheriff and his men can be summoned. Then you will be taken under escort to the town jail, and, in due course, you will be tried for murder.'

'It wasn't murder,' he said, hardly above a whisper. 'I didn't mean to kill her. I loved her. She was carrying our baby.'

Then, once again, he began to weep.

Chapter Fifteen

Josse and the Abbess walked side by side back to her room. Neither, it seemed, wanted to be the first to break the silence.

Josse wondered if she was experiencing the same feelings that he was. From what he could see of her face, and from the slump of her normally squared shoulders, he guessed so.

He was feeling – he was at a loss to name the emotion searing through him. It was a mixture, and, indeed, a mixture of elements which did not normally go smoothly together. There was anger – yes, anger was still there. But also an undermining, growing pity. And, to his distress, guilt; although he fought it, reminded himself again and again of those two pathetic dead bodies, he had the unwelcome sense that, by manhandling Milon up to the Abbey and throwing him in that cell, he had acted like a bully.

It was the lad's weeping that was so disturbing, damn it! You couldn't even call it that, really – it was like no crying that Josse had ever heard before. It was a quiet, high-pitched keening sound, like the wind blowing through thin reeds.

And, although the cell and the undercroft were now a considerable number of paces behind, it seemed to Josse that he could still hear it.

As much to drown out the echo of the sound as for any other reason, he said to the Abbess as they approached her room, 'I still think he did it. Killed Gunnora as well as Elanor, I mean. Whatever he says.'

He heard the Abbess's small tut of impatience. 'He didn't,' she said firmly. 'Whilst I am the first to agree that it would be a tidy solution were he responsible for both deaths, he isn't.'

'How can you be so sure?' Josse demanded angrily. God, she was a stubborn woman!

'I—' Slowly she went round to the far side of her table, as slowly seating herself and indicating for him to do the same. He had a suspicion she was using the time to gather her argument together, which was quite a daunting thought. 'It's all wrong,' she said eventually. 'I can imagine him putting his hands round Elanor's neck and gripping just that bit too hard. He's frightened, let's say, desperately worried because the careful plan seems to be falling apart. And, by his own admission, he's cross with her. He's not entirely in command of himself. They have just made love, and that can leave people in a vulnerable emotional state, especially the young.' He was surprised that she should speak so matter-of-factly on the subject. Equally surprised that she should speak so accurately.

He realised she was watching him, a slight suspicion of irony in the large eyes. As if she knew exactly what he was thinking. 'But,' she went on, 'no matter how I try, I cannot believe he coldly drew a knife across Gunnora's throat and made that appalling cut.'

'I can,' Josse said heatedly.

But could he really? Now that she was making him look at it rationally, he began to wonder. Did he believe in Milon's guilt, or was it merely convenient for the youth to have killed both women? Because it would save Josse looking any further for a second murderer?

Interrupting his thoughts, the Abbess said, 'Have you the stomach for food, Sir Josse? It is the hour for breakfast.'

He looked at her. 'Have you?'

The clear grey eyes met his. 'No, but I intend to make myself eat.' The wide brow creased momentarily. 'We need our strength, you and I, and going without food will not supply us with it.' She gave a faint sigh. 'This business is not yet over.'

*

He went down to his quarters in the vale after the meal, and, stretching out on his hard bed, went almost instantly to sleep. He was awakened by a tap on his shoulder; Brother Saul stood over him, and beside him, looking somewhat grubby and travel-stained, stood Ossie.

'I am sorry to disturb you, Sir Josse,' Saul said, 'but the messenger here said it was urgent.'

Josse sat up, rubbing at his eyes. It felt as if someone had thrown a handful of small, sharp grit into them. 'Thank you, Saul,' he said, getting stiffly to his feet. 'Ossie, good morning.'

'Sir,' the boy muttered, grabbing the floppy cap from his head, and twisting it between his hands.

'You have a message for me?' Josse prompted.

Ossie's face closed down into a frown of concentration and he said, 'My Lord Brice of Rotherbridge sends word to Sir Josse d'Acquin, presently residing with the sisters at Hawkenlye.' He paused, then went on, 'My Lord says Sir Josse called on him twice while he was from home. Will he try a third time, now that my Lord is here?' The frown deepened. 'Now that he is *there*,' he corrected himself.

Josse smiled at the boy. 'Thank you, Ossie. You have carried the message well. Aye, I will come.'

Ossie gave him a quick grin. 'I'll go and say to Master,' he said, beginning to turn away.

'I shall be behind you on the road,' Josse called after him.

Saul was still hovering, face alight with curiosity.

'May I have water for a wash and a shave, Brother Saul?' Josse asked. 'It appears that I have to go on another journey.'

He covered the now familiar miles to Rotherbridge in good time. The weather had turned, and was slightly cooler; it was a lovely morning for a ride.

Crossing the river where he had tactfully turned his head away from Brice's grief, he wondered how the man fared now.

Was he becoming accustomed to his wife's cruel death? Was he beginning to believe that, for a true repentant, there *was* forgiveness? Josse fervently hoped so; the prospect of being the guest of a man in such straits as Brice had been, that day, was not a happy one.

He reached Rotherbridge Manor, and rode into the yard. This time, it was not Mathild who came out to meet him, but a man. Well-dressed, in plain but good-quality tunic, hose and boots, the man was dark-haired and had a look of Brice about him. But, whereas Brice's hair had had that distinctive badger-stripe of white, this man's was smoothly dark brown throughout.

It must be the brother. What was his name? Yes; Josse had it.

'Good day, my Lord Olivar,' he called out. 'I have come at your brother Brice's invitation – I am Josse d'Acquin, and he sent me word at Hawkenlye Abbey, where I am lodging with the monks in the vale, and—'

The dark man was smiling. 'I know who you are,' he interrupted. 'Please, Sir Josse, step down. Ossie will tend to your horse. Ossie!' The boy, Josse reflected, was having a busy morning; he appeared out of the stable block, broom in hand, nodded to Josse and took away his horse. The dark man watched, then turned back to Josse. 'Come and take refreshment.'

He led the way up the steps into the hall, and waved a hand at the chair where Josse had sat before, when he talked to Mathild. Of her, there was no sight; probably, with the master and his brother at home again, she had her hands full down in the kitchen.

'Have you any idea, my Lord Olivar, why your brother wished to see me?' Josse asked, more for the sake of conversation than any urgent desire to know. Obviously, having summoned Josse, Brice would no doubt soon arrive, and explain himself to Josse in person.

The dark man was smiling again, as if amused at some private joke. Offering Josse a mug of ale, he said, 'I think, Sir Josse, that I must correct a misapprehension into which you have somehow fallen.' He raised his own mug, took a drink, then said, 'I am not Olivar. I am Brice.'

Josse's immediate, foolish impulse was to say, No you're not! You can't be, I *saw* Brice, down by the river, in the deepest distress over the death of his young wife!

He held the words back. Clearly, he'd made a mistake. Jumped to a conclusion on purely circumstantial evidence. Wrong!

But, if this were indeed Brice, then who was the grieving man? There was a resemblance, yes – it was perfectly possible they were brothers.

He said, 'My Lord Brice, I apologise.' Brice shook his head, still smiling. Josse continued, 'If it is not impertinent, might I ask if your bother Olivar resembles you?'

'They do say so, yes, although I do not really see it myself. We are both dark, however. Only he has a streak of white, just here.' He indicated above his left ear. 'He's had it since he was a lad of fifteen. It grew after he'd had a bad fall from his horse when we were out hunting. The physician said it was shock, but I've always doubted that. It takes more than a fall to shock my brother, Sir Josse.'

'Ah. Oh. Yes, I see.' Josse, aware of making the right responses, was thinking. Not a man to shock readily? Perhaps not, when it was a question of physical fortitude. But the man Josse had seen down by the river had been in shock all right. He'd been grieving so deeply that it had seemed he would never stop.

Olivar of Rotherbridge, then, had a secret heartbreak which, or so it seemed, even his elder brother was unaware of.

'I asked you to visit me,' Brice was saying, 'because I wish to make a donation to Hawkenlye Abbey.'

'You do?' With some effort, Josse pulled his thoughts together.

'I do. I was planning to pay a call on Abbess Helewise, but there are matters here at Rotherbridge requiring my attention, and I have already been away for some time.'

'Aye.'

'I was with the holy brothers at Canterbury,' Brice went on. 'Doing penance.'

'Aye, I know.' Josse felt compelled to admit it; there was no need for this man to punish himself further by giving the details to a stranger.

But Brice, it seemed, wanted to. 'I did love Dillian,' he said, leaning forward and fixing earnest brown eyes on Josse. 'We had our difficulties, as no doubt do all married couples. You are married?' Josse shook his head. 'She could be wilful and over-frivolous, and she would not address herself to matters of importance. But I was at fault, too. I dare say I was too old and serious for her, God rest her soul, and I admit that I was not always kind to her.'

He was relating his story, Josse thought, with an ease that suggested acceptance. If that were so, then the heavy-handed monks had done their job well.

'Her death was an accident, I'm told,' Josse said.

'Accident, yes. I know it was. But it was my rash anger which led to it. I have made my confession, and done my penance.' He gave a grim smile, as if at the memory. 'I am reliably informed that for me to go on heaping ashes on my head would amount to self-indulgence. And I am only to wear the hair shirt on Sundays.'

This time the smile was open and unrestrained. Josse, wondering if possibly he were being deliberately charmed, found himself liking the man. And, if Brice had won himself God's forgiveness for his part in his wife's tragic death, then who was Josse to go on condemning him?

'You spoke of a gift to the Abbey,' he said.

'I did. I was explaining why I asked you to visit me, which was purely because, unable to make the journey to Hawkenlye, I could scarcely ask the Abbess to ride over here. So, Sir Josse, I asked you.'

It was reasonable. 'I have no objection,' Josse said.

'Good. In that case, let us proceed to the business. My late sister-in-law, Gunnora of Winnowlands, would have been left the greater part of her father's fortune had she and the old man lived a little longer. He disinherited her on her entry into Hawkenlye. Alard wanted her to marry me – it was a sound match, both families would have felt the benefits, and I was not unwilling. But she wouldn't have me, Sir Josse, shouted out to all who would listen that life as a nun was preferable to being my wife. There was a degree of blackening of my name, or so I gathered. But she had her reasons.' He spoke lightly, and Josse detected no hint of pain or of resentment. 'That was her story,' he murmured, half to himself. 'By God, she needed a good one. So Alard made Dillian his heir' – he was addressing Josse again now – 'but, when Dillian was killed, Alard had to think again. Initially he left the lot to his niece Elanor and her stupid little boy of a husband, but I am told he was about to reconsider. I imagine it is likely that, even with Gunnora dead, he would have made some gift to Hawkenlye. However, death intervened, and his unamended will stands; Elanor will inherit. Good news awaits her, on her return from her visiting.'

They didn't know, then, at Rotherbridge, of Elanor's death. Indeed, how could they, when, as far as the rest of the world was concerned, the second Hawkenlye victim was a postulant named Elvera? Briefly Josse wondered just who *would* inherit Alard's fortune. Milon, since he was Elanor's husband? But wasn't there some ancient law from back in the distant past about a criminal not being allowed to benefit from his crime?

The resolution of that matter remained to be seen.

'I wish,' Brice was saying, 'to give to the Abbey a donation to compensate, in some part, for what they would have received from my late wife's father, had he lived a day or so longer. I make the gift of my own free will, although I confess that the good brothers of Canterbury did drop one or two hints.'

'I'm sure they did,' Josse murmured.

Brice was reaching for a small leather bag that hung from his belt. 'Will you give this to the Abbess, please, Sir Josse? With the compliments of Brice of Rotherbridge, in the name of Sister Gunnora?'

'Aye, gladly.' Josse held out his hand, and Brice dropped the bag into it. The bag was very heavy.

'What news of progress in the hunt for her killer?' Brice asked as, seated once more, he raised his mug. 'You, I am told, have the new King's authority to investigate the murder?'

'Aye.'

'I wondered at Richard Plantagenet concerning himself with a rural killing until I made the connection,' Brice went on. 'Your task, I imagine, is simply to persuade us all that Gunnora was not killed by one of these released criminals he's been busy turfing out of the country's jails.'

'She wasn't,' Josse said. 'I've known that from the first.'

'Quite so. I can't imagine that anyone with any sense would have believed otherwise. Prisoners hereabouts may be mean, stinking and hopeless, but few of them are murderers.'

Josse grinned. 'Aye. Trouble is, Sir Brice, your average man drinking his hard-earned wages in the local hostelry doesn't have very much sense.'

Brice laughed. 'So, you remain here to satisfy your own curiosity?'

'Aye.' And, Josse thought wearily, I'm still a long way from doing so.

He was draining his ale, thinking it was about time he got up and headed back for Hawkenlye – it wouldn't do to be out after dark with a purseful of gold tucked in his tunic – when something occurred to him. He might not have felt he should ask, except that, for the past hour or so, he and Brice had been enjoying a long conversation about the end of Henry II's days, and discussing what likelihood there was of as good a life under the rule of his son. It had, Josse thought, put them on a new level of intimacy. Or it might have been the ale, and the sharing of the excellent food which Mathild had provided for the midday meal.

Either way, he plunged on and asked his question.

'Your brother, Olivar,' he began.

'My brother.' Brice sighed, sticking his legs out straight in front of him and regarding his boots. As if he, too, now felt able to speak of more personal matters, he added, 'My poor suffering brother.'

So he *did* know of Olivar's grief!

'Suffering?' Josse echoed innocently.

'Indeed. He laments her every waking minute. All his hopes gone awry, all he's waited and prayed for these three years or more.' He sighed again. 'I blame her, although I know it is wrong to speak ill of the dead. But she was ever a cold fish. Calculating, so that you never knew whether her actions had an honest motive. Me, I'm sorry to admit it, but I usually suspected the opposite. She was a devious woman. I can't understand what the attraction was, but it was there all right. He adored her.'

'His hopes?' Josse had no idea what Brice was talking about. Had Olivar concealed a private love for Dillian? Hoped – although surely it must have been hopeless – that one day he would win her? But no, that couldn't be right – nobody had suggested Dillian was a cold fish; quite the contrary. And, if he were speaking of his late wife, would Brice sound quite so offhand?

'Yes.' Brice frowned. 'I thought you knew? Thought they would have told you?' The frown deepened. 'No. Of course they couldn't have done. They didn't know. Nobody did, except the three of us.'

'Three.' Brice, Olivar, and—

'They kept it hidden from everyone,' Brice said. 'I only knew because Olivar confided in me. He felt bad, I think, because she'd turned me down. Not that I minded!' He laughed briefly. 'Only my pride was hurt. I was prepared to marry her, as I said earlier, but, in all honesty, I never really cared for her.'

'Three,' Josse said again. He wished he had not drunk so much ale; just when he needed his wits, here they were all fuddled.

'Yes.' Brice's dark eyes were on him again. 'My brother and me, naturally, and her.' Then, as if Josse could possibly still be in any doubt, 'Gunnora.'

Chapter Sixteen

As if fully aware that this new topic meant his guest was in for quite a long spell of sitting and listening, Brice got up and refilled Josse's mug.

'Had you, before we met,' he asked his guest, 'formed an impression of Gunnora of Winnowlands?'

Josse, who had quietly and, he hoped, unobtrusively, pushed the full mug out of his reach, considered. 'To some extent,' he said. 'I sensed, from what I was told, that she was self-contained, lacking in warmth, manipulative.'

'How astute,' Brice murmured. 'She was all of those. I knew her from childhood – my father's lands bordered Alard's, and it was inevitable that our two families should be on terms of some intimacy. Gunnora was several years my junior, but, nevertheless, it was she with whom I learned to dance, she with whom I harmonised when we were summoned to sing our little songs for our parents.'

'You did not like her,' Josse said.

'Not greatly. I respected her, for she was intelligent and, when she put her mind to the task, capable. But' – the heavy brows drew down in an expression of intense thought – 'there was ever an air of superiority about her, as if privately she was thinking, "I am better than you. I only join in these inane activities because, just at present, it pleases me to do so."' He glanced at Josse. 'She could be cruel. One of her father's serving women had fallen for a groom – a handsome fellow, but brainless, some years younger than her – and he let her down. Gunnora, pretending to console the poor wretched woman, said that someone of her years and her looks would do better to set her cap at a man her own age.'

'Sound advice, surely?' Josse said.

Brice smiled grimly. 'Indeed. Except that she didn't content herself with that. She went on to suggest a suitable man, a half-blind old fool who was fat, stinking, and chronically indolent. Said he needed looking after, and Cat – the woman's name was Catherine – could do the job.'

'A little heartless.'

'More than a little, if you could have seen the two men, the one so attractive, the other so foul. Gunnora made it clear to Cat that she considered Cat's own looks more akin to the old man's.'

'I begin to see what you mean,' Josse remarked. It sounded like a gratuitous piece of spite. 'And Gunnora, was she beautiful?' He had seen her in death, and her features had seemed regular enough. But a dead face gave no clue to how it had appeared in life, when it was animated, crossed with a dozen emotions, and—

'She could have been beautiful,' Brice said. 'Her hair was thick and dark, her skin was perfect, and her eyes were large and deep blue, like her sister's. But her chin was too small. That alone would not have detracted seriously from her looks, but, in conjunction with her pursed, prim mouth, the effect was too strong to miss.'

'You studied her closely,' Josse observed.

Again, the quick grin. 'She was meant to be my wife.'

'But she was in love with your brother, and would not have you.'

Brice considered that. 'My brother, definitely, was in love with her. As for her . . .' He seemed at a loss.

'When did it start?' Josse prompted. Often, he had observed, people told a story better when encouraged to begin at the beginning.

'Well, when she had her eighteenth birthday, her father told her it was time that her betrothal to me should be formally arranged. My late father had long since persuaded me that the match was in my best interests, since, once I inherited Rotherbridge, an alliance with Gunnora would unite our estates with Winnowlands. It was a sound suggestion, I could readily understand that. And, as for marrying Gunnora, I had no particular feelings either way. There was no other woman I was in love with, but that, in any case, would not have been strictly relevant. And, as I have said, she was intelligent, good looking and capable.' He shot Josse a shrewd look. 'What more can a man ask for in a wife?'

'What indeed,' Josse murmured.

'But Gunnora wouldn't have it. She acted as if the whole thing was a total surprise, which it surely couldn't have been. Then she said she did not wish to marry me, and, when pressed for a reason, said she did not care for me as a husband. That was not enough for Alard, who began a campaign to make her change her mind. He shut her in her room, threatened to beat her, took away her pretty clothes and left her with cast-offs to wear, all of which she greeted with the same sort of twisted, self-punishing delight as a martyr shown the means of her martyrdom. She was bright enough to realise that, if she acted as if this punishment were satisfying some strange, perverse desire in her instead of driving her towards surrender, then it would probably stop. Which it did – Alard was a simple man, poor sap, and no match for his elder daughter.'

'And, all along, you think her real reason for refusing you was because she was in love with your brother?'

Brice looked puzzled. 'I don't know. It must have been, mustn't it? I mean, no matter what she might have said about not wanting to be a rich man's wife and plaything – and I was a rich man by then, my father having passed away – there had to be more to it than that. She knew me well enough to be aware I wouldn't try to make a plaything of her!' he burst out suddenly. 'I might not have had any love for her, but I respected her. And life as a rich man's wife is, I assure you, better than the alternative.'

'You don't have to convince me,' Josse said. 'Why didn't she say she wished to marry Olivar instead? Assuming he had asked her?'

'He did that all right, any number of times. She said her father would not accept that, that it had to be the elder son – the heir – or nothing.'

'Was that true?'

Brice shrugged. 'I don't know. I expect so. Anyway, I got tired of the whole exasperating business. One summer night, I took Dillian outside into the moonlight for a stroll – it was after a family celebration, when we'd all drunk rather too much for discretion. She looked so lovely, and the gillyflowers were scenting the air, and a nightingale was singing, just for us . . .' He broke off, a smile of remembrance on his face. 'Before I knew what was happening, we were kissing. I think it was probably at her instigation rather than mine, although it is perhaps unchivalrous to say so.' The smile deepened. 'She was a delightful girl, Sir Josse. I couldn't resist her – not that I tried very hard. It seemed a happy solution all round for the pair of us to be wed, and we were. The rest, you know.' Abruptly the smile vanished. Brice turned his back, leaning one arm against the great fireplace for support. Josse, observing the slump of the broad shoulders, felt it would have been cruel to press him further about that particular part of the story.

After what he felt to be a decent pause, he said, 'And then Gunnora entered Hawkenlye?'

'No,' Brice said, on a sigh. 'She'd already gone. It was, she said, the only way to stop her father's bullying. "I'm going to be a nun," she told him, "and then I shall be answerable to nobody!" Alard pointed out that she would be answerable to God and her Abbess, and she said that *she'd* worry about that.'

'How did Olivar feel about the woman he loved becoming a nun?'

'He told me she was only doing it to get out of marrying me,' Brice said. 'Silly, really, when you look back – if she'd waited a little longer, she wouldn't have had to bother, because I married her sister instead. Anyway, the plan was for her to stay at Hawkenlye for a year, then, when the time came for her to take the first of her permanent vows, say she'd changed her mind. She was going to start her life as a nun full of devotion and enthusiasm, then, gradually, start being less co-operative, less obedient. She was quite sure she could act in such a way that the Abbey would be quite glad to see the back of her.'

And, Josse thought, she succeeded. Brilliantly.

'Then she was going to come back and find Olivar?'

'That was the idea. She had guessed what would happen here, that, with her out of the way, I'd probably marry Dillian. She may even have known that Dillian quite fancied the idea. She probably observed it for herself, come to that – she didn't miss much.'

Josse sat back in his chair. Good God, he thought, Brice had been right when he called Gunnora manipulative! How many people's lives had been affected – deeply affected – by her plotting? Her father, her sister, Brice, Olivar. Not to mention Abbess Helewise and her nuns, who had welcomed Gunnora in good faith, believed in her vocation, done their best to help her adapt to the religious life.

Josse was beginning to find it not quite so surprising that somebody had cut her throat.

'But now she's dead,' Brice was saying, 'and my brother nurses a broken heart.'

'Is your brother at home?'

'He was. He came with me to Canterbury, you know, and was a tower of strength during my various ordeals. Then he accompanied me home, but he seemed unsettled. He had, I think, derived as much comfort from our time in Canterbury as I did, possibly more. The new shrine to Saint Thomas is most moving – have you seen it?'

'Not yet.'

'I recommend it, for those in distress. Anyway, Olivar said he was going back. I encouraged him to go – a man must seek comfort wherever he can find it.'

'Amen,' Josse said.

There was a short reflective silence. Josse, going over all that he had just learned – as well as he could, after the ale – knew that there was something he must ask. What was it?

Deliberately he let his mind go a blank, which wasn't difficult. But then an image flashed into his head. Yes! He had it.

'Your wife had a cross, a costly piece set with rubies?' he asked.

'She did. Alard gave them both one, almost identical. And a smaller one for their cousin Elanor.'

'Aye. May I see Dillian's cross?'

Brice looked surprised. 'If you wish. Come with me.'

He led the way to a stair at the end of the hall, drawing aside the tapestry that hung over its entrance. The stair, set deep in the wall, climbed in a spiral to an upper floor. Following him through an arched doorway, Josse found himself in what was clearly a lady's bedchamber, plainly but adequately furnished. Little seemed to have been tidied away; the coverlet spread on the woollen mattress was smoothed and straight, but a small pair of soft leather shoes lay in a corner, one upright, one on its side. A wooden chest had its lid slightly raised, and a colourful piece of silk, heavily fringed – a shawl? – spilled out. The room could have been only recently abandoned, awaiting the mistress's return.

It was strangely touching.

'She kept her jewels in this thing.' Brice was picking up a shabby velvet-covered box encrusted with glass beads. 'It's a tawdry piece, but she was sentimental about it. It was a gift from an old nursemaid, she said. I bought her that' – he pointed to a large and beautifully made silver casket that stood on the floor beside the chest – 'and she thanked me prettily and said she'd keep her gloves in it.'

Smiling, he opened the velvet box.

Inside was a pearl necklet, a brooch set with a sapphire, some amber beads and four or five rings. There was also a circlet of gold, quite plain but for a decoration in the shape of two hearts, picked out in tiny pearls.

'I gave her that for our wedding,' Brice said, touching it with his finger.

He seemed to have forgotten what he and Josse had gone up there for.

Josse hadn't. And it came as no surprise whatsoever that the cross was not in the box. He knew where it was.

'No cross,' he remarked.

Brice started. 'Eh? Dear God, but you're right!' He began rifling through the jewels, as if the cross might lie hidden. Then he flung the box down and picked up the silver casket, throwing out the gloves, then turning it upside down and shaking it.

'Do not worry, my Lord Brice,' Josse said hurriedly – silver caskets were not made for such treatment – 'I believe I know where the ruby cross is.'

Brice turned a furious face on him. 'Then why make me come up here to look for it?'

'I apologise. I was not entirely certain, until now.' That was a lie, but Brice wasn't to know. 'A cross was found beside Gunnora's body, and we – the Abbess Helewise and I – believed it to be that belonging to your late wife.'

'But Gunnora had one, too, I told you! Surely it would have been hers that lay by her?'

'No, hers she had entrusted to the Abbess for safe keeping.'

Brice was slowly shaking his head. 'Dillian's cross? *Dillian's* cross, found beside Gunnora? It makes no sense!'

But Josse thought it did. 'Who else would have known where she kept her jewellery?'

'Oh, anyone who knew her well. Her sister, her maid. Me, of course.'

'Her cousin?' Josse hardly dared say it.

'Elanor? Well, yes, I suppose so. She was a fairly regular visitor to Rotherbridge, and she and Dillian spent hours up here in Dillian's chamber.' He had picked up the gold circlet, and was turning it in his hands. 'She wore this over her veil. She looked so beautiful. So eager.'

Josse had learned all he needed to know. His impulse now was to get going, as swiftly as he could, back to Hawkenlye. He had already stayed longer than he should – he was going to have to hurry to arrive back by nightfall.

Brice was still deep in his memories. Feeling guilty – for it was his presence that had caused Brice's reverie, his questioning that had taken the man back into the pain of the recent past – Josse said, 'My Lord Brice, I regret, but I must take my leave of you. It is a long step back to Hawkenlye, and, with your gift on me, I wish to be there before dark.'

Brice turned to him. 'Gift? Oh, yes. Of course.' Then, manners instilled from childhood reasserting themselves, he said, 'Let me see you to your horse. May I offer refreshment to sustain you for your ride?'

I have had more than enough already, Josse thought. But it was surprising how his head had suddenly cleared. 'Thank you, but no.'

As he mounted his horse, he leaned down and offered Brice his hand. 'My thanks, my Lord. I will arrange for your late wife's cross to be returned to you.'

Brice nodded. 'I thank you.'

As Josse turned to leave, Brice called out, 'Shall you find him, this man who murdered Gunnora?'

And Josse said, 'I think I already have.'

All the way back to Hawkenlye he was thinking, it *has* to be him! Milon killed Gunnora, just as I've been saying. It all fits! He knew from the first that he would have to make her murder look like rape or robbery, or both, and so he instructed Elanor to get hold of Gunnora's cross, so that it could be dropped by the body. But Elanor went one better – maybe she thought it would be too difficult to get her hands on Gunnora's cross, once at Hawkenlye – and she stole Dillian's cross before she left home. It would have been easy, surely, to visit her dead cousin's chamber?

Damnation. He realised he should have asked Brice if such a posthumous visit had indeed taken place.

It must have done, he concluded, for how else could it have happened, that Dillian's cross ended up beside her sister's murdered corpse?

They were, he concluded, cleverer than he'd thought, those two. Milon and Elanor might seem like children burning their hands by playing with the fire of the adult world, but it had to be an act! How well-planned it had been, that first murder. And how brutal. Had Elanor turned away, when Milon slit her cousin's throat? Had the horror of the spilled blood affected the grip of those hands on Gunnora's arms, so that it slackened as Elanor swayed in a faint?

He would never know.

Turning his mind to the practical – how he was going to convince the Abbess that his version of events was the true one – he kicked his horse into a canter and raced back to Hawkenlye.

Chapter Seventeen

Helewise sat in the shrine in the valley, staring up at the Virgin Mary.

She was still feeling the after effects of the shock. Sister Euphemia had tried to make her lie down in the infirmary until she felt stronger, but Helewise had said firmly that she preferred to go and pray.

If Euphemia had assumed Helewise had meant she was going into the Abbey church – and so would be close to the infirmarer's help, should it be necessary – then that was unfortunate.

Helewise was finding it difficult to concentrate her mind on her prayers. She felt rather odd – light-headed, as if she might quite easily float up to the ceiling, or, once out through the doorway, away over the trees – and still more than a little sick.

'It's a very nasty cut,' Euphemia had said, bathing Helewise's right forefinger with gentle hands. 'What *can* you have been doing, Abbess dear?'

'I was trying an edge to see if it was sharp,' Helewise had replied, which was accurate, as far as it went.

'Oh, *dear*, oh dear!' Euphemia, clearly, had thought she would have had more sense, as indeed she should have done. It was just that it had been so unexpected . . . 'Next time, Abbess,' Euphemia had said, 'test your knives on something that can't feel pain!'

Helewise was feeling pain, that was quite certain. A great deal of pain. Euphemia had found it a tough job to staunch the blood – the pad of Helewise's finger had been cut neatly in two, right across the first segment – and it had been necessary for her to sit for some minutes holding her hand above her head, while Sister Euphemia pressed the cut edges together, before the blood had stopped pumping out. Then the infirmarer had applied a salve of white horehound, which had burned like hellfire, and bound the whole hand up tightly, instructing Helewise to try to remember to keep it held up against her left shoulder.

That, in fact, was easy to remember; the moment Helewise let the hand fall, the wound began to throb so violently that the pain increased tenfold.

It was the loss of blood that was making the Abbess feel so faint, or so Euphemia had informed her.

'Faint,' Helewise murmured to herself. 'Faint.'

It made matters considerably worse. Perhaps, Helewise thought, Euphemia was right, and I should go and lie down? Not in the infirmary – I couldn't bear it – but on my bed in the dormitory? But no! Abbesses don't do things like that, even if their whole hand has been cut off! Abbesses keep a stiff back and an upright posture, maintaining a dignified air of quiet authority at all times. Lie on my bed, indeed!

She fixed her eyes on the Virgin's statue and told herself not to be so feeble. She thought she saw the Virgin's head turn slightly – she's looking at me! – but, staring harder, realised she was mistaken. She wondered if she were hallucinating.

'Ave, Maria . . .' she began.

But the words, which she must have said thousands of times, refused to come. And so did the comfort she might have received from the saying of them.

Cradling her hurt finger in her other hand, she closed her eyes and waited, in the calming silence of the deserted shrine, for Josse's return.

*

Some time later, she heard him enter the shrine. Heard the sound of boots on the steps, so it must have been Josse, for the monks and the lay brothers wore soft sandals.

'You're back,' she said.

There was a grunt of agreement.

She opened her eyes and began to turn round to look at him, but it made her feel so sick that instantly she stopped. The shrine seemed to be whirling round like a spinning top, so she closed her eyes again.

She sensed him come close. Sit down beside her on the narrow form.

To her vague surprise – all her emotions seemed to be vague, she was discovering – she couldn't remember for a moment where he had been. Then she thought she recalled a messenger . . . Yes. That was right. A boy had come, breathless from haste, his words tumbling over each other as he'd announced that he had to see Sir Josse d'Acquin, he brought a summons for him, an invitation to visit Brice of Rotherbridge. She wondered what *that* had been all about.

'You found the Lord Brice in good spirits?' she asked.

There was no answer for some time. Then a voice which she had never heard before said, 'Aye, Brice is himself again. He has made his confession, done rigorous penance, and obtained absolution.'

There was such despair in those words that she felt her heart contract with compassion.

Opening her eyes again, very carefully she turned her head to her left and looked at him.

He was, she guessed from the unlined quality of his skin, in his late twenties, but looked far, far older. It wasn't only the dramatic streak of white threading through the dark hair, nor the weary, defeated posture. It was the eyes. Those dark eyes, heavily hooded, whose lids were swollen and which were circled with grey, as if someone had filled in each entire eye socket with smudged black powder.

No wonder he spoke with such hopeless envy of Brice's recovery; here, she was in no doubt, was a man suffering such torments, pursued by such devils of misery, that the happy state of absolution must seem as far distant as the moon.

Who was he? Someone, clearly, acquainted with Brice of Rotherbridge.

But first things first.

She said, very calmly and quietly, 'Are you here to pray, friend?'

A brief light of hope entered his eyes at her form of address, but, as quickly as it had come, it was extinguished.

'I cannot pray,' he said flatly. 'I have tried, others have tried with me. The monks in the holiest shrine in all England have done their best for me. But it is hopeless. I am beyond help.'

'No man is beyond God's love,' she said, maintaining the same level tone. 'That is Christ's message to us, that, with genuine repentance, we are to be forgiven.'

There was a silence.

Since he did not seem about to break it, she said, 'Will you pray with me, now? Our Blessed Lady is here, see? She will listen.'

It had worked with others at the very end of their endurance; Helewise had sat, up at the Abbey and down here in the shrine, with seemingly hopeless cases, talking quietly, listening to the outpourings that told of a life gone wrong, of one bad deed leading with dreadful inevitability to the next, until the downward spiral of sin upon sin spun away out of control. Then, when they were empty of words, cried out of tears, she would begin to help them back up the long and difficult slope.

Yes. She had seen men – and women – apparently far beyond God's love, brought back into the precious fold.

She watched the dark-haired man.

Slowly he raised his head until his sore eyes looked up at the statue of the Virgin. For a moment a half-smile spread over the handsome features, but then it was gone. His face falling, he said hoarsely, 'Here, of all places, I cannot pray. She – Our Lady there – is watching me, like she did that night. She knows what happened. She knows that, but for me, Gunnora would still be alive.'

He turned to Helewise, and his hands suddenly gripped at her shoulders with surprising strength. 'She promised me!' he shouted. '*Promised!* It was to be that night, she *said* it would, after all my years of waiting! I didn't rush her, I didn't try to persuade her out of coming here, for all that I felt it was wrong. You welcomed her, didn't you? Believed she really had a vocation, wanted to make a good nun! When, all along, it was just a place to hide away till the heat died down and Brice was safely married.'

Helewise's head spun with a dozen questions. But now, when this poor tormented soul was in the throes of spilling all the pain out of him, was not the time to ask them. She said, 'Yes, we made her welcome.'

He dropped his hands. 'I know, I could tell! You are good women. Too good for—' Too good for Gunnora? Abruptly he stopped, as if pulling himself up short of that betrayal. 'We should have told them, all of them at home, from the start,' he went on instead. 'It wouldn't have been easy, when her father was set on her marrying Brice, but I believe we could have won him round. He was a decent father, according to his own lights. I don't think he would have insisted on doing things his way, when everyone else involved wanted it to be otherwise. But Gunnora was not to be diverted.' He glanced at Helewise. 'For some time, at the start, I became very worried. I thought she might actually enjoy being a nun, and I was terrified that she'd decide to stay at Hawkenlye. That I'd lose her.'

As he spoke, Helewise noticed, his hands were gripping at a fold of his tunic hem, pleating it first this way, then the other, with such force that the material was crushed beyond recovery. There was a compulsiveness about the repetitive action that spoke of a deeply troubled man.

For the first time, she felt afraid.

Don't think of yourself, she commanded her quaking soul. Think of *him*.

It helped.

'She knew how much you loved her?' she asked. The man hadn't spoken of love, but she was quite certain she was right to assume it.

'Of course! I told her, over and over again!'

'And did she return your love?'

'Yes! *Yes!*' Then, after a pause, 'I think so. She once said she thought she loved me. But it would have grown!' He spoke very rapidly, as if he wanted to defend himself against a protest which he hadn't given Helewise the chance to make. 'It was enough, that she had the beginnings of love for me! Wasn't it?'

'Yes.' It was the only possible response.

'My brother said I was a fool,' he went on. 'Brice didn't mind Gunnora not wanting to marry him, and he could never see why I loved her so much. But we'd grown up together, you see. I'd assumed, like everyone else, that she'd marry Brice, but I always hoped something might happen . . . God forgive me, but once I found myself hoping he'd die, then she'd marry me. My own brother!' Tears sprang into his eyes.

'We all have bad thoughts sometimes,' Helewise said. 'But we don't mean them. Do we? You would never have turned your brief, private hope that your brother would die into reality, would you? Nor have failed to grieve deeply and honestly had he died?'

'No! No, of course not.'

'Well, then.' She gave him a quick smile, hoping to reassure. 'God sees into our hearts, you know. Give Him credit for that.'

The man nodded slowly. 'Yes. That's what the Canterbury monks said.' Briefly he seemed to brighten, but then, as if some further dread thought took over his mind, he said mournfully, 'But Christ and His Holy Mother won't understand about Gunnora.'

Offering a swift prayer of her own, Helewise took a steadying breath and said, 'I believe that *I* understand, now. Why not try them and see if they do?'

*

They told Josse up at the Abbey that the Abbess Helewise was praying. Not finding her in the church, he hurried on down into the vale and, for some unknown reason walking with exaggerated stealth, approached the shrine.

The door was ajar. Putting his face to the opening, he looked inside.

Down at the foot of the steps, sitting side by side on a bench that stood on the only flat area of floor, were Helewise and Olivar.

His instinct was to hurl himself forward; for some reason which he did not pause to analyse, he had the clear impression she was in danger.

He made himself stop. Stood perfectly still, listening.

Helewise had placed a heavily bandaged hand over Olivar's hands, folded in his lap. She was leaning towards him, and Josse heard the tail end of what she was saying: '. . . try them and see if they do?'

Olivar didn't respond for some moments and, in the brief pause, Josse wondered wildly what he was doing there. Had he come to mourn Gunnora, in this the nearest place of worship to where she had been murdered? Or – frightening thought! – had he somehow discovered that Milon was responsible for the death of the woman he had loved, and was here to find him and extract his own vengeance?

Helewise, good woman that she was, seemed to have calmed him; Olivar was looking relaxed, Josse thought, perhaps persuaded by the Abbess into believing that praying for Gunnora's soul was better than seeking out her killer, and that—

But just then Olivar began to speak, and Josse turned his full attention to listening.

'We were to meet here, in the shrine, in the hour before dawn,' he said. 'She would attend Matins, then return with the sisters to the dormitory. But, as soon as she thought they were all asleep, she was going to get up and creep out. I said I'd wait from midnight onwards – I didn't mind how long it was till she came, I just didn't want her arriving first. I got here while you were at your devotions.'

'You must have had a long vigil,' Helewise's soft voice said.

'Yes, but I was so happy at the thought of seeing her again that I didn't mind. It had been months since we'd had any contact – we'd only been able to make that tryst because of her silly cousin's fun and games. I gave Elanor a letter for Gunnora, you see. I said a lot, wrote of my love for her. I wrote too much, perhaps. But I didn't think it would matter – it was only for Gunnora's eyes, Elanor couldn't read. Nor could Gunnora, not really. At least, not very fluently. I suppose I was wasting my time.' There was the smallest suggestion of amusement in the voice. 'Then she – Gunnora – did as I suggested and left her brief reply hidden for me in a crack in the wall out there.' He waved a hand towards the doorway; Josse, afraid that one or other of them might turn round, swiftly moved back out of sight.

'That was how you knew she'd come,' Helewise said.

'Yes. I said in my message that the year was up, it was time for her to put our plan into operation and announce she was leaving the convent. I had hoped we would set a firm date, a time, even, then I could have been waiting at the Abbey gates for her and we could have found a priest straightaway and asked him to marry us. It wasn't what I wanted, this secret meeting down here at dead of night. I didn't want it to be so *furtive*. As if we were ashamed.'

'So, you waited, and, eventually, she came?' the Abbess asked.

'Yes.' Warmth flooding the bleak voice, he hurried on, 'Oh, I can't tell you how wonderful it was to see her again! I threw my arms round her, hugged her to me, tried to kiss her.'

There was a brief silence.

'Tried?' It was, Josse thought, exactly what he would have asked.

'She wouldn't let me, well, not on her lips.' Olivar gave a small laugh. 'She said she was still a nun, and that I must show due respect and only give her a brotherly peck on the cheek. And that was funny, because she didn't look much like a nun – she was wearing her headdress, but it was loosely draped, and the wimple was tucked into the front of her habit, not secured round her throat. I pretended to find it funny, her not kissing me, but I didn't really. I mean, it wasn't as if we had been – well, you know – intimate, before, but we had exchanged kisses. Very passionate, thrilling kisses.'

Josse, knowing what he now knew of Gunnora, found that hard to believe. Passion, from a woman like that? Perhaps she had been good at simulating it.

'Anyway, it didn't matter,' Olivar was saying, 'because we'd be man and wife very soon, and then we'd be able to kiss, make love all night if we wanted to. So—' his voice broke on a sob. Quickly bringing himself under control, he tried again. 'So I said, "How soon can it be? When do you come out of the convent?" And then she told me. Said she'd changed her mind about marriage, didn't feel that she wanted to be a wife after all.'

Helewise murmured something, but Josse couldn't catch the words.

'Yes, I know.' Olivar was weeping openly now. 'I couldn't believe it, you're right. I said, "Sweeting, it's me! Olivar! You haven't to be Brice's wife, he's married to your sister, remember?" I didn't tell her what had just happened to Dillian – I know it was wrong, but I didn't dare. Gunnora might have used that as further grounds for staying where she was – after all, she might have thought they'd have made her marry him, now that he was a widower. "It's us that are to marry," I said, "you and me, like we planned!" And' – again, the break in his voice – 'she just stood there, at the top of the steps' – he waved his arm, indicating behind him – 'and said she'd decided to stay in the Abbey a little longer. Or, failing that, she'd leave and get her father to reinstate her in his will, then live at Winnowlands on her own. Then she turned her back on me and made a dainty little curtsey to the statue of the Virgin.'

He paused briefly, collecting himself, then the grim narrative resumed. 'I was standing beside her, and I tried to turn her round to face me. I don't really know why – I think I thought that if I could just get her to kiss me – gently, you know, I didn't intend to *force* her – then she'd get a bit aroused and remember how sweet it used to be for us, before, when we embraced.'

You poor deluded man, Josse thought. What an optimistic hope!

'So – so – I took hold of her shoulder, and I said, "Gunnora, my dearest love, won't you hug me? Please?" and she twisted herself out of my grasp and said, "No, Olivar, I don't care to. I am going to pray." Then' – the weeping was loud now, each sob breaking out of him as if tearing him apart – 'then she started to go down the steps, almost dancing, as if to say, see how happy I am? See how I love to be a nun, to pray before the Holy Mother?'

It seemed unlikely that he could go on.

But he didn't need to; Helewise's quiet voice took up the tale.

'She danced down those slippery steps, and she missed her footing, didn't she?' Josse saw the young man nod. 'It's so easily done,' Helewise said, 'it's the condensation from the spring, it settles on the stones and makes them as perilous as ice.'

There was another, longer, silence. Josse was beginning to wonder if either of them would finish the story – was there, indeed, any need, when both appeared to know perfectly well already what happened? – when Helewise spoke again.

'You tried to catch her, didn't you?' Once more, the nod of agreement. 'I knew. We saw the little bruises on the tops of her arms – we thought at first that someone had held her fast while another person – well, never mind that. Someone did indeed hold her, but the marks were from your hands on her, trying to stop her fall.'

'Yes.' Olivar's brief monosyllable was so wracked with agony that Josse could have wept for him. 'But it was no good – she was already tumbling forward, and I couldn't hold her. She slipped out of my grasp, flew through the air, and then . . . then . . .'

'She fell against the statue,' Helewise finished for him. 'By the most terrible ill fortune, the plinth caught her across the throat. Didn't it?'

'Aye.' He rubbed at his eyes like a punished child crying at the injustice. 'I leapt down the steps after her, to see if she was hurt. I don't know what I expected – she was lying so still that I thought she'd bumped her head, knocked herself unconscious. Then I turned her over, and I saw.'

Helewise had her arm round him now, and he was leaning against her, the big body shaking. 'There was so much blood!' he cried, 'all over that horrible plinth, pooling on the floor under her, soaking down into the black cloth of her habit, and I didn't know what to do! I remember thinking I mustn't leave her there, for her life's blood to run into the holy spring water, so I picked her up and carried her outside. I think I intended to take her up to her sisters, but I'm not sure – it's all so hazy, that bit of it. She was getting heavy, and I felt very sick – I laid her down on the path, but it was all dusty, and I thought it wouldn't be nice if her poor hurt neck got dirty. So I carried her to the less-used path, where there was clean, damp grass at the edges, and settled her there. I'd brought her sister's cross for her, as a betrothal present – I knew Gunnora didn't have hers any more, she'd said she was going to give it to the Abbey. I didn't think Dillian would have minded – for all I knew, she might have left it to Gunnora anyway. I knew where she'd kept it, in that old box of hers, and I went up to her chamber and took it. It wasn't long after she died – everyone was in such a state, I don't think they ever knew what I'd done. I brought it with me, that night. When I came to meet Gunnora.'

He paused for some moments. It seemed to Josse that, having gone back in his memory to a time before the terrible death had happened, he was reluctant to resume his account.

Eventually he spoke again.

'After she – afterwards, I went back into the shrine and I cleaned away all the blood. It's a holy place, and I knew it wasn't right to defile it. It took so long. I took off my shirt and used it as a wash cloth, but I had to keep scooping up water to wet it, over and over again. And there was so little light, just a few candles burning, and I couldn't really see if I'd done it properly. In the end, I just had to leave it. I wanted to get back to her, you see. She was all on her own, out there in the dark.'

Helewise said something, her voice soft, soothing. Josse saw Olivar nod briefly.

'I said, "I'm back, Gunnora," then I bent over her, un-fastened the chain and put the cross round her neck,' he went on quietly. 'It looked so pretty, against the black of her habit. I was kneeling by her side, and I stayed there for a long time, just looking down at her. Then I ran away.'

Helewise was rocking him gently, crooning as if she were soothing a child waking from a nightmare. 'There, there,' the soft voice intoned, 'all done, you've got it out of you now. There, there.'

There was a silence. An extended silence.

Olivar said presently, 'Is she buried?'

'She is,' Helewise said. 'Tucked up snug and safe in her coffin, where no more harm can come to her.'

'Is she with God?'

Josse noticed Helewise's hesitation; he wondered if Olivar did. 'I expect she soon will be,' Helewise said. 'We have prayed for her soul, and we will continue to have Masses said for her. We will do all we can to shorten her time in purgatory.'

'She was good!' Olivar protested. 'She will not have many sins staining her soul, Abbess. Soon she'll be in heaven.'

Helewise murmured, 'Amen.'

Then, dropping her head down on top of the dark head resting against her shoulder, she began to pray out loud for the late sister of the Abbey, Gunnora of Winnowlands.

Chapter Eighteen

They put Olivar in the infirmary.

When Helewise had finished her prayer for Gunnora, he had straightened up, looked around him with an expression that suggested he didn't quite recall where he was, then, remembering, had slowly slumped to the ground. His face in his hands, he said, in a tone which had torn into the souls of both those who heard, 'She is gone. What is there left for me now?'

He had suffered some sort of collapse. Josse and Helewise, at a loss to know what to do, had half led, half dragged him up the hill to Sister Euphemia. Observing his extreme distress, she had prescribed a draught of her poppy mixture, strengthened with a little precious mandrake root. 'It is best that he sleeps, for now,' she said. 'To give him some of the blessed oblivion is, I fear, really all that I can do.' Her round face creased in concern. 'It's only a temporary solution, mind,' she added practically, 'the poor soul will find nothing changed for the better when he wakes.'

She found a corner of the infirmary for him, where he could lie screened by thin hangings, a little apart from the sights, sounds, and smells of the other patients. One of the nursing sisters placed a shallow bowl of full-blown roses by his head, and their powerful scent soon wove itself through the air. 'Roses are good for grief,' Sister Euphemia remarked, nodding her approval. As Olivar gradually relaxed into sleep, she stood over him for some minutes. Then, with a tender touch of her hand on his shoulder, left him.

Brother Firmin had presented himself and announced, although Sister Euphemia had given no indication of either wanting or needing assistance, that he had come to help her. He had brought a cup of the healing spring water for the patient. He waited patiently while Olivar was settled down, then, observing that Olivar had in fact gone to sleep, sent one of the sisters to fetch him a stool, which he placed at the foot of Olivar's bed.

'I will remain here,' he announced to Sister Euphemia. 'Yes, sister, I know full well that the young man sleeps. But it may be of help to him, in some way, that somebody is with him.'

Then, putting the cup of spring water carefully beside the roses, he closed his eyes, and, lips moving in silent prayer, he settled himself down to his vigil.

Josse had sought out Brother Saul and asked if he would make the journey to Rotherbridge. Brice had to be notified, and, this time, Josse felt that it was acceptable to ask another to set out on the errand. Josse had a suspicion that Abbess Helewise might prefer it if he were to stay at the abbey. He was trying, haltingly, to explain this to Brother Saul, when the brother put out a hand to touch Josse's arm and said, 'There is no need. I understand.'

Abbess Helewise, Sister Euphemia, Brother Firmin, Brother Saul, the unknown sister who had brought the roses, all of them, Josse reflected, so eager to help, so full of compassion, with willing hands, willing legs, hurrying to do what was asked of them, often before it had even been asked . . .

For the first time, it dawned on him what a *good* place Hawkenlye Abbey was.

Josse asked Abbess Helewise, 'How did you know?'

They were back in Helewise's room. She was sitting straight-backed in her usual place, but he had the impression that the effort of appearing normal was costing her dear.

She turned to look at him. She raised her bandaged right hand, waved it at him, then, with a wince, lowered it into her lap.

He shook his head incredulously. 'You ran your finger round the edge of the plinth? To see, I imagine, if it had enough of an edge to cut someone's throat?'

'I did.'

'Abbess Helewise, how reckless!'

'Don't *you* start,' she flashed back, 'I've already been reprimanded for my irresponsibility by Sister Euphemia, thank you very much.'

She managed to look both indignant and pathetic at the same time. Knowing her as he was beginning to, he knew the latter was not intentional; it was, he decided, the combination of her pale but resolute face and that damned great wad of wrapping on her hand.

'Does it hurt?' he enquired kindly.

'It does.'

I'll wager, he thought. It would have hurt badly enough before we staggered up here with a semi-conscious man. The dear Lord knows how *that* little adventure must have affected her.

He remembered his original question. 'Actually, that wasn't what I meant.' It was better to change the subject, he thought, to talk about Olivar and Gunnora, than to risk undermining her courage by his sympathy. Not that it was easy to ignore her state; her face was very pale, and the wide brow beneath the starched white linen headdress was beaded with sweat. 'I really wanted to know what made you suspect what happened,' he ploughed on, 'when I'd been doing my utmost to convince you that Milon was lying through his teeth and had killed Gunnora after all.'

'I went down to speak to Brother Firmin about the resumption of our services for pilgrims,' she began. 'The devotions, and the distribution of the healing waters. Life has to go on, you know, and we've had so few visitors since the murders. There will be unnecessary suffering, all the time we do not throw open our doors to those in need. While I was down in the valley, I thought it was about time I made a visit to the shrine. I have been guilty of allowing my worldly preoccupations to interfere with my devotions,' she said sternly.

Josse was about to say that he was quite sure the Lord would understand, but something about her expression made him change his mind. 'Quite so,' he muttered.

She shot him a glance, as if not entirely convinced by his bland reply. 'I went into the shrine' – fortunately, it didn't seem that she was going to pursue it – 'and I knelt to pray, right in front of the Blessed Mother's statue. I noticed that the plinth seemed to be very shiny, as if someone had recently been polishing it.' She bowed her head. 'I know that I should have been concentrating on my prayers to Our Lady,' she said, 'but, as I said, I am easily distracted at present.'

'Understandable,' he remarked. 'Wouldn't any abbess be, with two suspicious deaths among her nuns?'

'The very time an abbess needs to pray hardest for help!'

Oh, dear. She wasn't in the mood for understanding. Didn't, apparently, want to be released from her self-accusation. 'Go on,' he said. 'You were thinking how shiny the plinth was.'

'Yes. I got up and had a closer look, and I could see a stain of some sort running underneath it, right at the point where it adjoins the rock wall into which it's set. I touched the place, and the stain felt dry, sort of crusty. So I moistened the tip of my finger in the holy water and rubbed again. What came off was, I was almost sure, blood. I repeated the action, this time getting a good sample. Then there was no doubt.'

'And you began to see what might have happened?'

'I did. I thought of the steep, slippery steps, and, in my mind's eye, I pictured that terrible wound in Gunnora's neck. I saw that perfectly symmetrical cut. I'd always puzzled over that, hadn't you?'

'Aye.'

'I mean, if you're slitting someone's throat, even with an

accomplice holding them, surely you haven't the time to make such a perfect cut?'

'And nobody did,' he said. 'It was done by her falling against a circular edge. It *is* sharp enough?'

'It is,' she said with feeling. 'I ran my forefinger gently around it, and almost sliced off the top joint. We *must* have it seen to – I must go and tell Brother Saul to close the shrine until we've done so, and he ought to send word to the silversmith immediately.' She half-rose, as if she were going to go racing down to the vale there and then.

'I'll see to all that,' Josse said hurriedly. 'You have my word, Abbess.'

She looked doubtful.

'My word,' he repeated.

She bowed her head in acknowledgement, sinking back into her chair. 'It's sharper than any blade, you know, the edge of that plinth,' she said. 'For some reason, the silversmith cut off the skin of silver so that it overlapped the wooden platform. Only by a little. But it was enough to slice through flesh and sinew.'

'She would have built up a great deal of momentum in her fall,' Josse said. 'Those steps are quite high, and she'd fallen from the top. Right on to that perilously sharp circle of metal.' He shuddered.

Helewise must have noticed. 'It doesn't bear thinking about, does it? And just imagine that poor man, Olivar, trying to clean up. Believing it was his fault, that the woman he loved so devotedly was dead because of him.'

'The only small amount of logic there may be behind that is that it was he who requested the meeting,' Josse pointed out.

'But I don't think it was. When we were talking, he and I, down in the shrine, he said that it wasn't what he wanted, that secret tryst. *Furtive*, he called it. I had the impression it was something they'd agreed on before she even came to Hawkenlye, that, one day, they'd meet up and she would leave again. Only he, I think, was envisaging arriving at the main gates for her, having me ceremoniously put her hand in his. Going to the shrine was, I'm almost certain, her suggestion.'

'Why did she change her mind?' Josse asked, although not in any real expectation of an answer. 'Olivar's a fine-looking man, a man of substance, what's more, and she surely had no doubt of his love?'

Helewise was looking at him, one eyebrow raised in faint irony. 'Don't you recall what I said to you, in the course of our very first meeting?'

Most of it, would have been the honest reply; she had, he recalled, said quite a lot. But then he thought he knew what she meant. 'I do. Gunnora, you said, was not apparently bothered by the vow of chastity.'

'Indeed.' She leaned forward, as if eager for his understanding. 'I have noted it before in young women – not only young ones – who enter the convent. While in the world, they do not question the ways of the world; they know what their duty as women – as wives – is, and has to be. Whether they like it or not is irrelevant. But then, when they take the veil, suddenly all that changes. The realisation that, from the very day they join us, they will for ever more sleep alone, comes to some women, I assure you, as nothing but a vast relief. Gunnora, I strongly suspect, experienced that realisation. She did not want to be any man's wife. Certainly not Brice's, whom she never loved, and, she discovered, not Olivar's either.'

'Whom she did love?' Josse asked. He was reeling slightly from what the Abbess had just told him. He wondered if she would have spoken so freely were she not suffering from shock.

'Did she?' Helewise leaned back in her chair. 'I'm not so sure. I asked the same question of that poor young man, and he said that, in return for all his protestations, she once – once! – said she *thought* she loved him.'

More fool him, was Josse's instant thought, for pursuing her so singlemindedly.

But he didn't say it aloud.

'Her death was an accident, pure and simple,' he said decisively after a moment. 'I can't think that there is any necessity for him to be arrested and put on trial, since, as I see it, there's no question of his being responsible for her death. And, with the remains of the bloodstains under the plinth, what really happened can be proved. Do you agree, Abbess?'

'Yes, Josse, indeed I do.' It was, he noticed abstractedly, the first time she had called him simply by his given name. It was a timely moment for a move to more intimate terms between the two of them. 'We shall have to make our reports on the two deaths to both the Church and the secular authorities, I suppose,' she went on, 'but, like you, I feel that there is no guilt attached to Olivar. He is innocent of blame over Gunnora's death.' She paused, frowning. 'But I do not think we shall ever convince *him* of that.'

'We must!' he said, horrified. 'The poor man's life won't be worth living, unless we do!'

The cool grey eyes looked on him with mild pity. 'Do you think he'll ever find it worth living anyway, without her?'

'Of course! He's young, and she's not worth grieving for! She—'

'Every one of us is worth grieving for,' she said quietly. 'Yes, I know what you think of her, you who hadn't even met her.' He heard no reproof in her words. 'I feel the same. She was cold, she was calculating, she used people and she was not worthy of Olivar's love and devotion. But *he* thinks she was. He has waited several years to claim her, and his love seems to have grown despite the absence of any encouragement from her. Why, he hadn't even seen her, until the night of her death, for the year or more that she had been with us here!'

'I don't understand,' Josse admitted. He stared at her. 'Do you?'

'No.' She dropped her head into the palm of her unbandaged hand, kneading at her temple with her knuckles. 'Not really. Not that it makes any difference.'

'Does your head ache?' he asked sympathetically.

'A little.'

He stood up, moving round to her side of the table. 'Why not lie down?' he suggested. 'You've lost a lot of blood, you've solved a murder that wasn't, you're in pain from both your hurt finger and your head. Don't you think it's time, my dear Abbess

Helewise, to admit you're only human, and need a good, long sleep?'

Her head flew up at his words, and he thought she was going to tick him off for his presumption. But then, to his great surprise, she began to laugh. 'I don't see what's funny,' he said, quite offended. 'I was only trying to help.'

'Oh, Josse, I know!' She had recovered her solemnity. 'Between you and that old hen Euphemia, I don't think I stand a chance of staying here at my post for the rest of the day. So I think I might just give in. I must admit, the thought of lying down somewhere quiet, with a pleasant breeze to cool me, and one of Sister Euphemia's cold lavender compresses on my forehead, is increasingly appealing . . .' She stood up, too quickly, and he caught her as she toppled.

'Told you so,' he murmured close to her wimpled and veiled ear.

'I shall pretend I didn't hear that,' she remarked. Then, with her not inconsiderable weight leaning against him – she was, he'd noticed, broad-shouldered as well as tall – he helped her out of the room and across to the infirmary.

Chapter Nineteen

The coronation of Richard Plantagenet, second surviving son of Henry II and Eleanor of Aquitaine, took place in Westminster Abbey on 3 September 1189.

The new King, Richard I of England, was five days short of his thirty-second birthday. He had been in the country for a fortnight, and, even as the day of extravagant and lengthy ceremony continued, the greater part of his able brain was thinking ahead to when he could leave again.

Two years earlier, the Muslim leader, Saladin, had captured both Jerusalem and Acre from the Franks. Guy of Lusignan, King of Jerusalem, set about besieging his stolen territory, but it had become clear that the recapture of the Holy Sepulchre was not a task that he could do alone. Richard Plantagenet had been ready – more than ready – to go to his aid, and had taken the cross in preparation. However, the timetable of events in Outremer had not been drawn up to suit the Plantagenets; the everlasting intrigues and in-fighting between Richard, his father and his brothers continued to make it impossible for Richard to embark for the crusade in the east.

Now that he was King, however, all that was over. Even before the crown was on his head, he had demanded a muster of ships. And, across the Channel, his companion-in-arms, friend and ally, Philip Augustus of France, was waiting . . .

Henry II's thirty-five years on the throne had left England

sound. Unlike his son and heir, he had involved himself in all aspects of good government, and had managed to achieve that remarkable feat of integration simply because he had intelligent, informed help. His small group of administrators had shared with him the aim of making the country strong. And solvent: when Henry died, he left a substantial sum, rumoured to be in the region of 100,000 marks, in the Treasury.

Richard's magnificent coronation nibbled away at quite a lot of that. But, nevertheless, the remainder would have been a more than adequate inheritance for most kings.

Kings, that is, who were not champing at the bit with impatience to go off to war.

The raising of revenue was Richard's sole, driving purpose. His new kingdom, which he hardly knew, was no more to him than a vast bank, where, happily, his credit appeared to be good. Whether or not his demands were acceptable to his new people, whether, even, the majority of his subjects shared his fanatical determination that the Holy Land must be wrested out of infidel hands, were matters of supreme indifference to him. The important thing was to raise as much money as he could, as quickly as he could; he once joked that he would sell London if he could find a buyer.

Quite a lot of people didn't realise it was a joke.

In those hectic days of the new reign, it seemed that everything was for sale. Not even the highest in the land were exempt from demands; Henry's able and loyal advisors were made to pay heavily for the dubious privilege of the new King's goodwill. And, lower down in the establishment hierarchy, officials were thrown out of office to make room for incumbents who paid for their new appointments. Anyone whose money was a burden to him, went the ironic saying, was relieved of it; it was possible, at this extraordinary, country-wide market, to buy privileges, lordships, earldoms, sheriffdoms, castles, even towns; human nature being what it is, there were plenty of people more than ready to advance themselves the quick way, via their wealth, instead of the more noble but painstaking route of via their worth.

Richard achieved his immediate goal; money flowed into his crusade fund like the great Thames through his new capital.

But at what price?

Josse d'Acquin had duly reported back to the King concerning the deaths at Hawkenlye Abbey, although the King, understandably, perhaps, did not appear to remember who Josse was or what he was talking about; Josse happened to catch him during the time in mid-August when, freshly arrived in his new kingdom, he was re-acquainting himself with a country and a people he hadn't seen since early childhood.

'Hawkenlye?' he had said, when, at long last, Josse had managed to shoulder his way to the front of the queue of men eager for the new King's ear. 'Hawkenlye? A dead nun?'

Josse reminded him of the salient facts. Down on one knee, head bent in respect, his words were drowned by the general commotion all around; Richard's peripatetic court was settling itself into its new abode with characteristic, noisy exuberance.

He felt strong hands grasp his shoulders, and the King hauled him to his feet. 'Stand up, man, and talk so that I can hear you!' he bellowed impatiently. 'What's all this about released murderers?'

He recounted his story again, and this time light dawned on the King. 'Ah, yes, the abbey full of women, where the miracle spring was discovered!' he exclaimed. 'Indeed, Sir John—'

'Josse,' Josse murmured.

'I think I do recall . . .' Richard frowned thunderously at Josse, as if trying to draw intelligence from him.

But, just then, Richard's chief advisor, William de Longchamps, sidled up to the King and, standing on tiptoe, for he was a good head shorter than his sovereign, began to speak urgently and quietly in the King's ear.

Josse waited for the King to dismiss him, tell him to wait his turn; there was already resentment of the favoured position occupied by Longchamps, who, people were saying, the King was going to appoint as Chancellor. And the man was the son of runaway serfs!

But Richard did not dismiss him. Instead, with a wave of the regal hand, he dismissed Josse.

Walking away, too irritated to show the fawning respect that the occasion demanded, Josse was surprised, on reaching the outer chamber, to feel a detaining hand on his arm.

It was William de Longchamps.

'I know of your business here, Josse d'Acquin,' he said in a low voice. 'I will see to it that the King hears of your success.'

Josse was on the point of saying he'd manage very well on his own, without anyone's help, when he reconsidered.

Would it do any harm, really, to have the support of the man tipped to be England's next chancellor? No! Hardly!

And so what if the man wasn't of noble birth? Looking down at him, Josse did have to admit that the man didn't look a likely candidate for the dignity of high office. Still, he thought fairly, if any man were to trace his lineage back far enough, he'd probably come down to peasant origins.

And that included the King; hadn't his illustrious forefather, William the Conqueror, been the bastard son of a tanner's daughter?

'I thank you, Sir,' he said, making Longchamps a courteous bow. He hesitated; should he go on to tell Longchamps the outcome of his investigation? Yes, he decided, 'I sensed all along that the first death was somehow a family matter,' he began, 'but—'

Longchamps put up a hand. 'No need, Sir Josse, for this.' He smiled faintly. 'The tale is already known to me.'

'How?' Josse asked.

Longchamps seemed to grow suddenly taller; not by very much, but, in his case, every little helped. 'My Lady the Queen told me,' he said.

'Queen Eleanor?'

'Have we another queen?' Longchamps said, somewhat wryly.

'Oh. No, no.' Queen Eleanor? Had she, bless her, troubled

to follow up the matter? With everything else that must be on her mind at present, had she remembered this small provincial matter, unimportant, surely, as soon as it was clear that the perpetrator was not a prisoner released by her son's clemency?

She had. She must have done.

'I am indebted to Her Majesty,' he said, bowing as deeply as if it were Eleanor herself who stood before him.

'As are we all,' murmured Longchamps, 'as are we all.'

Then, with a curt nod in Josse's general direction, he scurried off back to the King.

Josse had expected to hear no more from either Longchamps or the King. But he had been wrong.

A little while later, he received word that he was summoned to the new King's coronation.

There were, Josse was wont to say afterwards, some distinctly odd aspects to the coronation of Richard I. Not that he was an expert on coronations, this being the only one he attended in his long life. But still, it made, he thought, a good opening to his oft-repeated account.

The first strange happening was that, for all that it was broad daylight, a bat was seen to come flapping and flitting into Westminster Abbey. Bold as you please, it did not content itself with a discreet circuit of the darkest recesses of the great building, but flew straight up the nave. Eventually, it found the sacred spot where the King-elect sat, stiff-backed, extravagantly robed, mystic symbols of monarchy in his hands. And there, around and around the noble brow, it continued to circle, until one of the presiding prelates came out of his pop-eyed trance and, flapping at the bat with his wide sleeves in a manner that threatened to make the small creature produce an unsavoury testimony to its fear, managed to shoo it away.

'A bat!' came the horrified whispers, buzzing around Josse

like the gossiping of women at the well. 'It's an omen! A *terrible* omen!'

Against his will – damn it, the bat was just a wild animal, neither good nor evil! – Josse found himself thinking of the words of Leviticus: *all flying, creeping things, going about upon all four, shall be an abomination unto you.*

God had said that, of one of His own creatures! A thing of the night, of the dark, of secret places, and an abomination unto the Lord . . .

In the Abbey, there was a disjointed, quiet muttering, growing in volume, as, on all sides, men tried to mitigate the potency of this evil omen by a few repetitions of the Paternoster.

With which, despite his attempts at rationality, Josse joined in.

There was no special place for Queen Eleanor at the long Westminster Abbey ceremony; she did not go. Which was, Josse considered, the other peculiar thing about King Richard's coronation.

They said she had refused to attend because she was in mourning for her husband, the dead King Henry.

In mourning?

Technically she was, Josse had to acknowledge; Henry had only died a couple of months ago. But everyone knew how the Queen had felt about him! Why, he'd had her shut up, a prisoner in her own house, for the last sixteen years! They *hated* each other, and, for her part, she must have been delighted to see the back of him.

And, as well, Eleanor had worked so relentlessly for her son's sake. Why, it was said she hadn't had a day's rest for the last few weeks, so determined had she been to leave no stone unturned in her efforts to make England welcome the new King. Was it not unexpected, to say the least, for her not to attend what was, literally, her son's crowning moment?

But, whatever the true reason was, Eleanor was not there.

Nor, Josse had noticed with growing amazement as he stared around the assembled multitude, was any other woman.

Richard's coronation was attended only by men.

Well, he thought, rationalising again, it's the men who hold the reins of power, why should Richard not summon them without their wives? And, perhaps, the King had thought that if his own mother declined to see him crowned, then no other woman in the realm ought to have that privilege.

Josse couldn't help wondering what Abbess Helewise of Hawkenlye would have said to *that*.

A week or so after the coronation – it had taken almost that long to get rid of the hangover; one thing you could say for King Richard, he certainly knew how to throw a party – Josse made his way home to Acquin.

There would inevitably be a sense of anticlimax in returning to his rural backwater after the various excitements; he had known that, and had prepared himself for it. Or so he thought. Indeed, as he crossed the Aa river and set his tired horse's head along the valley for home, he was actually looking forward to the peace.

The long, low roofs of the great courtyard appeared in the distance, the flint-slated tops of the watch towers on the two outer corners catching the rays of the westering sun and seeming to glisten. In the pastures either side of the little river, large cows grazed, the tearing sound of their mouths pulling on grass loud in the tranquillity. One or two groups of peasants, trudging heavy-footed homewards, nodded to him, some, recognising who he was, tugging a respectful forelock.

Home.

He encouraged his horse to a reluctant trot as he entered the tiny village that had sprung up around the spreading manor house. Past the church, along the track that led to the gates . . . and he was there.

The gates were closed; fair enough, it was almost dusk, and nobody knew he was coming. Still, he couldn't help feeling a slight sense of rejection.

He leaned sideways in the saddle and thumped with his fist on the stout, iron-banded doors. 'Open up! Open up, Acquin!'

After quite a lot more banging, a small aperture beside the gates opened, and he saw the cross face of his senior steward. 'Whadyouwant?' the man shouted, all in one word.

Then, seeing who it was, he reddened, muttered an apology, and closed the little window; very soon afterwards, the main doors opened. Between the one action and the other, Josse had heard him call out, in a tone not as full of joy as Josse might have expected, 'It's Sir Josse! The Master's come home.'

They welcomed him warmly enough, his brothers, his brothers' wives, his nephews, his nieces; at least, those among the children who were old enough welcomed him. The babies still at the breast took little notice. There being no fatted calf to hand, they fed him on tasty fowl and well-hung game, and his brother Yves broached a barrel of wine which he said he had been saving for just such a special occasion.

They listened politely to what Josse had to tell them of life with Richard Plantagenet, went 'Ooh!', 'Aah!' and 'Fancy that!' in all the right places, were suitably horrified at the deaths in the Abbey and were diplomatically reserved about the new King's determination to bleed his new realm of all – possibly of more than – it could afford in order to go galloping off to the Holy Land and boot out the infidel.

But Josse noticed that, the moment he had finished describing some exciting piece of news, that would be that. He was lucky if he got one interested question before the talk turned to other matters. To the harvest. The field down by the river that always flooded when it rained hard. The spotted cow's sickly calf. The prospects of a good autumn's hunting. The second-youngest brother's broken ankle, the senior sister-in-law's mad mother, even, God help them, the priest's haemorrhoids and the youngest-but-one baby's spasmodically tarry stools.

And the last two topics over dinner!

I had forgotten, Josse thought to himself rather sadly as he settled down to sleep on the third night after his arrival. I had forgotten how small life is here in the country, how footling the preoccupations.

Then, fair-mindedly, he corrected himself. Small and footling, perhaps, but the preoccupations were not unimportant. Acquin was a big estate, and, as well he knew, it took the conscientious work of all four of his brothers to keep it running smoothly. And that – its running smoothly – was vital, not only to the wellbeing and the fortunes of the immediate household, but to the vast number of peasant families who depended on them.

And after all, Josse thought, it was my decision to leave. Nobody ousted me, it was my own choice to test out my luck at the court of the tempestuous Plantagenets. It's hardly the fault of my poor family if, in terms of variety and excitement, life here at Acquin can't compete.

When at last on that disturbed night he managed to sleep, he dreamt that Richard Plantagenet had sent him an enormous cross set with rubies and ordered him to escort Queen Eleanor to Fontevraud, where, once she had stepped down from her horse, she donned a white headdress and a black veil and turned into Abbess Helewise. Terrified at the prospect of breaking the news to Richard that his mother had turned into someone else, Josse had ridden his horse so fast down a hillside that it had grown wings, thrown him off, turned into a huge bat and flapped away.

He awoke sweating and slightly shaky. And with the very beginnings of a plan forming in his mind . . .

The plan took several months to implement. Josse excused the delay, privately, by telling himself it was only fair, having disrupted his family by his return, to stay a good long time and make it worth everyone's while. To salve his conscience over being an intruder in his own home – although everyone tried very hard to make him feel that he wasn't – he turned his hand to anything that he thought might help. But, it became clear, his brothers and their servants were, to a man, better than Josse at most of the tasks commonly demanded by life on a big country estate.

The fact that he could handle a sword better than all of them put together was, really, not a great deal of use.

Still, the boar hunting was exceptional, and there was a pretty young sister of one of his brothers' wives who, having lost her husband to the ravages of smallpox too many years ago for it still to pain her, was only too ready for some flirtatious dalliance on a November evening, when the hangings rippled in the draughts and folk snuggled close together round the great flaming fire.

Christmas came and went.

Then, in February of the New Year of 1190, just when Josse was mentally gearing himself up to quit the family home and set off back to the King's court, the message came.

His brother Yves, who had received the weary and soaked messenger, brought him up to Josse.

Eyes alert with excited curiosity, Yves hissed to Josse, 'He comes from the King!'

Josse led the messenger a little apart, and the man, producing a folded and sealed scroll from inside his tunic, verified that he did indeed come from Richard, who was at present in Normandy.

The King, it appeared, wished to see Josse d'Acquin, to convey his personal thanks in the matter of the deaths at Hawkenlye Abbey.

Josse, making an effort to close his dropped jaw, remembered his manners and ushered the messenger down to the kitchens, giving the kitchen staff orders to feed, water and warm him.

Then he went up to his own quarters to try to puzzle out just why, after all this time, the King should suddenly want to thank him.

*

He had his answer as soon as, a week later, his name was announced and, once more, he knelt before his King.

For, sitting elegantly in a chair only a little less ornate than Richard's, sat the King's mother.

Josse had seen her only a couple of times before, and that had been at a distance. And, he recalled, calculating rapidly, probably twenty years ago or more.

But the old Queen carried her years well. She must, Josse thought, be almost seventy, but her eyes were still bright, her skin, although a little weatherbeaten from the many months spent travelling, still quite smooth. The remains of that legendary beauty could be clearly seen; it was not difficult to comprehend how that anonymous German scholar had been moved to write of her, 'If the world were mine from sea to Rhine, I'd renounce it with joy to hold the Queen of England in my arms . . .'

Dressed immaculately and fashionably, her fine linen barbette was secured by both veil and small coronet, and the sleeves of her samite silk gown were long enough to sweep to the ground. Against the chill of the day, she wore a fur-lined cloak, whose generous folds she had wrapped around her legs and feet like a blanket.

Honoured, delighted and humbled at being in the presence of a woman he had admired all his life, Josse half rose, moved to his right and, sinking down in front of her, bent his head low.

He felt a light touch on his shoulder; looking up, he saw that Eleanor had leaned down towards him, and was now extending her gloved right hand. In awe, he took hold of it and kissed it.

'My mother asks me to convey my personal thanks to you, Acquin, for the service that you rendered to us last summer, while we prepared for our coronation,' Richard said, experiencing, Josse noted, some difficulty over deciding whether he was going to use the first or the third person. Perhaps, Josse thought charitably, being King took a deal of getting used to.

'Any service I can do for Your Majesty, Sire, it is my joy to perform,' he replied.

Richard's broad, handsome face briefly creased in a smile, which he as quickly smoothed away. 'The foundation at

Hawkenlye is particularly dear to my mother's heart,' he continued, 'because of its similarities to the Mother House at Fontevraud, where my mother wishes shortly to retire in order to—'

'I'm not going yet,' said Queen Eleanor, 'and I do wish, Richard, that you would not speak about me as if I were not here.'

Glancing at the King, her face wore, Josse observed, the sort of chiding, indulgent and loving glance common to mothers looking at their favourite sons. In Eleanor's eyes, he thought, even a king like Richard could do no wrong.

'My Lord d'Acquin,' the Queen was addressing him, 'I hear tell of your efforts at Hawkenlye, and I thank you for your part in the resolution of a crime that threatened to upset the smooth running and the good work of our Abbey there.'

'It was not I alone, my lady,' Josse hastened to say. Credit where it was due, and it had been Helewise, really, who had solved the murder. The murder that was no murder.

'I am aware of that,' Eleanor said, 'and, indeed, I have already expressed my thanks and appreciation to Abbess Helewise. She is a fine woman, my lord, is she not?'

'A fine woman,' Josse echoed. He was trying to picture Helewise, presented with a visit from the Queen. Would she have started to flap and panic? Would she have been thrown into a ferment of anxiety, worked twenty-four hours a day to ensure that every little detail was perfect?

No. That didn't sound a bit like Helewise. He grinned briefly; she'd have been more likely to say serenely, 'The Abbey is as good as our efforts can make it, we can do no better. Let the Queen see us as we are.'

'You smile, Sir Josse?'

She might be nearing seventy, Josse thought, but the voice still had a power to make a man quake. 'Your pardon, my lady,' he said, 'I was thinking of the Abbess Helewise.'

'And your thoughts were such as to make you smile?'

He made himself look up and meet her eyes. 'A little, Your Majesty, although, I assure you, lady, I intended no disrespect.'

'I am sure you did not,' Eleanor said smoothly. 'You might be interested to know that the Abbess also, when speaking of you, could not suppress her amusement.'

She knew – she must! – that he wanted to know what they'd been talking about, those two formidable women. Why the subject of Josse d'Acquin had made Helewise want to laugh. And, flirt that she still was, having dragged that tantalising little snippet in front of him, Eleanor wasn't going to tell him.

Richard, it had become evident, was getting bored with this conversation about people and events of which he knew nothing. He had been drumming one hand on the arm of his chair, humming snatches of some song only just under his breath. Now, unable any longer to restrain his restless energy, he jumped up out of his seat, stretched, and said, 'My lady mother, why not just tell him?'

'My son is not a great one for sitting and listening while others converse,' Eleanor said, with only a small amount of irony. She gave Richard another of her loving glances. 'Particularly when the matter under discussion is not to do with armaments, warhorses, ships or the journey to Outremer.'

Richard glowered briefly, then – for she was his mother, and probably the only person in the whole world before whom he reined in his quick temper – said, 'We have in our realm of England many manors and estates which we have made available to our subjects, should they wish to pay a fair price.' Fixing his eyes on Josse, he broke off from what sounded like a prepared speech and asked, in a far more friendly and informal tone, 'What did you think of England, Josse? Did you like it?'

'Sire, I only saw a small corner of it,' Josse said, 'and I was preoccupied with a matter of some importance, and—'

'Yes, yes, yes, I know all that.' Richard waved his arms as if wafting Josse's words away. 'But it is a beautiful country, mm? Good hunting to be had, in all those forests, not a bad climate?'

It was on the tip of Josse's tongue to say, not a bad climate? You must have been lucky, Sire, in the few months you spent there!

But he didn't. Despite the friendliness, Richard was still the King.

Uncertain still about what this summons meant, although he was beginning to have an idea, Josse said meekly, 'I liked what I saw of England very much, Sire. My childhood memories served me well, and the impressions I formed on my latest visit served only to endorse the sense that it is a land in which I could happily live.'

Was that wise? If, as everyone guessed, the King was on the point of setting off on crusade, would it have been more diplomatic to plead to go with him?

But I don't want to, Josse thought. Dear God in heaven, but I've had enough of war.

'My son wishes to bestow on you a token of our gratitude, for your help in the Hawkenlye matter,' Eleanor intervened. 'He wishes to—'

'Would you like an English manor, Josse?' Richard said. 'There are a few choice places still in my gift, even some not too many miles from Hawkenlye, even if the Clares have got most of that area tied up tighter than a cat's—' He broke off, shooting a look at his mother. 'Er, a cat's eyelids. What do you say, eh? A modest place, maybe, you being a single man, and at a reasonable price?'

'Richard,' his mother said quietly. 'We agreed, did we not, that it was to be a *gift*?'

Her emphasis on the word, Josse thought, suggested that it was one that was somewhat foreign to her son.

'A little manor, then, as our gift to you, Josse,' Richard said, beaming. Then, the benevolent expression hardening slightly, 'Close to London, I suggest, so that you can be reached by me, when I am there, and by those in England who manage my affairs when I am not. For who knows,' he added, throwing out a dramatic hand, 'when another event will occur that threatens the peace of that particular corner of our kingdom?'

Aha, Josse thought. There had to be a price.

But was it a price he was prepared to pay? Would he, for the great prize of a manor – even a little manor – in King Richard's

England, be willing to become a king's man? Someone Richard could rely on, to watch out for him, leap into action, when necessary, on his behalf?

Richard, Josse thought, was proposing to set off for the Holy Land, where he planned, no doubt, to stay and fight it out until the Holy City had been wrested back from the Infidel and was once more in Christian hands.

And God alone knew how long *that* was going to take.

He needs men like me, Josse thought, with sudden perception. And I, who have just discovered that I no longer feel at home in my own home, have need of what he offers me.

Of the two, my need is by far the greater.

Richard, he realised, was watching him. Waiting for his reaction. And so was Eleanor.

'Well?' Richard prompted. 'Do you accept the terms, Josse d'Acquin?'

Josse met his eyes. 'I do, Sire. Right gladly, and with heartfelt thanks.'

'The thanks,' Eleanor murmured, 'are also ours.'

But Richard was calling for wine and probably did not hear.

The Third Death

Chapter Twenty

Very early one dull, foggy morning, when the season was meant to be spring but felt far more like dead of winter, the man let himself quietly out of the house and set off along the too-familiar path. He went on foot. The still, moisture-laden air seeming to cling round his lower legs as if trying to hold him back, he made his slow way back to the place where he had first broken down and cried out his grief for her.

The place he had visited and revisited so many times that he could no longer count them.

There was nobody about. Spring was late this year, and the promise of new growth was still but a hope. As if the world were being held back, halted in her year's round, the predominant feeling in the air was of dead things. Last autumn's leaves, choking the hedgerows and the ditches; old, dry stubble in the fields from last year's crops. Bare branches on the trees, with still no optimistic, tentative first show of green. And, within the houses, still the comforting household fires were lit; for it remained bone-cold, the strength and power of the waxing sun so late in coming.

The earth had endured her long winter sleep. Now, it should be spring.

For him, time, cruelly, seemed to have stood still since her death. His eyes saw the outward small signs of the passage of weeks and months, but his brain didn't accept what he saw. It was, and would ever be, the pre-dawn grey of a morning in July, when he ran in horror from what had happened to the one being in the world whom he had truly loved.

They had cared for him devotedly, the round-faced nun and the fussy old monk. The sister, looking at him with a mixture of compassion and exasperation, had treated him like a recalcitrant child, who, knowing full well what was good for him, yet refused to do it. In vain she pleaded with him to get up and go for a walk in the good strong sunshine, or to eat up this fine, strength-building food, how could he expect to grow better if he did not look after himself?

The monk, whom he had learned to call Brother Firmin, had placed his faith not in good food and hearty exercise but in the love of God. And in the holy spring water, a cool cup of which he brought to the patient every morning. And the patient had drunk it, more to please the old monk than for any belief that it would do him any good.

The Abbess herself had not forgotten him. Far from it; regularly, every day that she could spare the time, she would come to the infirmary and sit with him when her work was done, before the evening meal. Often she would just remain silently at his side, sometimes saying her rosary, sometimes not. Or, if he greeted her with any sort of animation, she would talk to him. Not in a way that demanded a response; merely a brief description of some element of her day that she thought might interest him. An encounter with a fractious visitor to the shrine; details of how a sick patient was now getting better; even, once, the peaceful death of the oldest monk in the retirement house.

And, for all that he rarely spoke a word, she did not abandon him, either.

Perhaps, he reflected, he had been a hopeless case. For none of the various treatments had been of any benefit whatsoever; he wondered, later, if he had made up his mind that they wouldn't be, even before those kind people's efforts had begun. In the end, because accepting their well-intentioned ministrations when he knew that nothing could make him better had started to seem a little callous, he had one day pronounced himself cured. Got up out of his bed, told them they needed it for more urgent cases. Gone with them one last time to church, where Brother Firmin, who seemed more inclined to believe in this sudden cure than did Sister Euphemia, had prayed in heart-felt thanks for God's blessed miracle.

Then the man had left.

But she had known. Abbess Helewise had known.

When he went to seek her out to tell her he was leaving the Abbey, she hadn't, thank God, tried to stop him. It was as if some practical part of her were saying, 'We've done all we can do, my monks, my nuns and I. If you are to be made whole again, it is up to God to make you so. You are in His hands now.'

He had knelt before her as he had taken his leave, and, in a whisper, asked for her blessing. She had given a small gasp, almost as if she read what was in his heart. Then he had felt the pressure of her thumb as she traced the sign of the cross on his forehead and said quietly, 'God go with you, Olivar.'

She had given him Gunnora's cross.

He had returned home to Brice, since that was the only place he could think of to go. Brice had adopted the tack of trying to jolly him out of his grief. Dear old Brice. Olivar smiled faintly at the memory of his brother, perplexed as ever before an emotion too deep for him to understand, suggesting they went off on pilgrimage together. 'We could go to Santiago, even to the Holy City, if the Infidel will let us in!' he said. 'Wouldn't you like that, Olivar? Wouldn't it be good, to get right away from here, to be on the road together, meet new people, see wonderful sights? I'm willing! I'd love it, truly I would. I'll go anywhere, if it'll help you.'

He'd meant well.

They'd told him all about that other business, with Gunnora's wild cousin Elanor. Olivar pitied both her and that foolish young husband of hers. They had been greedy and callous, yes, but whoever had imagined they killed Gunnora, Elanor holding her while Milon wielded the knife, had been quite wrong. Milon didn't have it in him to kill, of that Olivar was sure. Not coldly and calculatingly, anyway, although it did appear that he had strangled Elanor in the heat of an angry quarrel.

He had gone on trial for that. The Abbess and that big knight, who had been sent to investigate the deaths, had given evidence. Not willingly, or so folk said. Neither, apparently, had spoken out vindictively against Milon; they'd just answered the questions asked of them truthfully. Tried, as far as they could, to speak up for him.

But the truth had been bad enough to hang him. Murder. He'd murdered Elanor, his pretty, lively young wife. He had admitted as much as they led him out to his execution. He had gone to his Maker pleading for forgiveness, crying out that he hadn't meant to kill her, that her death had been a terrible accident, that he'd give anything, *anything,* his own life, even, to have her alive again, laughing and dancing by his side.

Olivar sympathised. Although, in truth, he had to admit that his beloved Gunnora hadn't been a woman to laugh and dance – bless her, she was not given to frivolity – still, he, too, would have willingly laid down his own life if, by doing so, she would live again.

But the laws of nature did not operate that way. And nor did the laws of God.

When Milon was dead and buried, Brice had made up his mind to put the whole wretched business behind him. Despite having lost his wife, having his wife's sister die through a terrible accident which continued to devastate his brother, and having his bastard cousin-by-marriage die by the hangman's noose for killing his bride, still, he had returned to normal life. With what some people were calling indecent haste.

Let them, Olivar thought. They didn't know Brice. Didn't understand his direct, uncomplicated nature, his lack of sentiment; even his own brother was tempted sometimes to call him shallow. No, he corrected himself, Brice wasn't really shallow.

He was practical, down-to-earth, a little unimaginative. But he was a good man. He would marry again, in time, although no bride, surely, would bring him what would have come his way, had Dillian not died before her father did. Few fathers-in-law owned estates like Winnowlands.

Other than Brice's gift to Hawkenlye Abbey, the entire Winnowlands fortune was going to the Crown. And there was a rumour, on the face of it unlikely but strangely persistent, that the new King, Richard, planned to award a part of the estate and a not insignificant manor house to that big knight . . .

I don't care if he does, Olivar thought as he neared the river. I wish the fellow well of it. Nobody was ever truly happy at Winnowlands, not in Alard's household, anyway. Let the man do better if he can. Me, I am beyond such things.

He clambered down to the water, and, pausing by the shallows, where the salmon ran in spring, he sat down on the soaked grass. They had come here often together, he and Gunnora. That was why, of course; why it had become his special place.

He had always thought she was intended for his brother. Brice, the elder son at Rotherbridge, would be betrothed to Gunnora, elder daughter of Alard of Winnowlands. Loving her from afar, as he had done for as long as he could remember, he had had to endure the spectacle of Brice and Gunnora together, stiffly and reluctantly leading the dancing, sitting together at table on feast days.

Then, quite unexpectedly, a tiny glimmer of hope had started to shine. Shortly before her eighteenth birthday, when, everyone expected, the betrothal would be announced, she had come to seek him out.

'I do not wish to marry your brother,' she had told him. Right here, beside the river, in this very spot. 'I do not love him, and I fear he would not make me happy.'

He had tried to read the expression in those deep blue eyes.

Why was she telling him this? Why, indeed, had she taken the trouble to find out where he was and come to find him?

Could it – could it *possibly* – be that she did not love his brother because she loved another?

Him?

He had stepped forward. Not to touch her – oh, no, not that, not then – and the tense silence had continued.

A lady could not be the first to speak in such matters, as well he knew. Had always known. So, heart thumping, mouth so dry that he could hardly speak, he spoke instead.

Said, simply, humbly, 'Lady, could you, do you think, love me?' She had made no answer, merely cast down those great eyes in a delicate gesture of modesty. 'I love you, Gunnora,' he had rushed on, 'I have always loved you! Will you agree to marry me?'

Then she had looked up. Met his desperate eyes with her own. In which, for a split-second, he had seen what was, surely, an unlikely emotion.

Triumph.

But then it was gone, and, in the unspeakable joy of taking her, at last, in his arms, he had forgotten all about it.

He had fallen in with her plan without a moment's thought, helped and encouraged her every step of the way. It had seemed such a clever plan! For her to retire behind the stout walls of a convent until Brice was safely married to someone else, then emerge for Olivar to claim her as *his* bride, what brilliance! And it was foolproof – Alard might well refuse his permission for Gunnora to choose a husband, but he could hardly argue with a daughter's pious intention of becoming a nun.

The year he had been forced to endure without her had been constant torment. Before, even though he had thought her out of his reach, he had had the dubious comfort of seeing her regularly. Speaking with her, listening to her voice, watching her graceful ways. But then, to be awarded the great prize of her love, only to lose her behind the walls of Hawkenlye, had been almost more than he could bear.

The night he went to meet her had been both anxious and terribly thrilling. He had not been able to eat for a week, and he had been subject to fearful headaches, which would come without warning, strike into one side of his forehead like the point of a dagger, and, while they endured, leave him good for nothing but lying in the darkness, periodically vomiting into a pail.

Then, at long, long last, they had been reunited. He had taken her in his arms, tried to kiss her, thinking that, after a year apart, she would be as ardent and eager as he.

He had known, really, when she wouldn't kiss him on the lips. Had known, only hadn't been able to believe it.

She had . . . No. Even to himself, he could not use the words 'betrayed him'. Even then, in his dire, dreadful disappointment, he could not bring himself to criticise her. She was mistaken, he told himself instead. That night, seeing me again after so long with the good sisters, she *thought* she did not want me. It was a shock, seeing me! And I should not have thrust myself on her, I should have had more sense. More patience.

It would have been all right. Soon, she would have remembered how she and I loved one another. And everything would have happened as we planned.

But it couldn't.

Because she fell down those steps and she was killed.

And, for all the satisfaction and pleasure that my life has given me since, I should have died with her.

After a long time, he got slowly to his feet. He had brought with him a stout sack, which now he unfolded and spread on the grass. Reaching down into the shallow water at the river's edge, he selected a collection of large stones, the heaviest that he could lift. He filled the sack, stood up, then, grunting with the effort, dragged it along the grass as he went on around the bend in the river.

Here, out of sight of the road above, there was a place where the strong, swift current had formed a deep black pool beneath the eroded bank.

He tied the top of the sack securely, then, using a strong length of rope, fastened it tightly around his waist. It bit painfully into his thin frame, but that hardly mattered now.

He stood for a moment, thinking of her. Of how she used

to smile, in those lovely, endlessly sunny days that long-gone summer, when, so unexpectedly, the future suddenly seemed to promise so much. Of her lips as he kissed her, the swell of her firm young breasts. Her eyes, which he had, he now realised, never really read. Of her long dark hair.

Gunnora.

My love. My lost love.

He had her cross around his neck. Taking it in his hand, clutching it in a strong grasp, he took one last look at the world.

On the opposite bank, a young willow was showing a faint hint of green; it looked as if, at long last, spring might be coming.

Olivar smiled slightly. Spring. Well, even if it was here, it was, for him, irrelevant.

Raising his eyes to the wide sky above, where somewhere, so he had been told, heaven was, he murmured a last prayer for her, and then one for himself. Mercy. Forgiveness. And, please, dear Lord, the chance that, one day, she and I may be reunited?

In the midst of that thought, he jumped.

The weighted sack did its work well. Within seconds, the waters closed over his head, and he disappeared.

READ ON FOR AN EXCERPT FROM
ALYS CLARE'S LATEST BOOK

ASHES
OF THE
ELEMENTS

AVAILABLE IN HARDCOVER FROM
ST. MARTIN'S MINOTAUR

Into the profound silence of the forest at midnight came a sound that should not have been there.

The man raised his head. Still panting from his recent exertions, he tried to quieten his rasping breath, the better to hear.

He waited.

Nothing.

Spitting on his hands and preparing to go back to work, he tried to summon a wry smile. It must have been his imagination. Or perhaps some night creature, innocently abroad. And his own nerves, plus the great forest's reputation, had done the rest.

Shaking his head at his own foolishness, he renewed his efforts. The sack was already getting nice and heavy; a little bit longer and he would—

The sound came again.

And this time it went on.

He stood up, the sweat of toil on his forehead and his back suddenly icy cold, his damp skin breaking out in goosepimples. In a flash of intuition, he thought, I should not be here. As if some dark and ancient memory were stirring, he realised, with sick dread, that the midnight forest was a forbidden place. For very good reason did people fear to venture into it . . .

Ruthlessly he stopped that terrifying train of thought before it could undermine him. Carefully putting aside the axe with which he had been hacking at the fallen oak's thick roots and lower trunk, he clambered out of the hollow he had dug under the majestic old tree. Then, using the thick ground cover of early summer to conceal himself, he gathered his courage and began to creep towards the source of the sound.

Because, if this were someone having him on, enjoying themselves at his expense, then he was going to make sure they knew he wasn't amused. If it were Seth and Ewen, God damn their eyes, sneaking out and spying on him—on him! the brains behind the whole thing!—then he'd get even. He'd . . .

But the sound was louder now, increasing in insistence so that the man could no longer block it out. Could no longer try to tell himself that it was Seth and Ewen, playing tricks.

Seth and Ewen couldn't make that sound. It was doubtful, really, that any human could.

The man ceased his furtive crawling. Ceased all movement and all thought, as the strange, eerie humming seemed to sweep over him and absorb him into itself.

He felt himself begin to smile. Ah, but it was a lovely bit of singing! Well, it was more like chanting, really, like the very sweetest sounds of some abbey choir, only better. As if it didn't come from men or women, but from the cold, distant stars themselves.

Hardly aware of what he was doing, he began to move forward again. He was no longer creeping stealthily through the undergrowth; enchanted, he was obeying a summons he barely recognised. Straight-backed, head held high, he strode through the ancient trees and the new green growth towards the open space that he could see ahead.

And stopped dead in his tracks.

Eyes round, mouth gone dry, he stared at the incredible sight. Lit by the full moon directly above the clearing, so that its bright rays bathed the scene as if intentionally, he watched in total amazement.

He'd never believed those old tales! He'd dismissed them as the ramblings of daft old women. Women like his own mother.

And, latterly, his wife, who'd tried to stop him disappearing into the great Wealden Forest, especially by night, nagging on and on at him, over and over again till he'd had to hit her. But, even when he'd done so—broken her nose, that last time—she'd still persisted. Gone on telling him it wasn't safe, wasn't right.

Hah! He'd show her! Her, and the rest! They wouldn't nag at him when they knew what he'd found!

And, anyway, even if there were some element of truth in their old legends, then it wasn't quite the way they said it was. Wasn't he here, now, witnessing with his own eyes the very proof that, for all that they still muttered about those dread things, they'd got it wrong?

He'd show them, all right! Just see if he didn't! He'd—

He felt the gaze upon him as if it were a physical assault. His braggart thoughts came to an abrupt end as, screaming through his numbed mind, bursting from his mouth like a wail of agony, came the one word: *'NO!'*

Turning, bounding over brambles and tufts of tough grass, he raced away from the clearing. Running, panting, gasping, stumbling, he heard sounds of pursuit. He sneaked a quick look over his shoulder.

Nothing.

Nothing? But he could *hear* them!

Forcing his legs to work, he raced on. Oh, God, but it—they?—was all around him now, quietly, stealthily, menacingly, surrounding him with such a sense of threat that his sobbing breath came out as a terrified howl.

For still he could see nothing.

Heart hammering, legs and lungs in agony, he spurred himself on. Half a mile, a mile? He could not tell. The trees were thinning now, surely they were! A little further—not much, oh, not much further!—and he'd be in the open. Out on the grassy fringes of this ghastly forest, out in the clean, cool moonlight . . .

There was brightness ahead. As he ran on, stumbling in his

desperate exhaustion, he could see the calm, sleeping land out there. As he passed the last few giant trees, he could even see the cross on the top of Hawkenlye Abbey's church.

'God help me, God help me, God help me,' he chanted, repeating the words until they lost all meaning. Then, suddenly, he was out in the open, and, after the darkness beneath the thickly growing trees, the moon made the night as bright as day.

Ah, thank God. *Thank God!*

Safe now, and—

But what was that? A whistling noise, close by, speeding closer, closer.

The agonising pain as the spear drilled through the man's body was intense but brief. For the spear's point was sharp, and, thrown with deadly accuracy, it pierced his heart.

He was dead before he hit the ground.

Helewise stood for some time, watching the Queen's party disappear down the road. As Eleanor had predicted, all those mounted men had indeed made an almost intolerable amount of dust. Thinking that a breath of clean air would be pleasant, Helewise delayed her return within the Abbey walls, and set out instead for a brisk walk along the track that led off towards the forest.

The warm air of early June was bringing the wild flowers into bloom, and a soft, sweet perfume seemed to fill the air. Somewhere nearby, a blackbird sang. Ah, it was good to be alive! Straightening her shoulders and swinging her arms, Helewise increased her pace and marched towards the first of the trees. She would not go far into the forest, she decided, because it was always dark in there; even in June, the sun did not seem to penetrate, so that the atmosphere always struck chill. She would just take a brief turn around the perimeter of the woodland, a mile or so, no further, then—

She almost trod on him.

Hastily stepping back, twitching the full skirt of her habit away from the blood pooled on the fresh green grass, she pressed her hand to her mouth to stifle the horrified reaction.

He was dead. He *had* to be. He was lying face down, and the long shaft of a spear protruded from his back; from the angle, it appeared that the point, buried deep in the torso, must have penetrated the heart.

He was dressed in the rough clothing of a peasant. The hose were coarse and ill-fitting, and the tunic had been patched and darned. Neatly; someone had taken care with those tiny stitches. He must have had a wife, Helewise thought, or maybe a loving mother. Some poor woman will be grieving, when she learns of this. If she were his wife, it will mean loss of husband and loss of breadwinner. A bad day for her, whoever she is.

As the initial shock receded, it occurred to Helewise to wonder what the man had been doing on the fringes of the forest. And had he been lying there long? Had she and her nuns been going about their business for some days, while, all the time, this poor wretch lay dead not half a mile from the Abbey?

She bent down and touched the back of the man's neck; it was, she couldn't help but notice, filthy dirty. There were lice active in his greasy hair; would they not have left the corpse, had the man been dead for any length of time? Surely such little blood-suckers only supped on fresh, uncongealed blood . . . The flesh retained some semblance of warmth, although, Helewise realised, that could be because he was lying at least partly in the sun. Tentatively she picked up one of the man's outflung arms: the limb was getting stiff. The rigor that came to the dead was beginning.

Had he died, then, during the past night?

Helewise stood over the corpse, a frown deepening across her brows. Then, abruptly, she turned away. Hurrying back towards the Abbey, she thought, I must get help. I must send word to the sheriff. This is a matter for him.

Breaking into a trot—not a dignified mode of locomotion for an Abbess, but she didn't notice—she reflected that it was just as well this death—this murder—hadn't come to light during Queen Eleanor's visit. Had it done so, then everyone would have been far too preoccupied for the Queen and the Abbess to have had their calm and private little tête-à-tête.

Hard on that thought came another: that it was scarcely appropriate to be pleased about such a thing when a man lay dead, brutally murdered. Her shame at her own musings adding haste to her progress, Helewise gathered up her skirts and sprinted down the track to the Abbey gates.

Sheriff Harry Pelham of Tonbridge was an odious man.

Helewise, sitting listening to his pronouncements on the murder, had to bite down her irritation. At having to listen to his opinions—grandly stated, as if he alone could be right, as if she, a mere woman, could not possibly have any valid contribution—and at having to tolerate his very presence in her room.

He was a big fellow. Solid, squat, a chest like a barrel, and short legs which seemed barely up to the job of supporting the rest of him. He was dressed in a well-worn leather overtunic, and, when he performed his frequently repeated mannerism of flinging out his chest, it was as if his intention were to draw attention to the battle scars which criss-crossed the tough leather. As if he were saying, look! See what perils my duties take me into! See what cudgel blows and broadsword thrusts I have fended off!

It had apparently been quite a job to make him leave his own sword and knife at the gates. Sister Ursel, so Helewise had been informed, had stood her ground like an aggravated hen with her feathers ruffled out, and told Harry Pelham that, sheriff or not, *nobody* bore arms into God's holy place.

The same observant nun—it was Sister Beata, who, as a nurse, was always observant—also reported to the Abbess that Harry Pelham's sword was stained, and his knife looked as if he'd recently used it to carve his meat.

And it is this careless man, Helewise now thought, listening to his booming voice, who is our sole protector of law and order. Efficient he might be—he *must* be, she corrected herself, for he was appointed by the Clares of Tonbridge, and they surely did not tolerate slackness in their officers—but, oh, what an oaf he is!

'Of course,' Harry was saying, leaning back on the little wooden stool so that its rear legs squeaked a protest, 'of course, Hamm Robinson was a well-known felon. Me, I'm not in the least surprised someone's done him in, no, no, not at all, ha, ha, ha!'

Unable, for the life of her, to see why that was funny, Helewise said in a cool tone, 'Felon, Sheriff? What was the nature of his crime?'

Harry Pelham leaned towards her, as if about to confide a secret. His fleshy nose had semicircles of little blackheads in the creases where the nostrils met the cheeks, and there were oily-looking creamy flakes in his eyebrows and at his hairline. 'Why, Sister, he was a poacher!'

'A poacher,' she repeated. 'My word, Sheriff, a dangerous man.'

Entirely missing the mild irony, Harry Pelham nodded. 'Aye, Sister, dangerous, desperate, all of that.' He hesitated, and she had the strong conviction he was wondering how far he dare exaggerate the details of what he was about to say. Leaning close again—she wished he wouldn't, he didn't smell any too fresh—he said, 'Come near to apprehending him, I have, on several occasions. Tracked him, see, through those old woods.' He jerked a thumb over his shoulder in the vague direction of the forest. 'Ah, but he was a sly one! Wormed his way through that undergrowth like some wild animal, he did, all silent and swift, like. Reckon he knew the lie of the land like the back of his hand.' Harry Pelham shook his head. 'Never could quite lay my fists on him.'

'Perhaps he heard you coming,' Helewise remarked neutrally.

The sheriff shot her a quick glance. 'Aye, that's as maybe. And it's also maybe my good fortune that I never did catch him, desperate man like him! Why, *maybe* I wouldn't be sitting here now talking to you, Sister, if I had of!'

'Yes,' Helewise murmured, 'he'd have put up a rare fight, of that I'm quite sure.' Deliberately she stared at Harry Pelham's broad shoulders. 'Was he a big man, would you say, Sheriff?' she asked, raising innocent eyes to his. 'I only saw him dead, and it was hard to tell.'

The sheriff went, 'Humph,' and 'Ha!' a few times, then grunted something barely audible.

'What did you say, Sheriff? I didn't quite catch it.'

'I said, he was big enough,' Harry Pelham growled.

'Ah.' Helewise bent her head to hide her smile. Then, straightening her face, she said, 'He was killed by the spear thrust, and, when hit, he was running from the forest. Yes?'

Another grunt. Then, grudgingly, as if he resented her awareness of even such bare facts, 'Yes. That's how it was.'

'And from that, you hazard the guess that he was killed by—what did you call them, Sheriff? The Forest People?'

'Aye. Forest People, Wild People, folks refer to them by both names.'

'And you know for sure that these Wild People were in the forest the night before last?'

'Aye. It's June, see. They come here in June.' He frowned. 'Leastways, they sometimes do. They have done in the past, anyhow.'

'I see.' It seemed, Helewise thought, slim evidence on which to convict this unknown, hitherto unsuspected group of people who, apparently, were wont to camp at certain times of the year, almost on the Abbey's doorstep. 'And—forgive me, Sheriff, if I seem to be questioning your actions, only what with the murder being so close, and—'

'And what with you finding him, Sister,' the sheriff interrupted her. 'Aye, I understand.' A patronising smile stretched the moist lips. 'You go on and ask me,' he said earnestly, 'anything I can tell you, to set your mind at rest so you and the good sisters can lie easy in your beds at night, I will!'

'How kind,' Helewise murmured. 'As I was saying, Sheriff,

you've been up into the forest, I take it? You've found evidence that these Wild People have been there recently?'

'Well, I . . .' Again, the frown. More like a scowl, really, Helewise thought, deciding that, frown or scowl, it probably meant that Harry Pelham was about to tell her a lie. Or, at least, try to get away with a fudging of the truth. 'There's not much point in looking for signs of the Wild People, see, Sister. They're cunning and canny, and they don't go about cutting down trees or hacking off branches to make shelters. They're more, like, open-air folk. They live under the trees, under the sky. They've been there forever, they have, carrying on in their strange ways. Old even when the Romans came, some say.' Remembering the point he was making, he repeated. 'No use looking for evidence. None at all. Although, of course, I sent some of my men up there anyway.'

'Of course.' A likely story! 'And they found nothing.' It was a statement, not a question.

Harry Pelham grinned. 'No. Like I said.'

Helewise carefully put her hands together, resting her chin on the tips of her fingers. 'What we have, then, Sheriff, is a dead poacher, whom, despite any evidence, you are quite sure was killed by these Wild People. Who, since you have not managed to locate them, cannot be questioned.' She shot him a direct look, and felt a totally unworthy pleasure in seeing him flinch slightly. 'Therefore you have no proof of their guilt, other than your own conviction.'

Harry Pelham rallied quickly. Giving her his most threatening scowl, he said, 'My conviction's quite enough for me!' As if even he realised the flimsiness of that, he added, 'Anyway, you tell me who else could have done it! Go on, tell me!'

'Not knowing anything of the man or his background, naturally, I can't,' Helewise said mildly. 'But, surely, that is your job, Sheriff? To discover how and where the man lived, if he had any enemies, if anyone would be likely to gain from his death?'

'Ha!' the sheriff cried, punching the air as if to say, got you there! 'I *know* who he was. He was Hamm Robinson, like I said. He has a wife—poor meagre little woman she is, Hamm bullied and beat her within an inch of her life, the good Lord alone knows why she didn't make off in the night—and, as for what he did, he was a poacher.' He pointed a grubby finger at the Abbess. 'Told you that, too.' He exhaled a big sigh, and said, 'If you ask me, the world's well rid of him.'

'Perhaps so!' Helewise cried. 'But he was a man, Sheriff! A living, breathing man, until someone threw a spear at him and killed him. Is he not as entitled to justice as any other man?'

Harry Pelham, she was certain, almost said, 'No.' That, she thought, would have been the truth. Instead, the fleshy, greasy face took on its patronising look once more. 'Like I keep telling you, Sister,' he said, 'I'd do what you want and go and accuse the Wild People if I could. Arrest them, bring them to trial, hang a few, if it was in my power! But how can I if they've gone?' He chuckled. 'Even I can't arrest a man if he's not there, now can I, Sister?'

There was, Helewise thought, little point in pursuing it any more. She couldn't make the sheriff do anything he didn't want to; clearly, he was far beyond being shamed into action by anything she said.

She let the tense silence continue a little longer. Then, rising to her feet, said, 'Very well, Sheriff. But, please, do let me know if your enquiries arrive at any sort of satisfactory conclusion.'

Realising he was being dismissed—which, judging from his expression, he didn't much like—Sheriff Pelham stood up. The Abbess opened the door, and he trudged out.

'You may reclaim your weapons at the gate,' Helewise told him. 'Sister Ursel will have taken good care of them. I wish you good day, Sheriff.'

He muttered something in reply. It could have been 'Good day,' but it could equally well have been something far less polite.

*   *   *

When she was quite certain he had gone, Helewise left her room and crossed the courtyard to the infirmary, where she begged Sister Euphemia to part with some of her precious lavender-scented incense. Despite her efforts to think charitably of the sheriff, still Helewise felt a very strong desire to fumigate her room of his presence.

Later that day, she went back up the track to the forest.

It was, she had discovered, very difficult to leave the matter there. A man had been brutally murdered right by the Abbey, and she had all but stepped on his body. It appeared there was no chance of his killer ever being brought to justice, and Helewise could see no way to alter that.

I must, she thought, striding up towards the trees, have one more try myself. Take one more look. See if I can find some clue that the sheriff and his men overlooked, and, the dear Lord knows, surely *that* wouldn't be hard.

She found the place where the body had lain. There were still bloodstains on the grass. She walked a few paces on into the forest, and thought she could detect trodden-down undergrowth where the dead man's running feet had passed. But what of the killer? Had he run in the dead man's tracks? He must have stood still to throw the spear . . . She wandered on under the deep shade of the trees, not really knowing what she was looking for.

Some time later, she gave up the search. It was, she realised, quite hopeless.

She went back to the place where the man had fallen. There was some flattened grass a few paces off; she went to look.

There, amid the brilliant green, lay the spear.

Someone—Sheriff Pelham?—must have wrested it out of the dead man's back and thrown it away. Its head and the first few inches of its shaft were still sticky with blood.

Helewise bent down and picked it up.

Carefully she wiped it on the fresh young grass, feeling, as she did so, an illogical but very strong urge to apologise for this act of desecration.

Then, when it was as clean as she could make it, she had a good look. The tip of the spear was made of flint.

Flint?

Helewise had lived for most of her life close to the South Downs, and she knew all about flint. One of her brothers had amused himself on a wet afternoon by making a flint knife, and had discovered that knapping wasn't as easy as one might think.

But whoever had made this spearhead was a master in the craft. The point was exactly symmetrical, and shaped most beautifully. Like an elegant leaf. The knapped edges were perfect.

And the point was as sharp as any knife.

Helewise—who had learned her lesson over testing the sharpness of worked edges—tried the spearpoint on a patch of dandelions. It seared through the leaves and stems as if they hadn't been there.

A flint spearhead, she mused. Why flint, in this age of fine metalwork? Did it mean that wretched sheriff was right, and this murder *was* the work of some band of primitive forest-dwelling people, who lived not in the present day but in the manner of their distant stone-working ancestors?

The idea sent an atavistic shiver of dread down Helewise's spine. And here I am, she thought, not ten paces from the forest.

She turned and hurried back towards the Abbey.

But, disconcerted or not, still she took the spear with her. Even if this did appear to be the end of the matter, it seemed a good idea not to throw away evidence.